EXPLOSIVE CHEMISTRY

PAIGE E. EWING

CITY OWL
PRESS

EXPLOSIVE CHEMISTRY
Liliana and the Fae of Fayetteville, Book 2

CITY OWL PRESS
www.cityowlpress.com

Cover Design by MiblArt. All stock photos licensed appropriately.

Edited by Lisa Green.

For information on subsidiary rights, please contact the publisher at info@cityowlpress.com.

Print Edition ISBN: 978-1-64898-433-4

Digital Edition ISBN: 978-1-64898-434-1

Printed in the United States of America

PRAISE FOR PAIGE E. EWING

"Paige Ewing has written a romp of a book in Precise Oaths. Liliana is an engaging, sympathetic heroine with a striking view of the world. One of the things I enjoyed was the way it made me look at being neurodivergent in a new way without once being preachy. What's more, Precise Oaths is tremendous fun. Liliana's quirky worldview is mixed with pure determination and ingenuity, along with a strong moral core. The writing is clean and flowing, with a host of terrific characters and great worldbuilding. It's hard to write a thought-provoking book that's also fun to read, but Paige pulled it off in spades." — *Angela Knight, New York Times Bestselling author*

"Liliana may not always know how to act with humans, but she has deep knowledge of the ways of the Fae and the Others. Some unlikely alliances and Liliana's abilities give us a rollicking adventure and set the stage for more stories to come. It's a lovely book and I look forward to reading the sequels. I need to know what happens next!" — *Nancy Jane Moore, author of The Weave*

"A delightful paranormal fantasy with romantic elements. *Precise Oaths* takes place in the not-so-distant future, when fae, shifters, and normals coexist in an uneasy reality. Liliana is spider-kin—a neurodivergent loner who tells fortunes and longs for connection with others. Thrust into a murder investigation, she ends up having to work with unexpected allies to find the real killers and keep her new-found friends safe. Liliana is strong and intelligent, but she's not good at peopling. Which makes sense, because she's not human. But she is kind, loyal, and determined to make things right. I was rooting for her right from the start. This is an excellent beginning to a new series by paranormal fantasy author Paige Ewing. Fans will adore Liliana!" — *Patrice Sarath, author of The Sisters Mederos*

To my husband, Joe, who has always had my back, and encouraged me to chase my dreams, even when it meant I spent far too many hours in front of a keyboard.

Chapter 1

Lunch With A Rabbit

The bloody image of two young women in military uniform being shot in the back of the head jolted Liliana awake. She sat up abruptly, her heart pounding, a pointless "No!" forming on her lips.

Her fourth eyes that saw things in other times and places were already open, the source of the ugly dream.

Who are they?

But her mental question did not elicit any new visions, just a repeat of the same horrors. She needed more information to have any chance of saving the women. Her fourth vision showed her nothing near them but a forest, trees, and grass. There was a pine leaning on an oak tree, and a bush with lovely white flowers beneath it. The oak tree had no leaves, so it must have been winter. The plant life looked like the local forests, but that same kind of forest could be anywhere for hundreds of miles around. North Carolina had a lot of forests, especially since paper, and for the most part, wood, had become obsolete.

The two women both had faces in her vision that shimmered with Otherness. They were not Normal humans, but that was all Liliana could tell about them.

Death overwhelmed her fourth vision under the best of

circumstances. When she slept, she didn't have as much control over her vision as she did when awake. She had no idea why the two women she didn't even know were suddenly in her mind, or if the vision was of the future or of the past. Oddly, it had a trace of the overbright reflections of the future mixed with the muted color tones of the past.

They can't die both in the past and in the future.

It made no sense.

She got up, feeling tired and achy, and determined not to let it stop her.

Liliana had taken a sick day after nearly being killed a couple days before. Much to her chagrin, she had been forced to take a second sick day by the inability to open her fourth eyes to see the past and future without waves of dizziness from her head injury. She could not get paid for her job as Madame Anna Sees All when she couldn't open the large swirly pair of spikder-kin eyes on her forehead to see anything.

The awful dream told the spider-kin seer one important thing: her fourth eyes were once again fully functional.

That meant she could get back to work. Which was good. She hadn't cancelled the appointments for the day, hoping that would be the case. Spider-kin healed fast and cancelling appointments was bad for business.

Liliana removed all the bandages and examined her injuries in the mirror. When she closed her six spider eyes, leaving only her first, human eyes open, her thick dark hair hid the tiny crinkles where they closed. The image in the mirror looked just like a petite young Normal. It was good camouflage. Normals outnumbered Others a hundred to one and tended toward violence when faced with "monsters." She nodded at the image. She could pass.

Her face and body still clearly showed that she'd been in a battle recently, though. The gash on her cheek looked particularly ugly. The wide, jagged slice made by a widow spider's spiked limb was closed but still a livid purple with mottled green and yellow old bruising over that side of her face. At least Doctor Nudd had taped the gash shut. That helped it heal more cleanly and quickly.

All of Liliana's small cuts from her and Pete's recent battle had healed to the point that only raised pink welts were visible. The swelling on the back of her head was much reduced. She could rotate her neck and open all eight of her eyes without her head feeling like it would fall off.

The only real pain was from her shoulder wound. She supported one arm with the other as she carefully tested how much she could move it. She closed all her eyes as a wave of sadness came with the pain of moving her arm. Stella, the widow spider, had stabbed clear through her shoulder, and Liliana had used that leverage on her limb to drag the brave warrior to her death over the side of a tall building.

Under other circumstances, she and Stella might have been friends. Liliana mourned the death of a fellow spider-kin doing what she must to protect her nest sisters. But if she had not killed Stella, the widow spider would have killed Liliana, so... She sighed. She killed only when she had to, as all three of her parents taught. As long as that was true, she would still find the image in the mirror acceptable, but that didn't mean she couldn't be sad about the necessity.

As she dressed, she cheered herself with thoughts of the people she'd met over the last few days. Doctor Peter Teague, a civilian bio scientist with the Criminal Investigation Division for Fort Liberty, and a deadly Celtic wolf-kin, accused her of murder and tried to kill her before becoming the closest friend she'd had in years. Siobhan, the little person and flower sprite who owned the custom weapons shop Emerald Arms, a few doors down from her own shop, had also tried to kill her. Then the sprite helped her and Pete survive their battle with the widow spiders, the real killers Pete mistook her for. The unseelie oak goblin, Doctor Nudd, had also tried to kill her, but he made up for that later by loaning her his homemade warm sweater and healing her injuries after the battle.

She had an odd way of meeting people lately.

On the plus side, she had been getting out more, and her life could no longer be described as either boring or lonely.

Opening her fourth eyes, the swirling opalescent lavender and teal ones set above her eyebrows, she took a quick look forward in time to check the weather like she did every morning. It would get chilly and rainy again later. Winter in Fayetteville tended to be sunshiny one day and cold and wet the next. She added cozy purple tights with her black leotard under her usual flowing, brightly colored, homemade skirt. She chose a blouse made of warm velvet scarves with wide, drapey sleeves like mini-wings that went all the way to the wrist. They would keep her arms warm without restricting the natural weaponry hidden in her forearms.

Her shoulder wound would take a week before she could go without a sling. She put the sling on her arm and frowned. The medical sling Doctor Nudd gave her was a plain, dull light blue canvas. It did not go well with the sapphire blue velvet top, and the skirt with glittery silver bead trim that complimented it.

Liliana took the sling off, chose a scarf from her chest of drawers, and tied it around her neck. She slipped her arm into it and looked in the mirror again.

The leafy-green, floral patterned silk scarf held her arm without pulling on her sore shoulder, and it looked much nicer than the plain canvas one. She nodded with satisfaction and walked into the converted dining room that served as her place of business, Madame Anna Sees All. She closed the door that led to the rest of her house and checked that the crystal ball was where it belonged, in the exact center of the round table in the middle of the room.

She had scheduled multiple appointments back-to-back, far more than she normally would in a day, to catch up. The first knock on the business door came only minutes later. She welcomed the pair of young wood nymphs who entered in a cloud of giggles and lilac perfume.

Bowing, she waved her arms to gesture them in, and chanted, "Madame Anna sees all. Pay me what you feel is fair for truth that cannot be seen by other eyes. I see what is, what has been, and what might be. Ask and the truth shall be yours."

Her first appointments went reasonably well. Everyone insisted on asking what had happened to her shoulder and her face. The gash on her cheek from Stella's last attack was the first thing everyone noticed. It didn't particularly bother Liliana until they mentioned it, unlike her shoulder injury that restricted her movements, or the persistent itch from the gash on her ribs.

When she answered, "I was stabbed by a giant spider," the nymph girls laughed as if she made a joke, even though they were Others. They knew that such things could exist.

Her second client, a Normal human who probably didn't know such things existed, rolled his eyes and said, "That's a good story. You'll have a hard time topping it later."

When her best client, Janice Willoughby, a rabbit-kin homemaker, came in, she took one look at Liliana, covered her mouth with her hand, and interrupted Liliana's usual client welcome speech to say, "What happened?"

"I was stabbed by a giant spider helping Pete on that case a few days ago. I am fine, though. The injuries are already healing."

"Oh, Madame Anna, you could have been killed. I heard on the news about the serial killers in Raleigh targeting soldiers from Fort Liberty. They weren't Normals, were they? What were they really?"

"A nest of widow spiders." Liliana shrugged. She looked at the shoulder strap of her client's purse, a soft-looking blue denim material with appliqued flowers. Liliana wondered if it was Janice's own handiwork.

Janice gasped and her face blanched. "A whole nest of them! I'd scream and run if I saw even one. It's a wonder you weren't killed."

"I did not die," Liliana reassured her favorite client. "The widow spiders died. I am fine."

Janice insisted that Liliana tell her the full story. As talkative as Janice was, Liliana also found her to be an excellent listener. The spider-kin felt an odd relief after she shared the story of Pete, the red wolf-kin, hunting her, how she defeated him in single combat, and later risked her life to save him and his friend, Sergeant Zoe Giovanni. It was as if she had been holding something heavy all by herself, and now Janice Willoughby held one end of it for her.

Apparently, having someone she could talk to honestly about her life was soothing in some way. She had noticed this with her clients—that they would often pay the spider seer to simply listen to them talk about their lives when they had no real questions to ask. That had always seemed odd to her. Now she understood.

Long after her appointment ended, Janice stayed and talked with Liliana. When Liliana started to feel hungry, she did something she had not done in a very long time. She invited Janice Willoughby into her home to share lunch.

After telling the rabbit-kin about the recent events in her life, Liliana had little else to say, but Janice didn't have any trouble filling up the silence. While they ate grilled cheese sandwiches and drank tea, she kept chatting amiably about her children and her husband, Lou. She also spoke about rapidly becoming close friends with Ben Harper, Pete's Normal boyfriend who was one of Janice's son's teachers.

Liliana was surprised to find that having her best client in her home did not bother her like she'd assumed it would. She enjoyed having the cheerful rabbit-kin sharing her personal space.

In fact, she thought perhaps, once she was fully healed, she should go out on a social visit herself, her first in decades. The thought made her stomach a little queasy with nerves, but Liliana was not a coward. She had promised Doctor Nudd she would return his sweater. She would not let fear stop her from keeping her word to the kind goblin.

In addition, having seen him fight twice now, it was clear to Liliana that Pete needed more training. He had all the raw materials of a great warrior—courage without bounds, an indomitable will, intelligence, and incredible levels of brute power—but he did not know how to use those strengths to best advantage. Beyond training, he needed two other things to survive the attack she'd foreseen from a pack of assassins from the Order of the Wolfhound:

something to defeat the protective magic of the crown collars the Wolfhounds wore, and allies.

Liliana picked up their plates and went to her kitchen to fetch more tea for herself and Janice.

Pete would be dead already without his allies. Colonel Bennet, who secretly watched over Pete, was even more secretly an unseelie Fae prince. He was also the only reason the first Wolfhound assassin who came to Fayetteville had not already slain Pete. Well, the Colonel's abilities plus a little help from Liliana.

The only reason she and Pete had survived their encounter with the widow spiders was the timely aid of Siobhan and her machine gun. The value of good allies was incalculable.

Doctor Nudd, in particular, would be essential to Pete's survival. If an eight-foot oak goblin stood with Pete when he fought, that would certainly improve his chances. Not to mention the doctor's healing abilities after the battle.

Liliana opened her fourth eyes and looked along the goblin's life path.

How can I make sure Doctor Nudd will be there to help when Pete faces the Wolfhounds?

She saw the gentle doctor pierced with a sword, blood bubbling from his lips as he died. The power and clarity of the image meant that it would happen soon and was nearly certain.

Oh.

The tea tray in Liliana's hands tilted without her noticing, spilling tea and cups all over her woven carpet.

Oh.

Janice jumped up from the chair and grabbed the tray from her hands. "What is it, Madame Anna? What did you see?"

Janice set the tray on the coffee table and gently guided the spider seer to the couch by one elbow.

Liliana would have missed the couch in her distraction without the help. "Doctor Nudd is going to be murdered."

"Oh! That's awful." Janice picked up the mostly unbroken tea cups off the carpet. "He's the nice goblin who fixed up your injuries, right?"

Liliana nodded. "He is also Pete's closest friend and mentor. Pete will die if Doctor Nudd is not there to fight beside him the next time he is attacked. And he will mourn if Doctor Nudd dies." After a moment, she added, "I will mourn too."

"Is that why he's going to be murdered, do you think? Because he's friends with the Celtic werewolf? There's a lot of Others who have a hate on for Pete's kind."

"It is possible. Let me look." With a feeling of dread, she opened her fourth eyes again to look into the life path of Pete and his other allies.

Sergeant Giovanni had narrowly avoided one death at the hands of the widow spiders, only to walk blithely toward another. "Sergeant Giovanni, who is also Pete's friend, has at least three possible deaths waiting for her, one very soon. In two weeks."

Colonel Bennet, the handsome Fae prince who had killed a Wolfhound to protect Pete would be dead in less than a year. His entire identity was wrapped in secrets, so Liliana didn't say anything about him out loud. Seeing him die sent a jerk to her belly that made her fight not to throw up her lunch.

She swallowed, then said, "Detective Jackson will die within days, the same time as Sergeant Giovanni. Or Pete might die trying to protect her from an Other killer." Detective Jackson had been with Sergeant Giovanni and Pete when they accused Liliana of murder, but she refused to believe Liliana was guilty with no evidence other than Liliana being spider-kin. The detective had been the only one who believed in Liliana's innocence.

Janice sat down on the coffee table facing Liliana. "Wow. That's a lot of murder all of a sudden."

So much death.

Liliana shuddered and wrapped her arms around herself. "I have not seen so many images of people dying all at once since I lost two of my three parents, two brothers, one sister, and all their families in the same year. And that was when Nazis were killing everyone."

"These are all the red wolf's friends, though. You know werewolves are trouble, and Celtic wolves even more than most. I hope Ben is safe."

A quick glance showed no near danger to Ben Harper, the Normal teacher who owned Pete's heart. "Ben is not involved in most of what I see. He should be all right." Although, he would have died, too, if she and Colonel Bennet hadn't already slain the first Wolfhound.

Janice bit her lip. "Are you in any danger yourself?"

Even knowing that it was a question she probably did not want to see the answer to, Liliana looked into her future. She saw a dozen different deaths. Each vision was flickery like a candle flame in the wind, shifting with uncertainty, but they all involved Pete in one way or another. "Yes, the more I am involved in Pete's life, the more ways I might die."

She closed all her eyes, overwhelmed. Clearly, becoming Pete's ally had a detrimental effect on one's life expectancy.

"Madame Anna, I know you've always been the one to give me advice, but it sounds like being Pete's friend is really dangerous. He doesn't think you're a killer anymore, so he shouldn't bother you." Janice patted her knee. "Maybe you'd be better off just going back to the way things were?"

Liliana considered Janice's advice. If the spider seer went back to her old life, to watching the future of Others, guiding them safely around obstacles, and staying out of the larger affairs of the Other community in North Carolina, she would probably live a lot longer.

"Pete and all my new friends would die." Her life would go back to being routine, boring, and lonely. "I do not want to be alone anymore."

Janice squeezed her knee and nodded. "I didn't even think about how lonely you must get never talking to anyone who doesn't pay you."

"I am also unwilling to be the kind of person who sees danger to my friends coming and does nothing." Even if it meant increasing her probability of meeting an untimely end. That was not the child her three brave warrior parents raised. That was not the woman she wanted to see in the mirror. "Also, Pete trusts me."

To her surprise, Liliana concluded that being worthy of that trust was more important to her than anything else, including increasing the likelihood of her survival.

Janice nodded and sat back. "I respect that. Okay, then. Is there anything you can do to help?"

Having saved Pete from the certain death she'd seen a few days before, Liliana felt confident that she *could* change the dark futures she saw, although it might cost her own life. "Changing fate is always dangerous. I must be careful, or I could make things even worse."

"Worse, how?" Janice asked. "Could something happen to other people?"

That was a disturbing thought. "Other people may already be in danger." Liliana had spent decades keeping her clients safe and guiding them toward happiness. Her clients made up a fair percentage of the Others in Fayetteville, and even a small percentage of the Normal humans. "I only looked at my friends' futures."

Is this tide of death focused, or will it harm more people I watch over as well?

Her fourth eyes showed her an ugly chain reaction, pushing outward like ripples spreading in a lake of blood. "Oh."

"What is it, Madame Anna?" Janice bit the cuticle on her thumb.

"If Doctor Nudd dies, then Pete dies, then Sergeant Giovanni and Detective Jackson die, then everyone those two police women, military and civilian, might have protected dies or has awful things happen to them with no one to stop it. This could be devastating to all of Fayetteville." The fate of her entire community was tangled with the fate of her friends.

"Where is all this coming from all of a sudden?" Janice got up and paced back and forth in Liliana's small living room. "You and Ben's man, Pete, stopped the ones who were killing those soldiers. That should have made us all safer."

Janice was right. Wiping out the widow spiders should have stopped the red tide of violent death, not made the situation worse.

Why is everyone still in so much danger? What did we miss?

Another quick flash of the two military women being executed from behind made her shiver. They must be key in some way.

How are they related? Why do I keep seeing them?

Her fourth eyes failed to see an answer. The deaths themselves clouded and overwhelmed everything else. As always. "I keep seeing these two women being killed. They're soldiers in uniform. Others of some kind. I don't understand how, but they're related to the source of the danger in some way."

Janice sat next to her on the couch. "Well, whatever you decide to do, Madame Anna, you watch your back. Those widow spiders hurt you pretty bad. Whatever is coming sounds like it's a lot worse."

Despite the lingering horror all the visions of death left her with, she smiled. "I will be careful." Janice Willoughby worried about her. It was nice that someone did.

Clocks chimed, telling Liliana it was almost time for her next appointment. She had to ask Janice to leave. She found that she did not want the rabbit-kin to go.

"I'll see you next week then, at the regular time," Janice said.

Liliana nodded, said, "Goodbye," as social rules required, and started to shut the door.

"Um, Madame Anna?" Janice said.

"Yes?"

"I'm glad you're okay. You be real careful helping your friends, and...I really enjoyed lunch."

Liliana smiled at Janice's tennis shoes. "I did too."

After she shut the door, Liliana considered the Fae Colonel, wondering if he could be the source of so much danger. Having a Sidhe with the potential to bond with the land on this side of the ocean was something she'd feared since she was smuggled into this country. The land always chose Sidhe Fae as rulers. So as long as there were no Sidhe royalty on this continent, all the Others who had fled here were safe. No non-native Fae had bonded with this land in over two-hundred years, and most of the native Fae had been killed or driven into hiding.

If the Colonel did manage to bond to the land and another Sidhe Fae opposed him, like his sister Aurore Principessa, who was known for her cruelty...

It was a recipe for war.

Maybe he is the source of the rising tide of death.

Letting the Colonel's fated death happen without interfering might be best for everyone.

But he is handsome.

The thought came unbidden and was supremely unhelpful in her attempts to find a logical way through the morass of death and intertwined fates.

But he *was* handsome, from his shimmering obsidian demi-stone form to the high cheekbones, full lips, and intense gaze of his human form. Regardless of her attraction to him, she could not condemn a man to death without knowing more about him. After all, he had protected both Pete and Sergeant Giovanni. Plus, he was strong and fierce, and had a smooth, deep voice that made her belly warm. While it might be wiser to do nothing and let his death find him, she would not find that at all easy.

The right kind of Fae ruler had, historically, caused the land to flourish and ushered in golden ages of plenty and peace. Arthur Pendragon had only been half Sidhe and therefore mortal. Yet his brief rule was still remembered.

Baba Yaga, on the other hand, blasted her own land to win a war. Countless died, both millions of Normal and thousands of Others. It took a century for the land to recover. Baba Yaga was gone now. The Green, the power and soul of the earth, did not take kindly to those who betrayed it.

Liliana did not know what sort of man this Fae prince was or what his ambitions might be. But he had nearly a year to live. Later, Liliana would decide if she should try to save the Fae prince.

First, she would have to save Sergeant Giovanni. Again. And

Detective Jackson, and possibly Pete as well. And then Doctor Nudd.

A knock on her business door let her know that her next client had arrived, a nice seelie Fae sylph. His wife was a soldier deployed overseas, and he worried constantly.

After work, she would explore future paths to find a way to change her favorite people's dark fates.

Chapter 2

Camp Killer

Two weeks later, Liliana carefully laid a trip line between two tree trunks across a hiking path in Carver's Creek State Park. She tied one of the nearly invisible cords of silk at ankle height, grateful that her ribs no longer ached when she bent over. Even her shoulder was finally back to normal. The other line, she could just walk under, with a brush along the top of her head. She ducked anyway since the silk was still damp and she didn't want it to stick to her hair.

That used to happen to her a lot when she was young. More than once, one of her mothers had to cut out silk that had become hopelessly stuck and tangled.

Her fourth eyes supplied an image from her childhood.

Little Liliana ran to her home wagon, left hand stuck in her hair by her own spider silk. "Mut, help," she said, hopping up onto the wooden steps. She pulled the carved door open with her free hand. She must have been eight or nine since her second eyes hadn't opened yet.

The scent from the bunches of drying lavender tied to the ceiling and the warmth of the close wagon interior washed over her. "Look what you've done, Liliana." Solifu's clipped Egyptian accent sounded annoyed. "Your silk is strong, not easy to break. You must not be careless with it." She set aside the safety net she'd been retying that would go under the high wire and trapeze when they did their circus acts.

"I'm sorry, Mut. I didn't mean to." Liliana stared at the floor, seeing her first mother's delicate feet in ballet slippers and her second mother's bare feet and harem pants of brilliant green velvet with sequined edges.

Liliana looked to Ixchel for sympathy, where she sat on the floor, her head resting on Solifu's knee. Her tall, lithe second mother simply shook her head in exasperation. "I'll find the sewing scissors." She stood and started rummaging through the storage cupboards that lined most of the walls inside the wagon.

"But I don't want my hair short again. It makes me look like a boney little boy." The other kids in the circus made merciless fun of Liliana the last time her hair had to be cut short.

Solifu's face was stern, immune to her child's whining distress. "If you would keep your silk out of your hair, we wouldn't have to cut it."

Ixchel sat on the bench built into the wall where they stored their clothes and gestured to the spot between her feet. "Come here."

Liliana knelt between her second mother's knees, back to her, facing her first mother, who went back to tying the net.

Ixchel carefully cut away the hair and silk to free Liliana's hand. The snick, snick near her ears made Liliana's eyes burn, but she was glad to have her hand freed.

"I could just cut away the pieces of your hair that are tangled with silk?" Her lilting South American accent made the words sound like gentle music.

"Yes, Mamãe. Please." Liliana's tense shoulders relaxed a little. At least she would get to keep some of her hair.

Solifu clicked her tongue in disapproval. "Your hair will be a dozen lengths. You will look like a crazy person."

Liliana's ears and cheeks heated. Insanity was a problem her kind was prone to that got spider seers killed. Women in her family who lost touch with reality had been killed by their own sisters.

"What do you want?" Ixchel's deep sympathetic voice rumbled next to Liliana's ear. "Shall I cut it all short?"

"Yes." Tears rolled down Liliana's cheeks, even as she said it. The scissors cut away the hair she had just started to grow out from the last time she got silk tangled in it.

Ixchel gave her a quick hug when she was done. "You look cute with short hair, Kitten. Ignore the other children."

Solifu nodded to her. "The opinion of others is far less important than your actions. Be careful with your silk from now on and you can grow your hair as long as you like."

Liliana left the caravan, ducked under two others, and wedged herself as tiny as she could against the wagon wheel of a third, not caring about the grit under her knees. Then she stopped suppressing the heartbroken sobs.

Her elegant adult sister, Isabella, stepped down from the wagon. She had her own caravan, as the great Madame Bella who could see your future in your hand or your stars. Liliana, both her mothers, her father, and her two youngest brothers, Jason and Petros, all shared their wagon. It was much bigger, of course, but privacy and quiet were impossible goals. Liliana gravitated toward Isabella's wagon. It often felt like a point of peace in her chaotic life. She had come here instinctively to nurse her pain.

Isabella squatted down beside her wooden step, carefully tucking her pretty skirts up out of the dirt, and peered under the wagon. "Why are you crying?" Her voice was flat, without inflection as usual. Liliana couldn't tell if her sister was angry or disappointed or merely curious.

When Liliana told her what was wrong, Isabella put her head to one side as she often did when thinking or remembering. "I had the same problem when I was little. Come. I have something to show you."

Liliana wiped her face with her sleeve and followed her sister into the shadowy interior of Isabella's wagon.

"Sit," she told Liliana, who slid into a built-in bench around the small fold-out table.

Isabella fetched a beautiful decorative glass bottle from one of the storage cupboards that lined the walls. She set it down on the table and sat next to Liliana.

"Watch, now." Isabella touched the spinneret in her wrist and pulled back her finger, extending a line of sticky fresh spider silk from the tiny hole. A quick twist of her wrist put the silk into her other hand. She carefully pulled and tied and played with the silk, making cat's cradles of it and tiny nets like the giant one of rope Solifu had been repairing.

Liliana watched, fascinated by the ease and grace, where she was so clumsy.

A final twist of wrist and hand cut off the flow of silk, leaving the little net free. Isabella wrapped it around itself until it was a tiny ball, never getting stuck.

Liliana nodded, imitated the movement of her sister's hands, without pulling out any silk. It would take practice, but knowing how to keep her silk under control would help a lot in keeping it out of her hair.

Then Isabella opened the pretty bottle. It smelled wonderfully of thyme and lavender.

"Now, for when you make a mistake." Isabella's hair was straight and sleek, shimmering like a raven's wing, where Liliana's dull black hair tended toward wild curls, and frequently, frizz. Isabella deliberately tangled sticky fresh webbing in that lock of shiny blue-black hair.

"No!" little Liliana exclaimed.

Isabella chuckled. "It's all right." She got a few drops of the nice-smelling oil on her fingers and rubbed it over the webbing, then finger combed her hair. The webbing let loose and came away easily. "There, spiderling. See? For you."

Reverently, Liliana accepted the bottle of oil from her sister.

Liliana blinked her fourth eyes and looked around the forest just outside the border of Fort Liberty. She stood still, frozen in the moment after she ducked under the line of webbing. She had no idea how long she'd stood there half bent over.

She had jumped time unintentionally. That hadn't happened in a few years. Instead of her wayward vision controlling her mind, Liliana had tamed her vision over many painstaking years of exercising her gift every day with clients to where her mind controlled it.

Most of the time.

She'd long since used all the oil her sister gave her, but the pretty little glass bottle sat in a place of honor on one of her bookshelves. She'd refilled it many times.

The fact that Liliana unwillingly saw visions of a treasured childhood moment with Isabella made her wonder if she might see her older sister again soon. It had been a long time, and when visions overtook her that strongly, they often indicated the hand of fate in action.

Or maybe that was wishful thinking. She hadn't heard from her sister in more than a decade.

Her two brothers who escaped Europe with her, Petros and Jason, had grown old and moved away to the North Carolina coast. She didn't know their surviving families.

Before Pete, Sergeant Giovanni, and Detective Jackson accused her of murder, she hadn't been lonely simply from a lack of friends. The remaining members of her once numerous and boisterous family had died, or faded and then scattered, leaving her behind.

Voices brought her fully back to the present. She ran through the bushes to a different path, then leapt and scrambled up into the branches of a tall hickory, barely in time to avoid being seen. She did not want to accidentally change something that would send the path of fate in an unpredictable direction.

Homicide Detective Shonda Jackson looked completely out of place hiking through the forest in a stylish modern synth silk suit with shiny silver electromagnetic buttons. She stepped carefully along the path leading to the small parking lot on the edge of the Bones Creek campground, Peter Teague following a half step behind her on the narrow hiking trail. "That's why I called you," she said, continuing a conversation with Pete. "Whatever did that, it wasn't human."

Pete shrugged. "The wounds seem clean and precise, nothing like the attack of an enraged beast-kin or Fae. I did some preliminary tests and couldn't find any sign of Other venom or contaminants. Couldn't it have been a Normal with a big, sharp carving knife?"

The policewoman twisted her lips in a way that looked like she tasted something unpleasant. "A human who managed to kill an entire family with a single clean horizontal slice along the middle back, without alerting the other family members, even though they were all within feet of each other?"

"It does seem unlikely." Pete rubbed the back of his neck where red hair grew short like fur. "But I've never heard of any Other that kills like this.

"Ever heard of an Other that removes the livers from its victims? They're all missing their livers. I had the forensics team check first thing."

"That's weirdly specific. Why would you—never mind, did you find their livers?"

"No, the killer must have taken them."

Pete's freckled nose wrinkled. "Or eaten them."

"Now, there's a cheery thought." Detective Jackson led Pete along the path that would soon run under Liliana's tree. "This is the second family we've found dead out here in the Carver Creek campgrounds in the last two weeks. The other family's deaths were called in as natural causes. We thought they'd eaten the wrong mushrooms or something. There weren't any slash marks on their backs like this."

"How were they like this family then, other than dying nearby?"

"At first, we thought they were entirely different too. They camped remotely enough that animals got to the bodies before the forensic team. We thought coyotes and vultures had eaten some of their internal organs, but one kid didn't have a mark on him. Only when the medical examiner autopsied the family did they discover his liver was missing. All of them were."

Pete stopped Detective Jackson on the path directly under the hickory tree with a hand on her elbow, so she looked back at him where he followed her on the path. "Wait, his liver was missing, but there wasn't a mark on his torso?"

"Exactly. Once we eliminated scavenger animal bites, we found slash marks on two of the victims, but none on the other two. Slash marks or not, they were all missing their livers. That's why I needed someone who specializes in 'biological anomalies.'" She made air quotes with her grim expression lightening. "You didn't think I'd call you and Giovanni in for a Normal killer who was knifing campers, did you?"

A woman with a long gray braid, wearing a buckskin dress that hung loosely on her old bones, stood in the path as they rounded the grove of trees. Dark eyes were all but buried in the wrinkles of her face, and her lips were smeared with red as if she'd been eating berries. She held her right hand in her left, clasped in front of her.

The spider-kin tensed. The path ahead of her friends had been clear when she looked a few seconds ago. Silently, she popped her arm blades out, the slightly curved blades that hid in almost invisible pockets in her forearms. They locked at right angles to her wrists, like a scythe, but with the razor-sharp edge outward.

The old woman spoke. "*Osiyo. Ani yunwiya hiwonihi?*"

"Hey there, where y'at?" Detective Jackson's tone was gentle, to avoid scaring the woman away.

The woman stood and stared at them for a moment, confused.

"What's your name?" Detective Jackson asked.

"U'tlun'ta." She waited for a moment, as if expecting them to recognize the name. The old woman snorted. "More whites."

The petite policewoman, with skin nearly as black as her hair, grinned. "Can't say I've ever been called that before."

"Where did the Ani' Yun'wiya, the real people go?" the woman asked in careful, halting English.

"Maybe she was with the family that died," Detective Jackson said softly to Pete.

"Maybe her mind isn't all there," he murmured back. Pete took a stride forward past Detective Jackson, standing a little hunched so he wasn't as tall and his broad shoulders didn't look as massive. "Were you with the family that camped back there?" He pointed back down the trail where he and Detective Jackson came from.

The old woman smiled, showing red-stained teeth. "I was." She cackled briefly as if remembering something funny. "Little girl wandered off in the trees. I found her." She walked toward Pete and Detective Jackson. "Are you friends?"

Liliana dropped from the trees into a defensive crouch, her arm blades high, with Pete and Detective Jackson both acting startled at her back. "They are here to catch the one who killed the little girl and her family. The one I am looking at."

The old woman stopped coming closer. She threw back her head and cackled in amusement. "So someone knows me then." She shrugged. "*Agi yosi. Hawiya awaduli.*" Then she switched to a song that sounded like a lullaby, with a broad shark's smile on her red stained mouth. "*Uwe la na tsiku Su sa sai,*" she sang sweetly in that strange language as she came closer. "*Su sa sai.*" She struck as fast as a rattlesnake, her right hand shooting forward, a long wicked-looking pointed flint knife where the first two fingers should be.

Lilana deflected the strike with her arm blade. "We are not such easy prey as an innocent child and her unsuspecting family."

The woman cackled. "You whites are all easy prey." She ducked into the woods, vanishing in the underbrush faster than a leaping deer.

Liliana looked over her shoulder at Pete and Detective Jackson, both staring with mouths wide. She flicked her wrists to fold her arm blades back into the hidden pockets in the flesh of her forearms.

Pete asked, "Did that old lady just try to stab you with something, Lilly?"

"With her right hand," Liliana answered. "She is the one who killed the families. Shoot her in the right hand."

Detective Jackson shook her head. "Shoot first is generally not how I do things, not even if the suspect is an Other. But if she just tried to stab you, I'd call her armed and dangerous. So—" She drew a pistol from a shoulder holster under her jacket.

Liliana smiled at Detective Jackson's Mary Jane shoes with thick soles, good support for running in any terrain despite their shiny surface. "She is always armed and very dangerous and now she is after your forensics team and Sergeant Giovanni."

The popcorn sound of pistols firing sent Pete and the detective running back down the path toward the campsite of the dead family.

The spider kin ran off the path, through the woods, rather than following them.

This part of the park was crisscrossed with hiking trails. She found another trail and ran down it toward the campsite from a different angle. She leapt over her own ankle height trip line and ducked slightly under the one just over her head.

The ground shook with a steady beat and a sound like boulders crashing together.

Liliana raced to reach the clearing by the lake where the young couple and their ten-year-old daughter had chosen to set up their tent.

A woman, still wearing a buckskin dress that now hugged her tightly and fell barely to her thighs rather than to the ground, took up half the clearing with her wide stance. She stood taller than some of the pines now. Her skin and hair were both charcoal gray streaked with lighter gray, and pale brown, the distinctive pattern of flint rock. Every step she took crushed stone beneath her giant form and made the earth tremble more than her mass warranted. She was a native Sidhe mineral Fae, the first Liliana had seen.

With her left hand around his waist, she lifted a struggling man wearing paper covers over his shoes, rubber gloves, and a black jacket that read POLICE in big yellow letters on the back. He shot her in the face with a pistol, and she cackled like it tickled.

On the ground, Sergeant Giovanni, Detective Jackson, and Pete all fired their handguns at the giant. Lieutenant Runningwolf, standing on two solid legs, fired an automatic rifle in her direction.

U'tlun'ta held up the man in her hand toward them like a shield, so Runningwolf pulled his muzzle up and stopped firing to avoid hitting him. U'tlun'ta kept her right hand hidden behind him, even though the bullets didn't seem to bother her.

From where Liliana stood, a few feet to the side and behind the giant's left knee, Liliana could see the long flint spear head on the woman's right hand where her index finger should be.

U'tlun'ta stabbed the man she held, slicing him open, and pulling out his liver, impaled on the point of the spearhead attached to her hand.

His eyes were wide in horror as he watched the giant woman pop his liver in her mouth.

She bit down on it. Blood filled her mouth and dripped off her chin, while the forensics man, gasping his last breaths, watched her eat his vital organ.

Liliana couldn't help him. No one could.

She drew out a line of silk and picked up a pebble, encasing the stone in silk on one end. She stepped back behind a tree trunk, waiting for the right moment.

In the clearing, Sergeant Giovanni, Pete, Detective Jackson, and Lieutenant Runningwolf surrounded the giant, shooting her from multiple angles. The bullets made tiny chips in her flint hard skin, no bigger than a mosquito bite.

U'tlun'ta laughed, holding the body of their now dead teammate in one hand, with the other behind it.

Pete tried hurling a few knives at the stone giant. When that had no effect, he reached to the back of his neck and pulled the machete from the sheath on his back.

Liliana shook her head. That would not help. If he had his sword maybe, but the machete would do nothing. He needed to shoot her in the right hand like Liliana told him.

With a whooped war cry, Pete hacked futilely at a stone thigh, the steel blade clanging *chang chang* against unyielding stone.

The giant shifted her grip on the dead body, so she held him by one leg, then swung the body at Pete and the others in a sweeping arc, ending with the body flying toward Runningwolf, who had an automatic weapon. His bullets had made more mosquito bite pockmarks in her stone skin than any other.

He dodged the flying body in a motion almost too fast to see, but it put him farther away from the stone giant.

Only Sergeant Giovani was left standing within reach. The tall, athletic MP aimed carefully and shot the giant in the eye.

U'tlun'ta blinked, rubbed her matt black eye with her left hand, the one that didn't have a long sharp spearhead attached. Then she reached for Sergeant Giovanni with that spear.

The military police sergeant ducked the giant's reaching bladed hand, turned, and ran for all she was worth straight up the trail Liliana hid beside.

U'tlun'ta's feet smashed everything in her path like massive boulders as she gave chase.

Sergeant Giovanni zoomed past, her long legs churning like an Olympic sprinter, but U'tlun'ta's longer stride rapidly closed the distance between them. Giovanni looked behind her just as the giant's hand reached forward...and the soldier tripped on one of Liliana's silk lines.

As Sergeant Giovanni tucked with the fall in a skilled reflex roll that Liliana admired, the giant's hand grabbed air where she had just been a moment before.

Liliana threw her pebble-weighted silk line around one massive flint ankle. It whirled around and around like a tether ball on a pole.

Sergeant Giovani rolled to her feet and kept right on running up the path.

The stone giant took one more running stride and encountered the line Liliana strung that was just over the petite spider-kin's head. Sergeant Giovanni had rolled under it. For U'tlun'ta, it hit just below her knee. The giant, who had already been leaning forward to grab at her prey, overbalanced forward and tried to bring her other foot up to compensate.

Liliana ran back around the tree trunk and dug in her ballet slippered heels, dropped her butt to the ground, held tight, and let the giant's foot drag her like a weighted ball on a chain. Her silk cord pulled around the tree, stripping bark as it went. Liliana's shoulder slammed into the trunk.

Unable to get her other foot out fast enough, the giant fell, knocking over mature pines, their trunks snapping like rifle shots. Her body shook the earth when it hit like a landslide.

Pete ran up the trail, Detective Jackson and Lieutenant Runningwolf on his heels. "Lilly!" he shouted.

She looked up at him, exasperated from where she lay beside the tree in the dirt of the trail, her skirt, leotard, and slippers all probably ruined. Her skin beneath the cloth scraped raw and burning. "Shoot her right hand."

"That makes no sense," Pete said.

The stocky soldier beside him said, "I'd swear that was U'tlun'ta, Spearfinger. But she's not supposed to be in this area. I heard she was killed in the mountains near Asheville a century ago."

"She is immortal." Liliana sat up and leaned backward just as the giant started to get up. The tree bent and cracked, but didn't break, so the giant tripped and fell again. "Killing her just makes her sleep in stone for a century and awake somewhere else."

"Lucky us." The big soldier grunted and looked at Pete. "We'll have to shoot her in the right hand. It's Spearfinger's only weakness."

Pete looked at him sharply. "How do you know that?"

Lieutenant Runningwolf shrugged. "I dated an Eastern Cherokee girl in college. We traded stories."

Lilly gave Pete a pointed look, too annoyed to be embarrassed to meet his eyes.

Pete's pale, freckled face, already red from exertion, might have turned a shade of brighter pink. "Sorry, Lilly." He sheathed the useless machete and pulled his pistol back out of the shoulder holster.

The giant yanked her foot hard. The tree snapped like a twig. The line Liliana held flung the little spider seer into the forest.

She released the silk cord and twisted her body to miss a tree trunk. She landed on her feet and rolled to take the momentum... right into a bunch of winterberry bushes.

Ow.

She groaned. New bruises and scrapes added their own shrill voices to the cacophony of pain her abraded skin and bruised shoulder were already singing.

As she extricated herself slowly from the bush's branches, which tangled in her clothes and hair, she heard an angry inhuman bellow mixed with the grating sound of stone on stone. Three rapid pistol shots cracked and the *brrrat* of a burst of machine gun fire. Then...nothing.

There was nothing more utterly silent than a forest with all the beasts hunkered down from fear. Not so much as a bird or a cricket chirped for a long moment.

Then somewhere a jay made its namesake call, and the normal forest sounds slowly returned.

Liliana worked her way around tree trunks and through brush to get back to her friends.

Pete, Detective Jackson, and Lieutenant Runningwolf now stood over the body of an elderly Native American woman in the path. Sergeant Giovanni had made her escape and was some ways farther down the path, unaware of her pursuer's temporary death.

Blood pulsed from the old woman's right hand into a broad pool, then sank into the earth. As Liliana got to them, the enraged, wrinkled face faded to dull, striated charcoal gray. The body solidified into a vaguely human-shaped outcropping of flint that ran across the path.

Liliana let her shoulders sag. Pain saturated her bones. It would be nice if she didn't have to fight any more giants until these new injuries healed. She took a deep breath and the adrenaline of battle started to fade.

Her friends had all survived the day.

She waved at Pete and Detective Jackson. "Please, do not put me in any reports. I was not here officially."

Pete nodded.

Detective Jackson looked quizzical. "Why is that?"

Pete answered for her, "Apparently her kind is almost extinct because people in power keep putting bounties on their heads. Most of her family and the rest of her race has been wiped out. She's afraid for her life if her refusal to die like all the other spider seers becomes known by the higher ups."

Liliana smiled. It was nearly word for word what she'd told him. Nice to know Pete was listening, at least sometimes.

"I see." Detective Jackson nodded gravely. "I never saw you."

"Genocide." Lieutenant Runningwolf's face made an angry scowl that looked like he'd like to shoot someone again. "You won't be in my report."

Liliana smiled at the broad soldier's belt. He'd just met her and immediately agreed to protect her most important secret. She liked him already. "Thank you all."

She took a different path so she could avoid the forensics team. That path brought her to a different clearing where she stopped and looked around. Something about what she was seeing seemed familiar. The pine on the other side of the clearing grew slightly slanted, and the oak looked like a friend the pine leaned on when drunk.

There should be a bush and a patch of flowers beside them.

In winter?

Liliana walked into the clearing, moving over to the right until her view changed, and she could see the branches of a dormant bush. The ground beneath was nearly white with blooming wild hellebores. Some people called them Christmas roses. She'd loved discovering the lovely, little, white native flowers that bloomed in winter when she moved to North Carolina decades ago.

Now, she sat down on a low mound of disturbed earth with broad flat stones on top and started to cry.

CHAPTER 3

WINTER ROSES

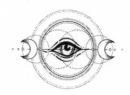

For an unknown, miserable time, Liliana sat on the flat rock holding her legs tucked up against her body, her human eyes leaking tears in steady streams down her cheeks. Internally, she upbraided herself for focusing so hard on her friends that she completely ignored the warning her fourth eyes had given her.

This day was not the victory she'd thought. It was a truly epic failure.

Detective Jackson's voice drifted down a hiking path that passed through this clearing. "I just want to check around the area, make sure there isn't anything we missed," the detective said to someone behind her.

"You want me to come with?" the voice of Lieutenant Runningwolf asked. "Watch your back?"

"I'm good," Detective Jackson said. "I seriously doubt there's more than one liver-eating giant stone woman wandering around these woods."

Liliana wiped her face off with a tattered sleeve. This entire outfit would have to go in the recycler when she got home, anyway.

"Hey, Madame Anna. I didn't know you were still here." Detective Jackson came around to her front, smiling, and got a good look at the spider seer's face. "Oh, hey now. What's the matter?"

Despite the dirt getting on her nice suit, Detective Jackson sat down beside Liliana on another flat rock.

"I couldn't save them," Liliana said. "I saw their deaths. I knew it would happen. I should have saved them."

"The family with the little girl?"

Liliana shook her head. "No, I couldn't have saved them or your Forensics man. I'm sorry. I didn't foresee their deaths."

Detective Jackson's lips went tight, and her chin trembled once.

Liliana wondered if the detective would cry.

Detective Jackson took a breath, and her jaw tightened. "Greg was a pain in the ass, but he was one of ours. I'm not looking forward to telling his wife."

They sat in silence for a few seconds, grieving for people they didn't like or even know.

Detective Jackson broke the silence. "I've been wondering what led you to be out in the same woods as a murderous stone giant on the same day as us."

"I saw that Sergeant Giovanni and you, or maybe Pete, would die here today."

"But you can see that we're not dead." Detective Jackson's voice took on a careful note, like she didn't want to upset Liliana. "So your visions are maybe not as accurate as you thought?"

"No. My vision was right."

"Did you see us dying later then?"

"I got between you and Spearfinger, drew her attack to me, and deflected it. If I had not been there—" Liliana shrugged.

Beside her, Detective Jackson's face became thoughtful, considering. "We thought she was harmless. If you hadn't been there, I wouldn't have been wary enough. She'd have stabbed me."

"Or Pete. Even Celtic wolves cannot survive without their livers. Or maybe she would have killed both of you if he tried to protect you but wasn't fast enough. Fate is determined by the choices we make."

"In that case, thanks for saving my life." Detective Jackson appeared to be thinking fiercely. "Let me get this straight. So, you saw us die, but we didn't die because you changed that?"

"Right."

"But you couldn't save Greg or the family because you didn't see it before it happened."

"Yes, I'm sorry."

Detective Jackson waved that away. "No one expects even a fortune teller to be omniscient. Does what you do to prevent something ever end up being what caused your vision? Like a self-fulfilling prophecy?"

Liliana shook her head. "What I see comes to pass if I do nothing about it. It is fated. If I alter the conditions that led to that situation, the visions change. Fate changes. Sometimes, all I have to do is decide to do something different and the vision will change. Sometimes, my actions make things worse, but always different. My visions show the future created by the sum of all likely choices, and sometimes I can see visions of even the results of unlikely choices. Fate is a collection of every choice made within the Green."

"That's kind of profound." Detective Jackson grinned at her, and it made Liliana smile a little as she stared at the scrape on her knee.

"So if you saw someone, say, about to be murdered, and told me, then could I save them?" Detective Jackson asked. "Or are you the only one who can change your visions?"

"If someone were about to be murdered, and I called a police detective who showed up and arrested the murderer before he fired the shot, then yes, that would change the victim's fate."

"But if I show up before a murderer killed anyone, I can't arrest them."

"You would have to find another way to save the person, but you would know they needed saving before you arrived, so you would do whatever was necessary."

"You know that's every homicide detective's dream, right?"

Liliana wiped her first eyes again and glanced at Detective Jackson. "It is?" The detective's face was almost exactly even with hers. The petite spider seer did not often encounter people her own size.

"Catching the murderer after some poor unlucky shmo is dead has always felt like a consolation prize to me. I couldn't protect them, but at least their murderer won't get away with it." She made a rude noise. "Better than nothing, but I wish I had your visions instead." Her face took on a glow of zeal. "That would be amazing, being able to save lives like that."

"It is always better to save a life than to avenge it," Liliana said softly. She remembered her first mother, her father, and her second mother all saying the same words to her at different points in her life. "And foreknowledge is often the weapon you need for that. It is good, except when you fail." It started the tears flowing again to know that she had failed so completely. "I had the knowledge, but they are still dead."

"Hey, hey." Detective Jackson started to reach for her, then pulled back. "Is it okay if I put my arm around you?"

Liliana nodded and leaned toward the detective, who put a gentle arm around Liliana's shoulders. She appreciated that the detective asked first. She didn't like being touched by people without her permission or unexpectedly.

"So you saved our lives," Detective Jackson said, squeezing Liliana's shoulder "You couldn't save the family or Greg because you didn't see it coming. Sounds like you did the best you could, right?"

Liliana shook her head. "I had another vision a few weeks ago. Two women in military uniforms. I didn't know them. They were shot in the back of the head. I didn't see by who. I couldn't even tell when because it was the oddest vision, shaded as if their deaths were happening in the future, but also like they had already died in the past."

"Not much to go on." Detective Jackson asked, "Did you see where it happened, or will happen?"

"It just looked like a clearing in the woods. It could have been anywhere, but..." Liliana pointed at the trees she recognized, "I saw that leaning pine and the oak with the bush over the ground patch covered in blooming wild hellebores."

The detective looked where Liliana pointed. "Yeah, that's pretty distinctive. So where are these two women now? Do you know?"

Liliana pointed at the ground. "Here."

Detective Jackson stood.

Liliana stood as well.

They both looked back at the mound of disturbed earth with large flat rocks on top that they'd been sitting on.

It was a grave.

CHAPTER 4

THE SPIDER AND THE PRINCE

LILIANA SAT FAR AWAY FROM THE GRAVES IN THE THICK branches of an old post oak growing by a glade where everyone parked their cars. She was cradled comfortably in some of the tree's stately limbs while the forensic team exhumed and studied the bodies she'd found, looking for clues.

Her clothes were still dirty and torn since she'd battled a giant in them, but she'd used the forensics teams sanitary wipes to get the dirt out of her scrapes and clean her face. As she sat in the tree, she carefully worked the broken twigs and leaves out of her thick curls. The rough bark of the old tree held her safely far away from the staring eyes of strangers.

Detective Jackson had convinced her that the day was still a victory, saying that she, for one, was very glad that Liliana had come. "As one of the people still breathing because of your intervention, I think you should count the lives you saved, not the ones you couldn't save."

Liliana still wished she'd done more for the military women. She'd been wracking her brain trying to figure out what course of action she *should* have taken, even though it wouldn't change anything now. Rationally, she knew that. But it didn't stop her thoughts from going round and round in circles.

Her fourth eyes watched the exhumation of the bodies as they were photographed and carefully moved. Sergeant Giovanni identified the bodies by the names stitched on their uniforms as two women who had been reported AWOL the day before when they didn't show up for duty. Their faces were half missing due to the exit wounds.

Pete told Detective Jackson, "They've only been dead a day or so based on the lack of decomposition, which matches Zoe's information. And it looks like they were standing in the hole when they were shot. Or the person who shot them was as tall as U'tlun'ta."

When Liliana first saw a vision of them, they'd been alive. It made no sense that the vision had been shaded both as if they were not yet dead and as if they were already dead. It could not be both. Clearly, they had not yet been dead two weeks ago.

What am I missing?

Her fourth eyes showed her a car pulling into the makeshift parking lot her big oak tree shaded. The spider-kin blinked several eyes as she saw someone she had not expected to see: Pete and Sergeant Giovanni's colonel, the Fae prince.

She didn't see him in the future. She saw him right then with her human eyes as well as her fourth eyes. He parked his urban camouflage-painted car with big knobby all-terrain tires between Pete's green van and Detective Jackson's unmarked sedan.

The military vehicle and the military man who drove it captured her full attention, as he always seemed to.

A part of her froze instinctively against the tree trunk. She was in the arms of an ancient oak and surrounded by miles of life in every direction. If the Sidhe prince blamed her for the deaths of his soldiers, he could kill her easily here. She would likely be no more effective at defending herself than the Wolfhound he killed by bringing a tree to life in Janice Willoughby's yard a few weeks before.

She didn't think he would make this tree eat her, though. Not with people here like Pete and Sergeant Giovanni, who both thought he was a Normal. A bunch of actual Normals were here as well, the whole excavation and forensics team, minus poor Greg. The Fae colonel certainly wouldn't use magic where they might see.

Every Other went to extreme lengths to hide their existence from the Normals who vastly outnumbered them. It was the one thing they all agreed on.

I need to talk to him.

Despite the inherent danger in a Sidhe knowing of Liliana's existence, and the fact that he might have been trying to kill her the first time they met, she had greatly enjoyed her previous encounters with the Colonel. They had spoken to each other twice, and she'd seen the tall, muscular, dark hair and skinned man in several visions. Yet, they had never officially met.

She'd side-stepped all the social rules and common courtesy before, due to the necessities of survival. Among other omissions, she hadn't given him her name or asked him for his. Those were essential social requirements.

Perhaps the Colonel would be willing to help her get on base so she could save Doctor Nudd on the day he would be murdered. Her direct help had the highest probability of saving Doctor Nudd's life, and the Colonel had full base access.

He had no reason to help her, though.

Last time, she had deliberately not bargained with him in the Fae way. He seemed to appreciate the exception, but this time, she really did need a favor and she had something valuable to trade. She'd seen a possibility that he would be hit by a car and die earlier on the day Doctor Nudd would. The probability of his death that day was low, but the probability of serious injury was high.

Also, his reaction to her request for help might guide her in her eventual decision as to whether or not to save him from the far more likely death that waited for him in less than a year. To decide whether to save him from his fate, she needed to know what sort of man he was.

A formal introduction was in order.

Liliana dropped from her perch, landing near the passenger side window of his car just as it rolled to a stop. The car was so tall that she stood on tiptoe so her whole face would be in the window when he looked. The interior of the big vehicle showed a lot of bare metal. It didn't look very comfortable.

She tapped lightly on the window, but the uniformed colonel still made a startled jolt.

His hand dropped to the butt of a gun in a holster on his belt. It was brand new. He hadn't had a sidearm the last time she saw him. It was probably Siobhan's handiwork, and therefore likely to be effective against a wide variety of Others. Liliana suspected that was why he'd been in the parking lot of Emerald Arms the day Pete accused her of murder.

The spider-kin carefully showed the colonel her empty hands.

He unsnapped the pistol holster with a flick of his thumb and pushed a button with his other hand that caused the window in front of her to roll down.

"It's you," he said, a single eyebrow high. "What is it this time?" His tone sounded curious, not alarmed.

"I wish to speak to you, to offer proper courtesy to a Sidhe of your lineage, and to ask for a favor."

Now, both dark eyebrows went up in surprise. The line of his mouth firmed. Not so much a loss of joy like last time, as a switch from casual to deadly serious. "What do you offer in exchange for a favor from me?" His voice was just as deep and smooth as she remembered, like a perfectly tuned cello, and utterly devoid of emotion.

A favor from any Fae held great value. From a Sidhe prince, a favor could be priceless. There were few things valuable enough to offer in trade. "Your life is in danger. There is a small probability that you will die within a few weeks or a higher probability you will receive grave injury on that day a few weeks from now. There is also a near certainty that you will die in less than a year." Liliana focused on his square chin, the closest she could comfortably come to eye contact. "If you grant my favor, I will make certain you survive the first danger uninjured."

His face didn't seem to change much, yet she sensed a shift in attitude, from something like surprise to something else. If she had to guess, she would say he was intrigued.

"Are you threatening me?" the prince asked her, voice sounding unconcerned, almost bored, but his hand tensed on the butt of the gun.

Liliana blinked her human eyes, the only ones currently open. That was not at all what she had meant to communicate. "I am doing the opposite of threatening. I am offering aid."

His hand relaxed. "I don't believe I need aid."

"Disbelief will not protect you from danger. May I sit with you in your car for a time and talk?" She made as if to reach for the car door handle but waited first for permission.

The prince's eyes flicked to the left for a fraction of a second, toward the trail that led to the excavation of the grave and the people investigating the bodies.

Liliana told him, "They will not be ready to give you information for another fifteen minutes."

One dark eyebrow went back up, wrinkling scar tissue on the right side of the prince's forehead. The scar ran along his temple to the ruined skin where his right ear once was. Above that, a white streak marked his military-buzzed, woolly black hair. He took the gun out of the holster and set it in his lap with one hand. The other hand pushed a button to unlock the door in front of Liliana.

He nodded an invitation.

Ignoring the strangely designed handgun with the short, wide barrel in the Fae prince's hand, the spider-kin joined him in the car. She had to climb up a tall step, nearly as high as the big tires, grabbing onto a handle on the inside of the doorframe. "Thank you, your highness."

Once seated, she wasn't sure what to say next. She fiddled with the ends of her tattered skirt, running the fabric between her fingers and watching the movement to try for calm. Social interactions were always challenging, and if she messed this one up, they might have to try to kill each other.

"Why are you here?" the prince asked.

"I helped to defeat Spearfinger and told them where to find the soldiers' bodies." Liliana felt herself relax now that she had a good question to answer. "Detective Jackson asked me not to leave until they were done exhuming the bodies, in case they had more questions for me."

To keep track of time, Liliana watched the digital satellite clock display on the dashboard. She didn't want to make the colonel late for Pete's report. It took her a moment to locate the clock among the tactical maps and side and rear camera images in the broad display surface that stretched from one side of the vehicle to the other. A bunch of knobs and tactile controls unlike anything in other cars ran in a line under the displays.

The second eyes on her temples peered through the curtain of her dark hair. They let her watch him beside her and the clock in front of her at the same time.

His expression was thoughtful as his gaze traveled over her tattered, dirty clothes and the scrapes on her skin. "You saved my life the last time we met. Your actions anticipated exactly what would happen, and you knew precisely when to act. You also seemed to know the answers to questions I intended to ask the Wolfhound." He studied her. "How?"

Liliana shrugged. "I know it the same way I know that you will be in danger in a few weeks and will die in less than a year. I know it the same way I know that you are not just an Army colonel, but also the son of Titania, the Queen of Air and Darkness. I am a spider seer."

"I've heard of your kind. Spider seers are supposed to be powerful and dangerous. But I thought they were extinct." The focus of his eyes sharpened on her face like the hot point of a laser sight. "I never thought I'd meet one."

"Now you have met a spider seer. I am Liliana." She nodded a sketchy bow in his direction. Letting a Sidhe know that her kind still existed was a huge risk, but she had to decide if she would save this man's life. His fate was closely tangled with Pete's, and with all her friends in one way or another. They respected and admired him and would mourn his loss. Her few brief encounters with him were enough to hint that given time, his life might become precious to her as well.

He nodded a half bow back to her from his seat. "I am honored." Old world manners surprised her from a new world soldier. "A spider seer could be a powerful ally."

"Or a powerful enemy, your highness. I must decide which to be. I need to know more about you to make that decision." Since he knew what she was and no one else could see, Liliana opened her third eyes, like tiny black teardrops under her first eyes, turned, and looked into his soul.

On the surface was order, complex and unrelentingly strong, like blue ice crystals in interlocking geometric snowflake patterns made of frozen steel girders. The red hue of passion tinted the crystalline order, but the strong desire was for civilized structure and fairness. Very unusual in a Fae, especially unseelie. Cold, ruthless logic ruled over that carefully controlled icy surface.

The spider seer looked deeper. There was far more to this man. What lay beneath the first layer was far from cold. His center burned with the black and orange charcoal fire of bitterness and rage.

So much anger. Why?

She opened her fourth eyes, too, and saw glimpses of his past. The proud prince on his knees in his youth, hands bound behind him, blood running from his nose, rage in his burning eyes. Another image of him face-down in the dirt, trembling with weakness, fighting to stand, with clothes tattered, while mocking laughter rang in his ears. This powerful prince had been humiliated. Someone had treated him like dirt beneath their shoes.

The many layers of his self were interwoven with an iron gray determination to never be weak again, to never be anyone's victim again. He craved power and respect like other men craved love and comfort.

A will of iron.

But she'd already known that. Her view into his heart told her a great deal about who this man was, but not why he watched over her favorite red wolf. His conscious mind, where his thoughts lay, was like the surface of a lake, reflecting distorted images back at her. *Shielded with magic.*

She sank so deep into contemplating her third eyes' view of this fascinating, multi-layered soul that she failed to notice as he moved his strange gun until the barrel touched her forehead, right between her fourth set of eyes.

"Get out of my head," he ordered her.

Liliana gave a slight nod of respect, all she could manage with the position of the gun barrel, and closed all but her human eyes. "As you wish." She waited for him to lower the gun, but he hesitated, still pointing it at her.

Her heart beat faster.

She couldn't know for certain now that she couldn't see his heart and mind, but he seemed to be considering whether to kill her right there and then. Nearby witnesses be damned.

This Fae prince feared loss of control and powerlessness above all. Liliana knew this now. In learning his deepest fear, she had unintentionally shown that she had the power to know his secrets. He could not stop her from seeing into him. She frightened him.

A frightened soldier with a gun pointed at your head was a very dangerous thing.

The spider-kin carefully did not move. She wasn't good with words, but they were the only thing that could save her life right now. "I am not the one who threatens your life, prince of shadows," she reminded him softly, hoping it was the right thing to say. "I seek a reason to save it."

His lips tightened, showing none of his fear, only a hint of the deep well of anger that lived at his center. "Don't do that again."

"You only have to ask. The gun is not necessary."

He set the gun back in his lap. "My apologies."

The spider-kin let out a quiet breath and some of the tension left her shoulders. "Accepted." Lately, people trying to kill her was a normal part of becoming acquainted.

Liliana glanced at the clock. "Pete and Detective Jackson will be ready to discuss the case with you in four minutes. You should go." She pointed toward the path through the trees.

She opened the passenger door and got out.

"You saw... me," the prince said as he got out on his side. "Who I am inside, I mean." Instead of looking at her, he looked at the hood of the car between them. His gaze avoided her face, like she tended to do. Then he squared his broad shoulders and faced her, chin lifted. "Are we enemies now?" he asked, shoulders tense, gun still in hand.

The Fae colonel was complex. There was coldness, anger, violence, ruthlessness, and pain inside him. But there was also a strong personal code of honor and a powerful desire for order and fairness. He was both a very good man and a very bad man. She had never met anyone so layered and balanced between darkness and light. "I have still not decided."

This Fae prince was not cheerful and dazzlingly bright like her favorite red wolf, but his soul held its own compelling intricate beauty that was just as dazzling. Where Pete was a bright azalea flower blooming in the sunshine, this prince was a velvet black night sky studded with sparkling stars. She would not wish to see such beauty destroyed. "May I ask your name, your highness?"

He looked at her now, brows drawn together in puzzlement. "You know what I am, my parentage, and the day I'll die, but you don't know my name?"

Liliana shrugged. "I only see what I'm looking for, and I didn't look for your name."

His lips curved in the barest shadow of a smile. He shook his head in amazement, then gave her what she asked for. "Alexander Bennet."

As she rounded the car, he took her fingers in his hand, a warm tingle accompanying the touch. She wondered if it was some sort of Sidhe power. She'd never been touched by a Sidhe before.

He bowed over her hand, and pressed his lips to her knuckles, his dark eyes never wavering from her face. He must find her attractive. His lips were warm and soft on her fingers, and the tingle went straight to more sensitive parts.

Her breath came faster, and she fought the urge to touch his face.

Oh. Probably not a Sidhe power then.

Chemistry.

She gave him a formal curtsy, completing a social ritual from long ago and far away, while looking at the eagle pin on his collar. Hopefully, the warm flush in her cheeks didn't show under her dark skin tone. She walked beside the tall prince past the trunk of the old oak that had sheltered her.

The top of her head barely reached the top of his chest. Standing beside him made her feel very small. He was not as tall as Doctor Nudd but taller than anyone else she knew. "If you will get me into Fort Liberty unnoticed a few weeks from now, I will make certain that you survive that day unharmed. Without my help, you will almost certainly be badly injured, if not outright killed."

"That's the favor you're bargaining for?" he asked, surprised. "With saving my life as the payment, you could bargain for almost anything. Why do you want on base?"

"Someone will die on Fort Liberty that day. I do not want it to be my friends." Detective Jackson and several others walked toward them from the other side of a broad open field, around the mound of excavated earth and through the knee-high grass. It was a fair distance, but they were closing it.

"If one of my people is in danger, I'll protect them." Colonel Alexander Bennet put a hand on her arm, stopping their progress in the shade of a pine tree, partially hidden from the people walking towards them. "Tell me who it is."

Liliana tilted her head sideways, looking carefully away from the prince and the Normals on the other side of the field before she opened her fourth eyes. "That won't work. They will die anyway, and then your life will be in even greater danger."

His jaw tightened and he dropped his hand. "I'm not going to smuggle someone I don't know onto my base."

Liliana sighed and nodded. Once he made a decision, she knew there was no point in arguing. The soul she'd seen was not one to bend easily to another's will.

So she had her answer. It was not the one she'd hoped for.

There was one other answer she really wanted from him, though. "Now that you know why your sister sent the Wolfhound, do you intend to order more Wolfhounds to come here to kill Pete and take his sword for yourself?" She held little hope that he would answer her since she had nothing left to bargain with. Neither Fae nor royalty were generally inclined toward straight answers for free.

A muscle in his jaw jumped, and his nostrils flared. "No."

She looked up directly at his face for a moment, surprised. That was certainly a straight answer. "May I look to see if you speak the truth?"

"I told you to stay out of my head."

She raised her hands to placate him. "I will see only what you think and feel in the moment. I will look for nothing more. You have my word." She always swore precise oaths. He seemed like a man who would understand what that meant.

He looked at her for a few seconds, then he nodded permission. "You've been honest with me so far, and you did save my life."

She opened her third eyes and looked only at his surface thoughts. The mirror shield of magical defense was lifted from them briefly.

He repeated his answer. "I absolutely have not ever and will not ever order Wolfhounds to kill Pete."

It was truth, very vehement truth. The white truth was colored with a blue-tinged possessive fondness for the Celtic wolf-kin and a lot of fire-orange anger.

They were out of time. There were too many people coming toward them. Liliana needed to get away.

She closed her third eyes to let the prince know that she no longer looked at his unshielded thoughts. "I will speak with you again some other time, Colonel Bennet." She bowed her head, giving him the respect he was due. What she'd learned of him told her that he deserved it.

"Wait." He put a hand on her shoulder and squeezed hard enough to hold her there. "Are more Wolfhounds coming to kill Pete? When?"

She looked at his big hand squeezing into her slender shoulder hard enough to bruise. He was too strong for her to break the grip. She could cut off his arm, but that seemed like an overreaction, and it would require her to reveal her arm blades where Normals might see.

The prince let go and held his hand up in apology.

"In less than a year," she told him. "Death will come for Pete shortly before it comes for you."

"Dammit! I knew Aurore wouldn't be stopped that easily." His hands clenched into fists, and he slammed the pistol back in its holster.

She didn't need her other eyes now to see that Colonel Alexander Bennet would never order anyone to kill her favorite red wolf. He really did like Pete, more than he craved whatever power he might gain from Pete's unique sword.

Liliana cocked her head to one side and opened her fourth eyes to look into Pete's future, looking carefully away from the prince and the Normals. Pete's death was still there, still with only a bit of flickering, a little uncertain, but unchanged.

The prince knowing ahead of time that the Wolfhounds were coming made no difference. "You cannot stop it this time," she told him.

He started to ask her something else but turned to look the other way as Detective Jackson raised a hand to wave at him.

Detective Jackson, Pete, Lieutenant Runningwolf, and four strangers from the military and civilian forensics teams were all getting far too close. Behind them, Sergeant Giovanni and a civilian police officer each unrolled an end of wide yellow tape with words on it, "Police Line, Do Not Cross."

Too many people. And strangers.

Liliana ducked behind the trunk of the big pine and scrambled up into its branches.

The prince turned back to where she had been as if to speak to her again, but Liliana was far above everyone's heads by then, well-hidden behind clouds of pine needles. He looked around quickly, then turned back to speak to Detective Jackson.

They would speak again another time, Liliana was certain.

CHAPTER 5

TEA WITH A GOBLIN

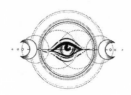

DOCTOR NUDD'S DEATH WAS THE NEXT ONE LILIANA HAD foreseen. If she could save this one life, she could possibly break the chain of death and save her entire community. But she hadn't yet found a path to safety for Doctor Nudd.

Three days later, after her new scrapes and bruises had time to heal, Liliana stepped out of a self-driving cab into the drizzle. After the last appointment of her workday, she'd caught a ride to the pine woods on the northern edge of Fayetteville just east of Fort Liberty, She held Doctor Nudd's bulky red and brown sweater, carefully cleaned. As the cab drove away, she slowly walked up the natural stone sidewalk.

Doctor Nudd's log-sided house with the grass on the roof seemed to get bigger and scarier as she approached. Her feet dragged anchors behind them with each step.

The spider-kin couldn't remember the last time she had gone to someone else's house. She cocked her head to the side, thinking. It had been nearly two decades ago when she attended the succession of the king of the lion-kin pride of North Carolina, Andrew Periclum. Then her brothers, Jason and Petros, and their grown children had been with her.

Somewhere along the path of her life, she had settled so deeply into her quiet routine that she had become a recluse, talking to no one but her clients. She hadn't intended to hide from the world, but sometimes the world could be overwhelming.

Hiding had been easy.

As she walked closer, the wooden door loomed impossibly large and imposing. The carving on it showed a pointy-eared elf dancing in a forest while playing a panpipe and wearing curly-toed shoes. It was excellent workmanship, but highly inaccurate.

Knocking on that elaborately carved wooden door would not be easy.

She pulled the teal velvet cape she wore more tightly around her shoulders in the chill of the light rain. If she left right now, she could advise her clients whom Doctor Nudd might have saved, or whom Pete might have protected, to move away. If she went home, closed her eyes, and kept on hiding, she would probably live longer.

While Liliana hesitated on Doctor Nudd's doorstep, music caught her ear. The cheery romp of Beethoven's "Kreutzer Sonata" for violin, accompanied in a strangely complementary way by an electric bass guitar. The music made her smile. She closed all her eyes and listened for several minutes, swaying on her ballet-slippered feet. Instead of cold, she felt uplifted. She wanted to fling off her cloak and dance in the wet grass.

Holding the thick, soft sweater to her nose, she inhaled the scent of the goblin healer, oak wood and hops with a faint tinge of rubbing alcohol. She had promised the kind goblin making such beautiful music that she would return his sweater.

Liliana kept her promises, even when it wasn't easy.

She knocked on the big wooden door.

The lovely music stopped immediately. Liliana peeked with her fourth eyes and saw the tall, gangly goblin doctor setting the violin down, while Siobhan set aside a modified electric guitar, small enough for her to play comfortably in her not-quite-four-foot, red-headed human form.

The sprite had a look of fear on her face. She scrambled to Doctor Nudd's bedroom and under his giant bed.

Liliana cocked her head. The sprite feared being found making music with the goblin. Since they were of opposing courts, Liliana had assumed that Doctor Nudd and Siobhan were merely acquaintances under an uneasy truce when she first saw them together. The jam session she interrupted indicated a deeper relationship.

On the other side of the ocean, such a friendship would have gotten them both executed by their respective rulers or lynched by their own people. Even on this continent, seelie and unseelie Fae rarely mixed. There were some who would enforce that separation with violence if necessary.

Liliana's urge to turn around and go home increased as she saw the goblin walk toward his front door. She focused on the texture of the hand-knitted sweater in her hands and held her ground, even while every instinct urged her to flee. She looked down at the intricate patterns of the weave and tried not to let her nervousness drive her away from the ally who needed her, even if he didn't know that he did.

Doctor Nudd opened the door.

Quickly, Liliana closed all but her human eyes.

His curly brown hair brushed the top of the oversized door frame. He looked out, then down at Liliana's five-foot-two-inch form. "Oh, um, hello?" he said, like it was a question.

She'd never heard "Hello" stated as a question. She scrambled for the proper social response but came up with nothing.

Looking into him might have made this less awkward by giving her clues to the meaning behind his words, but she kept all but her two human eyes firmly closed. Her six spider eyes disturbed many people. Liliana did not want Doctor Nudd to be disturbed by her.

She thrust the sweater into the startled goblin's hands. "I washed the blood out of it. I told you I would give it back."

"Ah, excellent. Thank you!" Doctor Nudd said with obviously genuine feeling. "I never thought I'd see this again."

"I keep my promises," Liliana stated in her usual flat inflection.

"Oh, of course, I didn't intend to imply that you wouldn't,

um..." The goblin seemed flustered and uncomfortable. She must have said something wrong, but she wasn't sure what offense he could have taken to a plain statement of her level of honesty.

Liliana sighed with frustration. She should just go home. She was terrible at socializing. But she remembered the image she had seen of the goblin healer dying, a sword thrust through his chest, and the raw grief on Pete's face when he was minutes too late to save his dear friend. They would both die if she gave into fear now.

The goblin stood in the doorway uncertainly. "Um, well, thank you again. For bringing the sweater back. It really means a lot to me."

"You're welcome." If someone said thank you, she was supposed to say, "You're welcome." But she should add something to keep the conversation going. "You gave it to me because I was cold."

"Indeed. I did," Nudd said and stopped talking again.

Liliana fiddled with the hem of her cape, running it through her fingers and watching the movement of the bright fabric. She wanted to go into the goblin's house, but she hadn't been invited. She knew the rule, but the goblin doctor seemed to have forgotten it.

That was okay. She understood. She forgot that rule, too, sometimes.

"Was there something else?" Nudd asked.

That was close enough. "Yes." She walked under the goblin's long arm and into his house.

He closed the door behind her.

She was supposed to say something complimentary. "I like your music. It makes me want to dance in the grass."

"Um, thank you, I suppose."

"I didn't, though. Maybe next time." Liliana walked into his large, open living room. "I don't like beer much, but I like tea." She had seen that when Pete came to visit, the goblin always offered him beer. She sat down on his overstuffed brocade couch near the crackling fire.

"Well, just make yourself at home then," Doctor Nudd said. His lips twisted funny, and his voice implied that the words didn't quite mean what they said.

Liliana ignored the possible double meaning and took the words at face value. "Thank you. I like your house." She closed her human eyes and listened to the deep-toned tick, tock, tick of his big antique grandfather clock while he went into the kitchen and made her tea.

His kitchen was on the far end of his rambling house. Liliana explored with her fourth eyes without leaving the couch. Like Liliana, he had a section of his home dedicated to his work. Some rooms were like guest bedrooms, but with narrow, high beds. All empty now. His kitchen, on the other side of that part of the house, even had an autoclave, the big metal dishwasher that sterilized surgical instruments.

Every window in his house was open. It let in the cool, damp night air, so it almost felt like a sheltered glen in the woods, rather than a house.

His living room was relatively small and filled with a big, overstuffed armchair that looked like it was at least a century old and the worn, but comfortable couch she sat on. The couch and chair surrounded the fireplace, burning merrily to chase away the chill. The ticking clock calmed her nerves, and the crackling warmth seeped into her bones, until she almost felt relaxed. Doctor Nudd's home was a good place, filled with peace and music and the welcoming scent of a hearth fire.

"I already know you are here, Siobhan. You don't have to hide," Liliana commented to the empty room, loud enough that the sprite should hear even in the next room under the goblin's bed. She closed her fourth eyes so as not to disturb the sprite.

Siobhan popped her head up from behind the couch. "Wasn't hiding." She came around to face Liliana, hands in fists on her hips. "You going to tell anyone I was here?"

Liliana shrugged. "My father taught me it was dishonorable to tell other people's secrets."

"Who else's secrets do you know?"

Considering, Liliana tilted her head. She could not think of any answer to that which would not, in itself, give away other people's secrets. "That is not a question I will answer."

Siobhan grinned at her. "Good answer, spider girl."

When Doctor Nudd came back and handed her a cup of tea, Liliana said, "I like your clock a lot." The tea smelled of cinnamon and orange peel, two of her favorite flavors. And it was properly brewed from hot water and tea leaves, not produced instantly from powder or syrup like some things that passed for tea these days.

"You like old clocks?" Siobhan asked.

"I love clocks." Liliana smiled.

"Clocks are class." Siobhan ran a hand down the carved and polished wood of the old clock, watching the brass pendulum swing back and forth for a moment. "All that intricate interwoven delicate machinery, just to keep track of time. Normals invent the most amazing things."

"I like the sounds they make," Liliana said. "And they always know the time. I don't always know when I am."

"I think I almost understood that." The flower sprite perched on the arm of the couch to Liliana's right. Sitting up there put Siobhan's eye level even with Doctor Nudd's as he settled in the big armchair by the fire to sip his own tea.

"You must remove the needle from the badger." It was one of the turning points in the goblin's future that Liliana had seen.

"And you're speaking nonsense again, spider girl," Siobhan said. "Is that a requirement for fortune-tellers?"

"Not you." Liliana ignored the irrelevant question. "Doctor Nudd. You must remove the needle from the badger."

Doctor Nudd's broad face scrunched at the bushy brows. "I'm afraid that makes no more sense to me than it does to Siobhan."

"You don't have to understand," Liliana told him. "Just remember." She was afraid he wouldn't remember her advice at the crucial moment. She needed him to remember.

The spider-kin reached across to the big armchair and touched the back of his hand. "You gave me your sweater because I was cold and took glass out of my skin. I don't want you to die. Remember to remove the needle from the badger." For a moment, she looked at the goblin, forcing herself to meet his big, wrinkled, oak-brown eyes with her dark blue first eyes.

Doctor Nudd's deeply tanned face managed to look flushed. He looked down at her small hand on his gnarled fingers. "I shall certainly do my best, madam."

Liliana nodded and patted his hand, smiling. He would remember. It would buy him time. She would take care of the rest.

She sipped her tea contentedly, enjoying the warm peace of the gentle goblin's home. This social visiting thing wasn't so hard, really. She could do this.

Doctor Nudd sipped his tea too.

The ticking of the clock and the crackling of the fire seemed strangely loud in the silence.

Siobhan downed half a bottle of dark beer in a few gulps. "Well, as much of a barrel of monkeys as this is, I'm going to dash."

Liliana looked around the room, confused. She didn't see any monkeys.

Doctor Nudd's eyes widened. "Oh no, no. No need to rush off so soon."

"Well, you know me. Places to be, toys to tinker with." Her nimble feet got her to the door before Nudd could lever his large frame from the armchair. She didn't take the bass guitar with her, so Liliana assumed she would return another time and play music with Doctor Nudd again. Maybe they would let her come next time they played and dance in the grass.

"You really don't need to leave me here." A note of something urgent entered Doctor Nudd's voice. "You should stay for a while." The note turned to pleading.

Doctor Nudd must really like Siobhan. Liliana wondered if they were lovers. It was forbidden, of course, for two Fae from opposing courts to have a relationship that close, but it still happened sometimes.

Siobhan left with a mischievous grin and a blown kiss. "Best of

luck to you, Doc." To Liliana she gave a cheery wave. "*Slán go fóill,*
spider girl."

"Goodbye," Liliana said as social rules required.

The tall, gangly goblin closed the door behind the flower sprite
slowly and made his way back to his armchair.

They sat in silence while Liliana sipped her tea.

The goblin tapped his fingers on the arm of his chair.

He crossed his legs.

He uncrossed his legs and crossed them the other way.

His foot tapped in the air.

"So was there something else you wanted to tell me?" Doctor
Nudd asked when her tea was gone and she set the cup down.

Liliana considered the question. In addition to sharing one's
home space and sharing food or drink, friendship building usually
involved some sort of sharing of personal information. She could
find out pretty much anything she wanted to know about the
goblin simply by opening her eyes and looking, but he knew almost
nothing about her.

"My father was lion-kin," she said. "He told me about fighting
as a gladiator in Rome many centuries ago. But he was an animal
tamer in the circus when I was little."

"Oh?" the goblin said, perking up a bit. "Rome's heyday was
before my time, actually. I've never heard of a beast-kin living that
long."

"They don't, normally. But my father did."

The clock ticked pleasantly. Liliana enjoyed looking into the
flickering light of the fire. She wished her little house had a fireplace.

Doctor Nudd tapped his fingers on his armchair again. "So
you're a pride-child then, one of Andrew's subjects."

She nodded. "I swore fealty to Andrew Periclum when he
became king after his father died." Andrew Periclum's father and his
father's father had been pride-kings in North Carolina. It was
expected that the only son would take his father's place. "It was a
surprise to everyone when the old king died. Andrew Periclum was
barely twenty, very young for a pride-king."

Doctor Nudd grunted agreement. "Not many people die in car wrecks anymore."

Liliana remembered her brother Jason telling her that no one would challenge Andrew Periclum when they had arrived in the broad glade outside of Fayetteville where the succession was to be held. A tree stump had been carved generations ago into the shape of a throne that looked like it simply grew there.

Back then, she had looked at the skinny twenty-year-old who was to be the new King of Lions. "That's good," Liliana told her elderly brother. "Because he does not look very formidable."

Petros chuckled beside her. "Neither do you."

Challenging the new king was generally only done when the old king had no sons, so combat was necessary to determine who would succeed the dead king. The only other reason for a challenge was if the eldest son, the obvious heir, was considered unfit to rule for some reason.

One sturdy, determined-looking lion-kin in work boots and a plaid shirt had called challenge, much to the surprise of all the other lion-kin, hyena-kin, and other pride related people who had come to witness the succession. The man shifted to demi-lion form and roared, "I am the King of Lions and my word is law!"

A few members of the pride backed the challenger by transforming and roaring agreement that he was the king, not Andrew Periclum.

Since there were now two claimants to the throne with pride members backing both, this meant that the ritual combat had to be fought to determine the new ruler.

There was a whoop of excitement from the crowd, who had come to witness the succession. Several pickups and one large moving van all carried sturdy steel triangles of various sizes and power tools. Liliana had wondered why until that moment. Many hands lifted the triangles out and brought them to the center of the glade.

A muscular giant of a man with night dark skin directed the many volunteers with a booming voice and an air of respected authority. She heard those building the traditional arena call him Mr. Magoro.

Andrew Periclum simply stood by the carved throne, waiting as if bored by it all.

Liliana wondered why Mr. Magoro wasn't going to be the new king, as he seemed far more suited to leading, but he hadn't challenged Andrew Periclum.

Within an hour, the triangles were put together like a three-dimensional puzzle into a huge dome. Once completed, the dome of triangles resembled some playground equipment Liliana had seen, but was far larger, over twenty-feet tall in the center. Two smaller domes were attached to it on opposite ends. Melee weapons were placed in the smaller domes–swords, maces, axes, knives, and shields.

The people who came to witness the succession now jostled for the best vantage point around the dome, an air of excitement like the audience at a sporting event taking over the crowd.

Liliana melted into the space between her two elderly, but far larger brothers, never comfortable in a crowd of strangers, but even less so as they got rowdier and noisier and pushier.

Jason and Petros bracketed Liliana, each putting an arm around her, sheltering her with their big bodies as they had since they were children together. Their wives and grown children surrounded them in a clump.

Surrounded by family instead of strangers, she opened her fourth eyes and watched the succession combat from the safe space. Her fourth vision was unimpeded by the many large lion-kin bodies between her petite form and the dome.

Andrew Periclum entered one of the domes through a hinged doorway, and the stocky man who had challenged him entered the other. One person accompanied each of them. The man with the slender, young Periclum was huge, with claw scars across his face. He also looked far more formidable than the skinny, barely grown boy, even though they were about the same age.

Each opponent stripped off their shirts and shoes and chose

weapons from those available. Andrew Periclum chose a sword and shield. His opponent chose a two-handed axe. The big man with the scarred face hooked the shield onto Andrew Periclum's arm, nodded, and opened a hinged section of triangles leading into the big central dome.

The stocky challenger and Andrew Periclum faced each other. Both transformed to big, demi-lion form, with full, shaggy manes falling to the middle of their backs, and fur covering their bare torsos. Andrew Periclum's mane was scraggly and short. It would probably fill in more when he got older.

They roared, big fangs bared at each other.

The crowd all transformed and roared with them. Liliana felt her brothers shift to demi-lion on either side of her, becoming far larger and furrier. She was used to them doing that, though, so it didn't disturb her. The sound of so many lions all roaring in one place was gut rumbling and nearly deafening, but oddly comfortable. Lions were family.

When that sound died down, the big man with the scarred face who had helped arm Andrew Periclum shouted, "Begin."

The crowd shouted a loud whoop and growls of excitement in anticipation of a good fight.

The stocky lion-kin swung his big axe at Andrew Periclum, who ducked neatly, and brought his sword up to the other man's neck in a single motion.

Stocky lion-kin's eyes widened. He dropped his axe and raised his hands.

The crowd suddenly got quiet as everyone there held their breaths.

Liliana gasped in surprise. At only twenty, Andrew Periclum was a far more formidable fighter than Liliana would have thought.

"I yield," the stocky challenger said.

Andrew Periclum chuckled darkly. "You shouldn't have challenged me in the first place." And he slashed across the other lion-kin's throat.

Blood spurted, but Andrew Periclum side-stepped so it didn't splatter on him.

As the lion-kin who called challenge dropped to his knees, clutching his throat, blood spurting between his fingers, Andrew Periclum turned to the crowd, and roared, "I am the King of Lions and my word is law! Any who say otherwise must face me here!"

After a moment, the crowd erupted in roars and shouts of, "Andrew Periclum is the King of Lions!"

Liliana's brothers did not join in the shouting. She could feel the rumble in their big furry bodies as they both growled low.

Simon of Nemea, their father, had always taught that it was the height of dishonor to kill after someone had yielded.

Slowly, in the center of the dome, the stocky lion-kin shifted back to human form as he died. A man in worn blue jeans, bare torso stained with blood lay on the grass in the glade.

Her third eyes were also open, and Liliana had rarely seen so much disgust and anger in her brothers' auras.

Jason and Petros were both too old to call challenge themselves, but she knew they considered it.

Jason had no sons, only daughters, and it was not traditional for lionesses to lead the pride.

Petros's son stood watching beside his father. He was already middle-aged but had married late in life. He shook his head when his father looked at him. His arm went around the waist of his pregnant wife. His aura showed a mix of protectiveness and fear.

Petros nodded understanding. His son would not risk death in the dome if death meant abandoning his wife and unborn child.

Liliana blinked, bringing herself back to Doctor Nudd's home with the crackling fire and the sonorously ticking grandfather clock.

Liliana, her brothers, and their families had all sworn fealty to Andrew Periclum on that day about two decades past, even though they didn't like him, or truly want to serve him. He was the new king of the lion-kin pride of North Carolina, and by extension, leader of all beast-kin in the area. Both her brothers moved away from Fayetteville after that, taking their families with them. They didn't want to be where the new king would call on them for service to the pride. They feared what he might order them to do.

Andrew Periclum had never asked for any service from Liliana, for which she was glad. She didn't even know if the pride-king remembered that she was the daughter of a lion, and therefore a pride-child.

Since Liliana had already sunk roots in Fayetteville, her business thriving, her clients counting on her to advise them, her brothers had left Liliana behind. That was the last time she saw them. They had already been old men. She hadn't watched them after they moved to the coast, not wanting to see her strong brothers wither and die of old age. Lion-kin did not live for thousands of years without the venom of a spider-kin to keep them young.

Liliana's sister, Isabella, her brother-in-law, Rizke, and niece, Ariadne, were all the family she had left now, and they were far away in Europe somewhere.

Doctor Nudd cleared his throat. "I'd heard that spider seers tend to choose mates from the fiercer Other species."

Liliana nodded, pulled from her melancholy thoughts. She was pleased to find someone who was familiar with her kind. "Yes. My grandfather was an oak goblin, like you. Only from my first mother's stories, he was more inclined toward bashing things than tending wounds."

"Right, well, the goblin reputation is not entirely un-deserved." He fell silent for a moment. His brown eyes widened suddenly. "You're not looking for a mate, are you?"

The unexpected question startled Liliana. "I have nearly four years before my first blood fire time, when I will be old enough to bond with a life mate."

The goblin seemed to relax. "Ah, all right, then."

"But I would like to choose one before my blood-fire time. Once that happens, hormones and chance will choose, and I would rather make a choice for myself."

Doctor Nudd swallowed, and set his teacup down a bit roughly, endangering the delicate china. The goblin doctor understood some of the nature of spider seers. So he was probably familiar with the blood-fire time. She could understand why discussion of such out-of-control behavior would bother anyone.

For the second—or was it third—time that month, Liliana found herself thinking about when she would be biologically compelled to find a mate and produce a child. She hadn't thought about it much in the last half century, but now, she felt the pressure of it coming up fast. Her first mother hadn't had the chance to teach her much about the blood-fire time, except that the overwhelming urges would be temporary. She must simply choose a male and ride it out. The more she thought about it, the more Liliana found the whole idea of being compelled to mate disturbing.

She had no one she wished to make a child with. She wanted to carefully choose the father of her daughter, as her mother had. Solifu loved and kept the man who fathered her children, and also the woman they both loved. She used her venom to extend their lives as long as her own. Liliana's three parents had been happy together for centuries. Liliana wanted that, not the random forced choices of a biological imperative.

She stood up suddenly, no longer comfortable in the goblin's home. She had returned his sweater and given him the necessary message. They had shared tea and conversation and gotten to know each other better. "I'm going home now."

The goblin followed her to the door. "Well, then. Thanks for stopping by, unexpectedly, in the middle of music practice, for no apparent reason, without even calling."

"You're welcome." Liliana paused at the door, thinking about what he said. "Would you prefer that I call first next time?"

"That would be a nice change." The goblin's voice seemed to almost always have that hint of mixed meanings. Again, she chose to accept his words at face value. Without looking into the goblin's mind, she had no idea what else he might mean.

Liliana nodded. "Okay." The cab pulled up just at that moment to pick her up. She had looked ahead before she left home, seen when she would leave on the goblin's grandfather clock, and told the self-driving car exactly when to come back for her.

Doctor Nudd shook his head as she walked away, muttering, "Red wolves, flower sprites, spider seers... What's next, dancing bears?" as he closed the door behind her.

Well, that had gone very well, Liliana thought, pleased with herself for overcoming her fear. She opened her fourth eyes and looked ahead. It hadn't been enough. The goblin would still die in a few weeks. She had only bought him a few extra moments of life on the crucial day.

It was a beginning, but Liliana had more work to do.

CHAPTER 6

HOW TO TRAIN YOUR WOLF

A FEW DAYS LATER, ON A SATURDAY MORNING, LILIANA
sat in the branch of a tree in a part of the pine forest not far from
Doctor Nudd's house, near Smith Lake. The cold snap had let up
and the February day promised to be warm and clear.

The Green glowed deeply here. She could see with her third eyes
the rivers of energy flowing like healthy blood vessels in the skin of
the earth. She listened to the wind in the leaves, the birds singing,
and the occasional drip of water from the early morning dew. The
air smelled of leaf mold, growing things, and the first hints of spring
to come.

The world had changed a great deal in the last three decades of
Liliana's life. She remembered even this relatively rural area as
having the stench of pollution in the air and living under the
constant threat of the super-storms of global climate change. The
green rivers of light her third eyes saw in the ground had once been
faded and sluggish.

Liliana was amazed at how a few technological breakthroughs
had changed the face of the world and brought back the waning
power sleeping in the earth. Modern batteries were lightweight,
made from readily available materials, and capable of storing and

putting out power reliably. Modern solar cells could charge those batteries faster than the power could be consumed.

In the mid-teens of the new century, the US Navy had needed a cheaper and more reliable way to get fuel for their ships. They found a way to make hydrocarbon fuel out of seawater in a carbon neutral process. Solar energy could also split seawater into unlimited supplies of hydrogen and oxygen that burned clean. This made even internal combustion engines produce clean water, not unwholesome poisons. The use of hydrocarbons had all but ceased. In the mid-thirties, the global warming trend completely reversed. The earth had begun to heal.

And more than heal. To thrive.

Liliana took deep breaths and reveled in the beauty that this new age brought with it. She spent far too much of her time inside her house. She promised herself that she would come to this place again. Many times.

She felt a little guilty for liking this new resurgence of nature.

Many powerful people once depended on the scarcity of hydrocarbon-based fuels for their livelihood. Political upheaval had been violent, both in the United States and in countries abroad.

In the States, some rejoiced in the new, cleaner, cheaper sources of power, but those powerful, wealthy few who depended on the status quo were not so happy. They paid enough to fuel propaganda that swayed many to their side. The country had nearly erupted in civil war.

The frequent need for martial law to quell riots led to the power of the military to act within US borders being significantly increased by a frightened Congress.

In the end, there was no way that the energy companies could put the genie of cheap, limitless power back in the bottle. Many of the mighty had fallen. New leaders had risen to take their places.

Wars still raged around the world, the echoes and aftershocks of economic upheaval. American soldiers still bled in many of those wars. And their families looked to Liliana for reassurance and guidance.

For Others across the globe, the changes were a breath of oxygen for people who had been suffocating. Gaia's favored children felt their ancient strength returning.

Liliana would not have been entirely surprised if the tree she crouched in, which had an unusually bright green soul, one day yawned and stretched and regained a human form it hadn't worn since the industrial revolution.

Young beast-kin like Pete didn't even know what it was like not to have comfortable ease with their three natural forms. Liliana remembered years and places when her brothers couldn't reach full lion form at all, and only attained demi-lion form when the moon phase was favorable.

Liliana wondered what other effects the resurgence of nature's energy would have on the world.

After maybe an hour of sitting silently in the tree, thinking, Liliana heard two familiar men's voices and a high-pitched feminine voice slowly coming toward her. They were deep in a friendly debate over the merits of various types of knives. For three people moving through wilderness, making no attempt to be stealthy, the wolf-kin and the two Fae made surprisingly little sound aside from their conversation.

Doctor Nudd and Pete strolled into the clearing near the spider-kin. Siobhan walked at their heels.

"This looks like a good place to practice," Doctor Nudd said. "No one around for miles." He hung a large grapefruit as a target from a branch of the tree that Liliana sat in. Behind it, he draped a quilted packing blanket that should catch stray blades that missed the fruit, so they wouldn't get lost in the leaf mold.

Siobhan hung back a bit, turning her head from side to side with a furrow between her carrot-red eyebrows. Flower sprites tended to be deeply in touch with the plants around them. Liliana didn't fit the normal pattern of this forest. The flower sprite looked up finally, saw Liliana, and opened her mouth to say something.

Liliana put a finger to her lips to ask for silence.

Siobhan grinned and shifted form, becoming far smaller. Bright purple and fuchsia double wings like a dragonfly's sprouted from her back, emerging through slits in her bolero-style leather jacket. As she shrank, the jacket stayed the same, looking more like a trench coat to the tiny woman with the hot pink mohawk. She fluttered up into a large branch of a nearby tree with a good view, then settled in to watch the show.

"You're not going to practice, Siobhan?" Pete asked.

"I'm good. You go ahead." She popped a small pistol apart into her lap, produced a tiny set of tools from somewhere, and did incomprehensible things to the gun.

Pete practiced throwing knives at the swinging fruit from various distances and angles, standing with feet wide apart, taking his time to aim carefully. Liliana recognized it as a good stance— steady, stable, and highly unlikely to be attainable in the middle of an actual fight. Pete's marksmanship with throwing knives was excellent. Doctor Nudd pushed the hanging grapefruit to make it swing wildly so it became a more difficult target. Pete's accuracy still required them to replace the fruit several times.

Pete seemed fairly pleased with his ability. Liliana shook her head in frustration. That would not do.

Pete removed a few dead lower branches with his old sword. He wielded it with raw force and a lack of finesse that would have been more appropriate with an axe.

If that was sword practice, then Liliana was a boggart.

He followed with some friendly wrestling with Doctor Nudd, both in their human forms. Pete's strength and speed, even as a human, were impressive, but his form was awful. Liliana's father would never have tolerated such sloppy footwork. Pete was off balance more than he was on.

The goblin was worse. Doctor Nudd depended entirely on his strength and long reach. He fought like a barroom brawler: all offense and zero finesse.

Liliana's father taught her toe-to-toe fighting with various weapons and without. He made certain that his daughter became an expert in the grappling dance of balance against balance of Greek wrestling, and the brutal but flashy weapon styles of the gladiator. Her first mother taught her the fighting style of the spider seer. Set traps, wait patiently, entangle the enemy. Her second mother taught her the fighting style of the jaguar-kin. Stalk silently, ambush from above, kill the enemy with lightning-quick merciless attacks.

Liliana used all three styles, depending on the situation. For the most part, it was her first mother's style, the fighting style of the spider seer, that she had used to defeat Pete. The sacrifice wrestling throw she'd used to defeat Stella was one that her father taught her.

Now that she no longer feared the red wolf, she realized that she could have defeated Pete in any of her fighting styles.

Any of the three beast-kin who raised Liliana would have destroyed this red wolf without breaking a sweat. Far too soon, he would face four Wolfhounds, all strong and properly trained. Even if he had magic to pierce their protections, Pete didn't stand a chance. Not without allies, and not without training.

When she felt like she'd seen enough, and the two men were starting to look a little winded from their inadequate practice, she dropped onto Doctor Nudd's shoulders from above. He fell on his face in the soft grass with a yelp of surprise.

Pete reacted instantly, drawing one of the throwing knives he had been practicing with and striking down at her.

Liliana blocked his arm with hers, set her foot behind his ankle, and shoved.

The red wolf landed on his butt in the grass and leaves next to the goblin. Her arm blade was at his throat before he could even begin to fight.

His bright blue eyes widened nearly as much as they had in her vision of his death. "Lilly! Where the hell did you come from?"

Liliana felt an odd sort of thrill in her belly that the red wolf showed only surprise, no sign of fear, even though her blade was at his throat. He really did trust her. Was it a good thing or a bad thing that the Celtic wolf-kin no longer feared her in the least? She really wasn't sure. But it wouldn't help him survive. Pete needed a little fear.

He tried to get up, but she added a knee to his belly to shove him down on his back and cause him discomfort. "Hit the fruit now."

He blinked at her in confusion for a moment, then his eyes flickered to the swinging target.

She nodded.

Pete hurled the knife awkwardly, at an uncomfortable angle. He missed. The heavy blanket backdrop kept the knife from getting lost on the forest floor.

"This isn't exactly an ideal throwing position," Pete said.

"When enemies come for you, any position you can hit them from is ideal."

From the tree above them, a small choking sound became increasingly louder. At that moment, Siobhan erupted in full-fledged guffaws. She pointed at them and squealed with laughter. She laughed so hard tears ran down her cheeks, and Liliana worried she might fall out of the tree.

Liliana sighed and flicked her wrist to sheath her arm blade back in the natural pocket in her forearm. "You are not helping," she told the little sprite. "Pete and Doctor Nudd must take training more seriously."

Siobhan choked out, "Your faces!" before dissolving in giggles again.

The spider-kin turned back to Pete. "You must practice throwing from your back, while running, while falling, while off balance, while surprised. Your enemies will not wait while you take careful aim."

She extended her hand to the wolf. Pete took it, and she helped him to his feet.

Doctor Nudd got to his feet on his own and brushed leaves off his thick sweater.

"Why are you here, Lilly?" Pete asked.

"I will train you."

"Pardon me, madam." Doctor Nudd said, "I am training this young wolf." The tall goblin glared down at her small, slender form, probably intending to be intimidating. The goblin undoubtedly felt she was impinging on his territory. That, she understood. Lion-kin like her father and brothers tended to react the same.

In a single motion, Liliana stepped forward diagonally past the goblin's position, placed her hip behind his thigh, and pushed with her arm across his chest, the main force on the opposite shoulder. He flipped over her hip and landed on his back in the grass again. Tall men were much easier to throw than short men or women, because of the higher center of balance.

Doctor Nudd snarled and shifted to his Fae form so that the teeth he showed her were yellow and pointed. His skin hardened and roughened like the bark of the trees around them. His lanky body filled out with lumpy muscles the density of oak hardwood and added a foot to his already impressive height. He leapt to his feet far faster than seemed possible based on the wrinkles around his eyes.

Liliana snapped her arm blades out. Each blade was a foot of curved, slender stone-hard bone that angled outward from her wrists in a position useful for both defense and offense, with an outer edge sharp enough to part falling silk.

The oak goblin swallowed. He brought his legs together and twisted his hips away from her instinctively. Then he put his hands up and shifted back to smoother human skin. "Perhaps we could simply discuss this."

"No talking. Defend yourself." Liliana slashed at him, deliberately missing.

Doctor Nudd flinched, arms up defensively. "I was under the impression that we had come to an accommodation of sorts, that we might even be considered friends."

She slashed at him again. "You must learn to fight properly so you will not die."

Doctor Nudd looked up at Siobhan, who had stopped laughing. "A little help, perhaps?"

The sprite shrugged. She waved her reassembled pistol. "What do you want me to do, shoot her?"

"Whoa, whoa, no one is shooting anyone here," Pete said. "Lilly, what the hell are you doing?"

Liliana slashed at Doctor Nudd again. "Stop me, Celtic wolf. I could kill your friend."

Pete grabbed her shoulder.

Liliana twirled, freeing herself from his half-hearted grip, and punched him in the face, hard enough to rock him back on his heels. He would not fight until she made him take her seriously.

Doctor Nudd tried to grab her while she faced Pete.

She sheathed one arm blade so she wouldn't accidentally stab the goblin, stepped back between his legs, hooked his ankle, and elbowed him hard in the belly, just below the ribs. At the same time, she threw her weight back. Her second mother, Ixchel, taught her that when people grabbed you, they expected you to try evasion, not to attack them.

The goblin's breath whooshed out, and he fell backward, but one of his long arms hooked Liliana's belly as he fell, pulling her over with him.

She flipped her legs up and over her head as she went backward, landing her full body weight hard on the goblin's chest just as his back hit the ground. He wheezed, coughed, and his grip loosened.

Her roll continued into a back somersault onto her feet. While the goblin made choking sounds, she leapt over him toward the red wolf, one blade out front as if she intended to decapitate him. She swung backhanded at Pete. On her blades, the sharp edge was outward. If she hit him, it would be with the blunt inner edge.

Pete ducked. His reaction had been lightning quick. If she had struck in earnest, Pete would still have his head.

Very good, she thought, but it wasn't enough. He didn't follow up the defense with an attack. He still held back.

She spun, snapped out her other blade, and struck him hard with the blunt edge in the back, about shoulder-blade level.

Pete grunted in pain. "Damn it, Lilly. This isn't funny."

"No one is laughing. Fight, or you will bleed."

"I don't want to hurt you."

"I am not hurt. You are." She considered for a moment, head tilted sideways. The red wolf refused to fight her. He didn't fear her, nor would he hurt her, even to save himself pain, as long as he believed she intended him no real harm. She swung a few backhanded blows at him while she wracked her brain for a way to motivate the compassionate wolf-kin. He dodged her attacks but didn't follow with any of his own. This would not do.

The way he practiced with Doctor Nudd was more like the rough play of boys. Pete needed to bring his skills to a higher level to survive. But with her, he refused to strike. He would only defend.

A solution was as simple as understanding Pete. He had to see blood—and not his own. Pete defended those he cared about far more fiercely than he defended himself.

Liliana leapt straight up into the tree sheltering Siobhan. The spider-kin caught a branch and swung. With a half-hearted kick to the wolf's face to keep him at a distance, she flipped up onto the branch.

She came nose to barrel with Siobhan's miniaturized pistol.

"Don't even think about it," the flower sprite said. "I'm not part of your little game."

Liliana nodded respect to the tiny warrior, still wearing her fuchsia pink petal-winged, demi-plant form that stood less than two feet even on tiptoe. Of all the people in the red wolf's sphere of influence, Siobhan had the best chance of survival.

Doctor Nudd would have to be the target then. Liliana leapt off the branch and landed next to Doctor Nudd.

The goblin had just gotten his breath back and was climbing to his feet, dusting leaves off his clothes.

Liliana cut his forearm, drawing blood, but not doing serious damage to more than his sweater.

"Hey! That hurt!"

"Fight me! Or I'll cut you again deeper. And again, and again." She swung her blade at Doctor Nudd in a serious slash, not a feint.

He leapt backward, farther than a human would have been able to, and snarled. "You will not."

Liliana grinned. Doctor Nudd would fight her now. He wasn't about to let her shed his blood again without a fight.

And neither would Pete.

On the day he would die, Liliana had foreseen Doctor Nudd with a shield in his hand. The goblin hadn't known how to use the shield properly. She'd brought two of her father's old shields, so they should be big enough even for the goblin.

She drove Doctor Nudd back with fast slashes toward the tree where the shields leaned, partially hidden by brush.

Doctor Nudd shifted to his tougher, stronger form and snarled at her through pointed teeth like sharp wooden stakes. He retreated steadily from her attacks, but his dark eyes looked for an opening to strike back.

Liliana smiled and opened her second eyes, so she could see in all directions. Now, things were getting interesting.

Doctor Nudd spared a quick glance for Siobhan, still sitting comfortably in her tree, while he braced his hands on his knees and gulped in air. Sweat dripped from his twiggy hair and ran along the bark of his cheek. "Are you just planning to sit there and watch?"

"My mother didn't raise any idiots. I am not getting in the middle of that." She waved her pistol negligently, clearly enjoying the show. "You boys have fun with your lesson."

Pete sprang at Liliana's back while she was distracted, no doubt intending to tackle her.

Liliana saw him coming with her second eyes. She jumped high and backflipped, tucked in tight, right over Pete's head. When she landed, she shoved him so his forward momentum continued until he ran into Doctor Nudd.

Nudd's bark-covered arms grabbed onto Pete so he didn't fall, then shoved him to one side as Liliana struck with her blade at the wolf's unprotected back.

Liliana nodded approval. Now, they were taking her seriously.

The back of Nudd's heel bumped against one of the shields Liliana left leaning against a tree.

For a moment, she backed off to give the wolf and the goblin a chance to pick up the shields.

Both men panted with exertion. They were tired before she began.

"Why are you doing this?" Pete asked while he strapped the shield to his arm. His voice was gentle, even as he prepared himself for her attack.

"You both must learn to fight better, or you will both die." The words came out flat, as her words always did, but she felt her throat close a little on the last word. She risked a single peek into the future with her fourth eyes, hoping to see something changed. Images of their deaths flashed in her mind again. She flinched.

Once seen, she could never unsee. Even if she changed their paths, even if they survived, the vision of their deaths would still haunt her nightmares.

She swallowed the lump in her throat. The visions she had seen would not happen. The nightmares would not become real. She would not let them. She had to make Pete and Doctor Nudd understand why this was important.

Pete approached her slowly, not as if he intended to attack, more like she was a frightened wild animal he didn't want to scare away.

Her watery human eyes watched a blurred image of his feet. Her domed green chrome second eyes on her temples saw everything in their oddly distorted, color-shifted way.

A hand came up and pushed her thick black hair gently from her face.

She wasn't sure why, but she let Pete do it.

"What did you see, Lilly?" Pete asked her gently.

It was rude not to answer when someone asked a question, but she couldn't form words. She met his gaze for just a moment. Her human eyes were hot and swimming with tears she refused to shed. She would not weep for her friends. These two men that she valued were not dead. And she would not let them be.

When she dropped her gaze back to Pete's boot toes in the grass, he nodded as if she had answered the question. "Okay. What do we need to know?"

Liliana's shoulders loosened tension she hadn't realized was there. Pete would listen. He would learn. Maybe he would live.

"Hold your shields high like this." She mimicked the proper position. "If I aim a blow low, drop your elbow only, keep your fist up. And don't just defend. Each defense of a blow should flow into an attack of your own."

"Attack with what?" Doctor Nudd asked. "The weapons are over there." He pointed a fair distance away, where they had been practicing before she pounced on them.

"Fight with what you have. A shield can be a weapon for offense as well as defense. You also have fists, claws, feet, sticks, trees. Everything is a weapon. When you can, find a way to move the fight to where more effective weapons wait."

Liliana fought them hard, both at once, so they learned to fight as a team, to protect each other's backs. She struck, jumped back, circled, and struck again. She jumped into the trees, leapt down, and struck again, using jaguar-kin tactics. She let them guide her toward Pete's weapons, and practically cheered when Doctor Nudd picked up a mace and swung it full force at her head.

Both men dripped with sweat and panted like overheated dogs.

For just a moment, she let them breathe. She needed a moment to catch her breath as well. But only a moment. "Doctor Nudd, fight as my ally now."

"You must be joking."

Pete wiped sweat off his forehead. "It's getting late, Lilly. I think we've done enough for one day."

"No, not enough. Now, you are tired. Now, you practice for real. Doctor Nudd and I will both try to kill you. Don't let us. Take us down. Use your knives. Use your sword. Do not hold back. We are both tough. As long as your strike is non-lethal, we will heal."

The tall goblin looked at her like she'd lost her mind.

Pete only hesitated for a moment. He looked at Liliana's determined face, then shrugged. He opted to set down the shield, which was not a weapon style he was comfortable with. Instead, he drew a long knife from the back of his belt, drew the ancient sword from its battered sheath, then shifted to his more formidable demi-wolf form, and nodded readiness.

Immediately, Liliana attacked.

Doctor Nudd followed shortly after. The tall goblin fought with ferocity, as if he truly meant to kill the red wolf. He shoved Pete clear off his feet with inhuman strength.

Liliana smiled.

Pete lost his grip on the sword when he fell but sprang to his feet before they could press their advantage. He was not just strong. The wolf defended with surprising agility, accuracy, and speed, even while winded.

His claws shrieked against Doctor Nudd's shield, and his long knife swished over Liliana's head, and clanged against her arm blades. The fight went on for a while until Pete used one of the goblin's long arms as leverage to slam Doctor Nudd into a tree trunk.

A foot sweep from Liliana while Pete was distracted and off balance sent the red wolf falling to the grass.

Even as Pete fell, he twisted and threw his knife at her.

The blade barely scratched Liliana's cheek and embedded itself in the trunk of the tall pine behind her, the same tree where Siobhan perched.

"Oi! Watch that!" Siobhan shouted.

Liliana laughed. "Now, it is enough."

Pete shifted back to human form and grinned at her; white teeth and blue eyes vibrant, shining soul fierce and triumphant.

Stunning.

In all her life, in all her different kinds of sight, she had only ever seen two souls so beautiful—Alexander Bennet's and Pete's. His shine took her breath away. For a long moment, she just stared at him with first, second, and third eyes all at once.

His smile faltered, and his brows drew together in question.

Liliana shook her head to clear it. Pete's heart belonged to another. She was his friend, and she would be a true one. She extended a hand to help him up, then bent to retrieve his sword for him.

In her second vision, the sword still glowed softly like she remembered from when she held it after her first battle with Pete. The hilt conformed to the grip of her small hand, just as well as it had to Pete's large human hand, and even larger, clawed demi-wolf hand. The balance was beyond perfect, as if the sword wanted to become part of her, like her arm blades. The urge to keep the sword hit her again.

She hadn't thought to look into a sword with her third eyes the first time. Weapons generally didn't have thoughts or feelings or souls.

This one did.

It had a presence like a sleeping person, swirling strong-willed gray and emerald green with power. It shone as bright as Pete's soul, but not as pure and good. If it had been a person, she would have judged that person to be strong, instilled with the Green through and through, but neither evil nor good. The sword held a power without conscience. It would be up to the wielder to determine how that power would be used. Her third sight also showed her hidden script in Ogham, running all the way to the tip of the blade in glowing, passionate red.

She touched the blade hesitantly with her fingertips, just above the curved flair of the hilt. It felt like normal steel, but as if it had just been submerged in a body's warmth, or as if it were alive. "Where did this sword come from?"

Pete shrugged. "It's been in my family for generations. It's the only thing my mom left me."

Liliana tilted her head, considering. A weapon that emanated heat passed down for generations in a Celtic wolf pack. This sword must be the reason that Princess Aurore sent an assassin after Pete. Liliana couldn't read Ogham. The ancient Gaelic script was not one of the languages she knew, but its existence along with what she could see, and what Pete told her about its history, was enough to identify the blade.

Freagarthach. The Retaliator. The Sword of Truth and Air that can cut anything, command the winds, and compel truthful answers to any question.

Liliana swallowed. No ordinary sword indeed. A great many people had died trying to find this sword.

In the wrong hands, Freagarthach had the power to wreak untold havoc. She swallowed and considered if she should give in to the sword's urging and take it from Pete. Keep it safe.

In the hands of a Sidhe with a cold heart like Princess Aurore, this sword could devastate entire continents. Liliana shuddered and carefully did not open her fourth eyes to see what would happen if Aurore got her hands on this sword.

Pete had no idea what he possessed. He only knew that it was a good sword and his long dead mother gave it to him. He valued it for those reasons alone. He had no ambition for greater power.

In fact, Liliana's favorite red wolf sought only to protect both humans and Others of all kinds and had an overwhelming aversion to being ordered to kill anyone without good reason. Pete was the best kind of person she could imagine wielding a sword of power. He was, fundamentally, a better person than Liliana.

"No," she said to the sword. "You are Pete's."

Her friends stared at her oddly for talking to a piece of metal, but she was too busy thinking about the ramifications to worry about that now.

It seemed that Pete would not need any sort of extra help to pierce the Wolfhounds' protective spells. No armor, no defensive magic, and no natural resistance to harm could stop Freagarthach. When awakened, Pete could cut through solid stone with that sword.

In Liliana's vision of his death, Pete did not have the sword. She knew how to save him now. She had to ensure that when the time came, he would have it, and he would know how to use it.

She laid the blade across her arm formally, hilt toward Pete.

"This is a sword of great power. Guard it with your life. Learn to wield it with skill, and it will keep you safe."

Pete gave her a sheepish smile as he took it. "My mom was the sword master in the family. She never had the chance to teach me much more than 'the pointy end goes in the enemy.' I just swing it like a bat, and it does the job."

Siobhan hopped off her tree branch and fluttered down until her feet touched the grass. "I can teach you the art of the sword."

Pete and Doctor Nudd looked at the little sprite with surprise and skeptical doubt on both their faces.

Doctor Nudd spoke first. "I was not aware that you were skilled with a blade."

"I thought you only used weapons that went bang," Pete added.

"There are a lot of things you don't know about me, lad." The little sprite winked and twirled her miniature two-shot pistol like a Wild West gunfighter. "Weapons like this didn't exist when I was a sprout. I had to stay alive somehow."

Liliana had considerable sword skill herself and had intended to teach Pete. The spider-kin looked with her third and fourth eyes at the flower sprite.

How skilled are you with a blade?

The images of lightning grace and deadly precision convinced her in moments. "Tomorrow, we will add sword drills to our practice. Siobhan will lead them. I will assist."

Doctor Nudd groaned. "Tomorrow?"

Pete chuckled. "It's going to take us a week to recover from one day of this."

Liliana nodded. "That is why we must do it again tomorrow. Tomorrow you will hurt. You will be sore and tired."

"That's a good thing?" Pete looked at her quizzically.

She considered how to explain it to him. "A smart enemy will exploit weakness and attack when you are most vulnerable. My father taught me that when you are injured and exhausted, that is when you must be most prepared to fight. Imagine if you and I had stopped fighting when we were hurt and tired while facing Lady Daphne and Stella."

Pete's jaws tightened and his lips pressed together. "Good point."

With her third eyes, Liliana watched images flash through Pete's mind like glittery fish in a river. His dead parents' faces first in smiles of approval with back-pats and hugs, then in frowns of disapproval, shaking their heads.

"If your parents had lived, I think they would have taught you themselves." Liliana touched the back of his hand with her fingertips. "Even if you did not choose the path of a mercenary soldier, they would have wanted you to be prepared to defend yourself against those who would count all red wolves as enemies." She had not known his parents, but she was certain this was true.

Pete turned his hand, caught her fingers, and squeezed gently. Gratitude glowed in his aura. "Tomorrow then."

Doctor Nudd groaned. "Some days, I wish I'd never met you, Pete."

Shocked, Liliana looked at the goblin, but her third eyes were still open. She saw he didn't mean what he said. He glowed with pride from Pete's trust in him and excitement. Doctor Nudd looked forward to cutting loose again. As much as he enjoyed his civilized life, it felt good to let his goblin wildness run free now and again.

She looked at Pete to see how he took the apparent insult.

Pete grinned at his goblin friend. He already knew that Doctor Nudd's grumbling was meaningless.

Liliana shook her head, baffled. She would never understand why people said one thing and meant something completely different.

As Siobhan shifted back to her four-foot human form from her tiny demi-plant form, the black leather jacket she wore went from big and roomy to tight and cropped. Even in human form, Siobhan was over a foot shorter than Liliana. The sprite grinned up at her. "Thanks for the show, spider girl." She opened her mouth to say something else, then closed it. She ran her fingers through her short red hair, fiddled with a jacket zipper, and shuffled her feet in the grass.

Liliana's third eyes clued her into what the odd shift from the sprite's usual confident body language indicated. Siobhan wanted to ask her something but was embarrassed. "What is it, tiny warrior?"

"Right, see, I never saw much point in someone as small as me trying to learn unarmed combat, but watching you put Nudd and Pete on their bums a few times makes me rethink that."

Liliana shrugged. "Being large is not required to be fierce, but it certainly helps. I could train you to use what strength you have to best advantage."

Siobhan chuckled. "People have tried to convince me before that I could still fight effectively at my size unarmed. You're the first person who made me believe it. I'll teach the boys which end of a sword to hold if you'll teach me how to fight when I've got no weapons left."

Liliana nodded and smiled brightly at the grass between the sprite's feet. "I would be honored."

The spider seer left her friends in the woods and headed toward home. She was a bit sore and tired herself. It had been a while since she had had such an intense workout. It was fun, in a strange way. Combat practice with live opponents was yet another aspect of her life that the red wolf, the goblin, and the sprite had reminded her to miss. She hadn't even noticed how dull her life had been before they made it so much more interesting.

As she leapt from tree to tree, she opened her fourth eyes and looked ahead to the red wolf's death. The vision of the Wolfhound pack killing Pete was still there, far more solid now that his death at the hands of the widow spiders was no longer a possibility, but it flickered a tiny bit. Pete would, without doubt, be there to protect Janice's husband, Lou. The rabbit-kin mechanic would survive. That was solid with certainty. The red wolf's death was no longer completely certain, though.

Other possible outcomes of that fight flickered in and out of vague possibility. In a few, barely there glimpses, Liliana saw her favorite red wolf holding the ancient Fae sword of power, Freagarthach, standing victorious over the bodies of his enemies. In those few faint flickers of possibility, Doctor Nudd stood bloodied but triumphant at his side.

If they both lived, the paths of everyone in Fayetteville would shift. The people she watched over would live better lives. Many would survive who might have died without protection and healing from the two men.

Liliana smiled in triumph. She was right. Pete needed training, his unique sword, and allies to win.

Unfortunately, the ally in question had a low probability of surviving long enough to help Pete defeat the Wolfhounds.

When she peeked quickly, she saw that Doctor Nudd's death, which was very close in time, was still overwhelmingly likely. The tall goblin would fight with more skill, but it would make little difference. He would still almost certainly die.

Extra training would not be enough to save the goblin healer.

Her smile faded.

She had to do more.

CHAPTER 7

THE MAN WITH THE SILVER ROSE

A WEEK AFTER LILIANA STARTED TRAINING PETE AND Doctor Nudd, she got dressed and prepared for her customers in the morning. She had only two meetings scheduled. One was with Janice Willoughby, her favorite customer, and the other wasn't until late in the afternoon. Liliana cooked mushroom soup with lots of onions, rosemary and butter, but didn't add bacon as she normally would. Janice Willoughby was a vegetarian. Liliana made sure to cook enough so that the rabbit-kin could stay for lunch if she wished.

She had a little time to tend her neglected herb garden. The weeds in the small patch by her back porch had gotten away from her. Oregano, mint, sage, and rosemary were easy to grow here, but she had to work a little harder for thyme. Parsley and cilantro seeds, and tubers from her ginger plants were in her refrigerator until she could plant them in spring. In Fayetteville, spring came early, though, so she might be able to plant as soon as late March. She'd have to watch for when the last freeze would come.

She still had not found the path of choices and fate that would lead to survival for both Doctor Nudd and Pete. Time was rapidly disappearing. She trained with them as often as they could, but she knew increasing their fighting skill wouldn't be enough.

One thing Pete had to have when the Wolfhounds came was his sword. Without it, no amount of training would be sufficient to defeat them. Each assassin in the Order of the Wolfhound wore a black leather collar embossed with a silver crown, bespelled by Titania, the Queen of Air and Darkness herself, to make the wearer impervious to harm. The unseelie queen created the crown collars specifically to make her assassins effective against Celtic werewolves like Pete, who traditionally served seelie rulers. Pete refused to be anyone's mercenary, but that didn't mean he could automatically pierce magical protections specifically meant to defend against his kind. Not without his extraordinary sword, anyway.

Liliana tied a purple silk scarf around her forehead to hold her hair back, and incidentally, cover her fourth eyes. Since they didn't need to be uncovered to see, it meant she could open them without risking any of her Normal neighbors seeing them while she pulled unwanted plants.

What will keep Pete from having his sword when the Wolfhounds come?

A rose made not of living petals but of silvery metal on the hood of a sleek electric sportscar cruised into her vision. A man stepped out of the car in one of the lots on Fort Liberty. The brown sign in front read "Provost Marshal's Office." The slender man in his mid-thirties had long, stylishly cut black hair. He wore dark glasses, an emerald green tailored shirt, neatly creased khaki slacks, and a sleek, modern wrist phone. He carried a fancy box in his hand, wide and flat with gold designs that glittered like foil.

Liliana had an odd sense of déjà vu, as if she had seen this vision before, but couldn't remember when. It had the bright clarity of the present. She saw what was happening in the moment that she looked.

While Liliana pulled weeds, the man with the silver rose went into a building, signed a screen with a stylus, and placed his thumb on it for scanning. He chatted with a woman in uniform at a desk, then went further inside.

He put the glittery box behind his back as he came to an office with the door open, tapped on the frame, and grinned widely.

Liliana recognized Pete's friend, the pretty military police sergeant, Zoe Giovanni.

She stood with an answering smile and hugged the handsome man, who produced the flat box with a flourish. "Chocolate!" she exclaimed. "I can't remember the last time anyone brought me chocolates."

"You deserve them. They're almost as sweet as you." He pushed his sunglasses down for a moment and winked, so she could see the striking green eyes that matched his shirt.

Sergeant Giovanni giggled like a much younger woman, and her cheeks flushed pink.

Liliana quirked her lips and rolled her human eyes. She was not overly experienced with dating, but even she had heard that line before.

"The old man in?" the handsome man in the sunglasses said. "We've got some business."

"Yeah." Sergeant Giovanni said. "The Colonel's in a good mood too, William. If you want to sell something, now might be the time."

The man, William apparently, chuckled. "I only move stuff around creatively. I have nothing to sell but my organizational genius."

"Organizational genius sounds a lot better than Logistics Consultant. You should print new business cards."

"An excellent suggestion, lovely lady. I just might." He gave her a quick peck on the cheek before leaving her office.

Liliana wondered why her fourth eyes showed her Sergeant Giovanni's boyfriend when she asked about Pete's sword.

William went down a hallway to a larger office and knocked on the closed door.

"Come," a deep voice said.

As he opened the door, Colonel Alexander Bennet's tall form stood from behind the desk. He walked around to greet the newcomer. His uniform was impeccably pressed and spotless. A broad politician's smile lit his face. "Ah, Mr. Eliot. I assume you wish to speak to me about the training operation next month."

"Yes, of course, Colonel." William Eliot closed the office door and strode forward. The tall, slender consultant pushed the more powerfully built colonel hard on the chest when they met. He all but slammed Colonel Bennet against the office wall, making medals and citations rattle in their frames.

The colonel allowed it, his smile broadening to something real before William Eliot's mouth met his, devouring hungrily in a kiss that looked hot enough to lead somewhere they couldn't go at a place of work.

Liliana's eyes widened in surprise.

Oh.

She remembered now when she'd seen this vision before—the day she met Sergeant Giovanni. She warned her not to fall for the man with the silver rose since he desired another.

She could have used that advice herself. She remembered the warm tingle of the Fae prince's lips touching her hand and how it had traveled, making her cheeks flush warm.

Alexander Bennet is already involved with someone.

For a moment, disappointment crushed the joy out of the sunny February day, surprising her with its intensity. She barely knew the handsome Fae prince.

But she'd seen inside Colonel Bennet's deeper self and had not seen the love that glowed in Pete. Alexander Bennet was not committed to this man like Pete was to Ben.

Also, when he'd kissed her hand, Liliana had seen the spark of attraction in his eyes. Alexander Bennet desired her, or at least he wanted her to think he did.

She watched the two men's passionate kiss with her head cocked to the side.

Perhaps she had been wrong to warn Sergeant Giovanni away. Perhaps William Eliot wanted both her and her commanding officer and was trying to win them both.

Liliana sighed, touched by a wistful wish that she could find herself in such a situation.

Her parents had been a happy triad, so she tended to consider that the ideal. But unlike her mothers, she was attracted only to men. Women didn't interest her the same way. For her, a happy triad would involve two men who loved each other as well as her. But finding even one man who would be right for her was hard enough. Finding two such men, who also cared for each other, seemed far too much to ask of fate.

And yet, here were two men who desired each other, and at least one of them had also indicated interest in her.

They were both physically stunning men. Potentially, they could be exactly what she wanted, a more perfect match for herself than she ever thought to find. From the flirting chemistry she'd felt, Alexander Bennet wanted her, and clearly, from the steamy kiss she just witnessed, he also wanted William Eliot.

William Eliot was a complete unknown, though. Was he deceiving Sergeant Giovanni with his attentions to get closer to Colonel Bennet, or was he wooing both? Deciphering complex relationships was not her strong suit.

She wished to know more, especially about the man with the silver rose. William Eliot's face shimmered as Liliana studied him.

Not a Normal then. What kind of Other is he?

An image appeared of him standing near a pond in the elaborate garden of a grand antebellum house, possibly one of the old plantation houses outside of town. A huge old oak spread its limbs above him, and stars sparkled in the sky. He dripped his blood into the shallows of the pond. The water lifted into the shape of a small four-footed transparent creature where the drops fell. The creature ran off when he waved his hand casually.

The working did not show any signs of draining his energy. He didn't even look visibly tired.

A water mage. A powerful one.

How does he come by his ability to do magic and his affinity with water?

A quick image flashed with the faded colors of long ago. An asrai, an unseelie Sidhe Fae whose element was water, with long black hair, dressed in an emerald green samite gown, kissed a human man dressed in a fine plaid kilt and saffron shirt with a jeweled broach on his shoulder. The shimmer of moonlight gave the kiss a romantic feel, but Liliana knew asrais were universally nocturnal. Any kiss with an asrai would be at night.

The land around the asrai's lake was rocky and steep, and a path led up from the water's edge to an old castle wall, not like anything in the North Carolina area.

Probably overseas. Scotland, judging by the kilt, and nearly a century ago judging by the style.

In older times, humans who ruled an area in Europe would sometimes wed the local land-bonded Fae to legitimize their own rule. In this case, water-bonded, rather than land-bonded, would probably be the right term. The water Fae were only ever chosen by bodies of water, but bonded asrai could be very powerful within their limited realms.

Swift flashes passed Liliana's fourth eyes of the asrai presenting a swaddled babe to her human laird. The babe had eyes of green like the deep water. A man in expensive late nineteenth century finery with green eyes shaded by a big hat married a pretty woman in the garden of the same plantation house Liliana saw before, but it was still being built and the oak tree beside the pond was a sapling.

William Eliot had an asrai ancestor, his grandmother. She had been a powerful bonded ruler of a body of water in Scotland and married the human ruler of the land surrounding it. So William Eliot had deep magic and noble ancestry. He was handsome, and Alexander cared for him, even though they were not yet committed to each other.

Liliana disliked the idea that Eliot might be dishonest to Sergeant Giovanni, not telling her about his feelings for her commanding officer. The passionate sergeant was bad enough at choosing her mates without someone toying with her heart. Besides, all three of her parents taught Liliana that honesty was essential in any long-term relationship, but even more so when the partners went beyond two.

If Alexander valued this man, then Liliana would do her best to give him the benefit of the doubt, at least until she knew him better.

She went back to current time and checked in on Alexander and William Eliot.

Alexander chuckled low and caught the wiry man's hands as they reached for the buttons of his uniform shirt. "Not here."

William Eliot grinned. "Spoilsport. No one would know with the door closed."

"I would know." Alexander firmly pushed his hands away. He straightened his shirt as he went back around his desk to sit down. "What have you learned?"

"Wow, one kiss and straight to business." William Eliot sat in a chair and leaned his elbows on Alexander's desk. "You wound me." He put a hand over his heart but did not look overly hurt.

Alexander chuckled. "Well, don't bleed on my reports. Why does my sister want Pete's sword?"

"I have no idea."

Alexander's fierce frown would have intimidated most men.

William Eliot leaned back in his chair and shrugged nonchalantly. "The only thing I've found out from the pretty sergeant is that your pet Celtic wolf has a sword that is very old, and that his mother gave it to him before she died when he was too young for her to tell him much about it."

"So Pete may not even know why Aurore would send Wolfhounds after him to get it." Alexander scratched absently at the scars on his cheek. "See if you can get it anyway. Without Pete knowing, of course. If he doesn't have it, then my sister will have no reason to send more assassins after him."

William Eliot wrinkled his nose. "Still don't understand why you don't just kill that red wolf and take what you want. If he knew what you were ..." The slender man shuddered dramatically.

Alexander's stoic face showed a shadow of uncertainty. "Pete and Nudd are friends, even though Nudd is unseelie."

"Weird." William Eliot shook his head. "Almost as weird as Nudd thinking he's your Merlin, despite not being a wizard."

Alexander shrugged. "Healing is a powerful gift. It may be the only one he has, but the ability to save lives is no small thing. And he has collected a lot of wisdom over the centuries."

The water wizard waved that away with a long-fingered hand. "When your sister brings war to you, the ability to take lives is what will win the day."

Colonel Bennet gripped the pen in his hand. "I still have hope that the word is 'if' not 'when.'"

The wizard stood and put his dark glasses back on. "I will be at your side either way." He leaned across the desk and planted a lingering kiss on Alexander's lips. "Always," he whispered against them.

A knock on the door had William Eliot standing swiftly, and Alexander writing something on a piece of paper as if he'd been taking notes. "Come," he said in his normal, deep voice. "Get me that report on the training exercise requirements by the end of the week."

"Will do, Colonel." William Eliot left with a smile at Sergeant Giovanni as she walked in.

Liliana let that vision go. What she needed to know was what sort of person William Eliot was.

Are his feelings real for Sergeant Giovanni?

For a moment, she saw the wizard give Sergeant Giovanni a locket some time in the future and got an overwhelmingly bad feeling related to it. She remembered a vision she'd seen before of that locket. The young military police sergeant would die if she wore it.

William Elliot wove dark magic into it. His hands closed the clasp on the chain, hanging it around her neck.

Is William Elliot the source of the tide of blood I saw coming?

Green eyes flashed in her fourth vision like they were made of fire, then vanished. She couldn't see anything directly related to the wizard after that.

An odd afterimage of the fiery eyes persisted in front of her fourth eyes. She blinked repeatedly, trying to get rid of it.

Magic. The wizard must have some spell to protect his actions from seers that activated as soon as she focused on his actions, not someone or something adjacent to him.

But she'd seen enough. William Eliot was using Sergeant Giovanni, not wooing her. And it would end in her death if Liliana didn't change something.

She wondered if the wizard was similarly using Alexander Bennet, or if his feelings were any more sincere toward the Fae prince than they were toward the sergeant.

But when she tried to look, all she saw was that flash of eyes of green fire, then nothing again but a painful afterimage.

Frustrated, she yanked out a particularly stubborn chickweed and got to her feet.

CHAPTER 8

WINGS ON THE WINDSHIELD

LILIANA WENT INSIDE AND TOOK A QUICK SHOWER TO get the garden dirt off well before her first client appointment of the day. After that, she had some time with nothing to do.

Her favorite client, Janice Willoughby, would come at noon. If Liliana stayed in her converted dining room turned business, then she would not risk disappointing her best client. But it was only 10:52, according to her many old-fashioned clocks, and one digital satellite clock that she used to keep them all accurate and in sync.

Once she lit the jasmine incense to give the right atmosphere, Liliana had some time to let her eyes wander in the peaceful tick, tick, ticking.

She considered continuing to sit at the little round table in the center of her converted dining room and looking into the crystal ball as if there was a client across from her. It had become habit for her to look into it when she used her fourth eyes in her business space. Habit was comfortable.

But she felt physically restless.

She worried that Colonel Bennet might be in danger in the same way Sergeant Giovanni was from the wizard. Visions of Alexander Bennet's face, both human and polished obsidian in his demi-stone form, appeared in front of her fourth eyes every time she opened them without focusing on something else.

It might not just be worry that made her see his handsome face all the time.

But she felt uncomfortable watching the Fae prince. She most wanted to see him in private moments, and her father taught her that kind of spying was dishonorable.

She should look at someone else.

The fancy jar that people put pay cards into hadn't been emptied in some time. When she removed the lid, she was surprised by how many cards were in it, each with some unknown denomination assigned to it, the modern equivalent of cash. She dumped the cards out into her skirt.

She took the pay cards out of her business space through the door into her house, leaving it open so she could hear if her client knocked on the business door early.

The seelie daylight Fae, Siobhan, intrigued her in an entirely different way. The little sylvan Fae had nearly defeated Liliana on her own chosen ground after the fight with Pete. The spider-kin respected that level of combat prowess. Then, her help with the last widow spider had turned the tide from a battle that felt like it was already lost to one she and Pete rapidly won.

Everything Liliana knew about flower sprites—they tended to live in rural areas and be non-violent artistic, creative people with no interest in technology—none of that fit Siobhan. Even sprites from the unseelie night court powered by the Green of midnight and the dark moon were reputed to be merely mischievous, rather than dangerous.

Siobhan did not seem like a harmless flower. She reminded Liliana of tales her second mother, Ixchel, told about jaguarondi, tiny relatives of the jaguar. Siobhan's fierceness matched the tiny predator's.

Liliana braced her feet on either side of her closet doorway, legs in a Y a few feet above the ground. From there, she could reach the ceiling. She slid a small section aside and placed the cards in between the ceiling joists to join a fairly large pile already there. She probably ought to get those down and count them at some point.

Once she put them through the reader that told her how much money each card held, she could calculate the total. The last pile she'd counted still had several cards left, though, plenty to buy groceries and such for a while, so she didn't feel any urgency.

I wonder how Pete and Siobhan met?

Her fourth eyes immediately landed on a panicked flight through the shifting black shadows of a nighttime forest. The vision had the faded look of something happening years in the past, but Liliana wasn't certain how many years.

The spider seer placed the ceiling tile back into place, making sure she kept enough attention on her first eyes to see what she was doing. Then, she dropped to the floor as she watched Siobhan fleeing with her fourth eyes.

The sprite's dragonfly-like wings beat frantically, their bright colors leached by the wan moonlight. Her short green and brown dress showed slashes from branches, or maybe claws.

Sweat tangled the little sprite's long, bright pink hair. Her bangs fell in her wide frightened eyes as she looked behind her. She pushed them away repeatedly.

A gnarled hand with cracked, dirty nails shot out of a clump of foliage as the sprite flew close. It snatched at her tiny bare foot.

It took a burst of wingbeats and a frantic kick to push the little Fae just out of reach. Mud and blood streaked Siobhan's legs around multiple scratches.

This was not her first close call.

Gibbering laughter echoed around the sprite.

A malevolent hairy creature with long arms and hungry yellow fangs leapt down from a high branch.

Siobhan swooped to the side.

The cedar boggart fell past her, but sharp nails caught in her full skirt, dragging her sideways off course and ripping the cloth.

Fragile wings fought to stay aloft, stuttering and falling lower.

Four boggarts closed in on the struggling flower sprite. Two chased her from tree branch to tree branch, two ran along the ground under her.

Cruel laughter followed her from all sides.

The tiny sprite dipped and swerved between the trunks and branches of trees, narrowly avoiding again and again the grasping hands of the boggarts.

Liliana held her breath as the frantic beats of flower-petal wings staggered with weariness, dropping the sprite closer to her pursuers on the ground.

"No," Liliana whispered, even knowing that what she watched in the moment had already happened some years ago. Time didn't much affect what her fourth eyes saw, just a subtle difference in tint and brightness of color that she'd learned to identify as an indication of future or past, and an extra crisp sharpness that indicated present.

Boggarts squealed with excitement in her vision.

Siobhan burst out of the dense trees and into open air.

Hanging back, the boggarts stopped their chase at the edge of the forest.

The sprite used the respite to put as much space between her and the unseelie pursuers as she could. She gave up altitude and skimmed just a few feet above the tall grass to put on the only burst of speed her weary wings could manage.

A brilliant light sliced through the darkness and blinded Siobhan. Liliana saw her wings light up vivid translucent fuchsia and violet in the white light.

SMACK!

Liliana flinched as the under two-foot sprite with the ten-foot wingspan splatted into the windshield of a green van. The van swerved wildly.

Siobhan's wings draped over the entire windshield, completely blinding the driver and covering the auto-drive sensors. One bright translucent wing snapped in the middle at an almost right angle over the roof of the van.

The accident recovery program kept the vehicle on four wheels as the van slid off the road into the dirt edge of the forest.

Shaking his head, the driver staggered out, a very young human man, perhaps less than twenty years with bright red hair.

Normally, a Fae would go to extreme lengths to hide her true nature from a random Normal human, but Siobhan was too badly injured to do more than stare blearily with one eye as the human reached for her. Her left eye was drowned in blood, her cheekbone crushed. Her left arm was smashed so badly it was hard to identify as an arm.

Lifting her in gentle hands, the human murmured apologies. He moved her carefully to a more comfortable position on the hood, straightening her damaged wing.

Liliana gasped as she recognized a much younger Pete. She twisted between her hands the cloth of one of her blouses hanging in her closet as she watched. That was certainly an unusual way for two life paths to cross.

"I'm so sorry. I couldn't stop in time. You came out of nowhere," Pete told the injured Fae. "Don't worry. I know someone who can help. You're going to be okay." He pushed the shaggy mop of bright pink hair away from Siobhan's bloody face.

The flower Fae's one functional eye widened in horror.

"It's all right. I'm not going to hurt you," Pete assured her.

"Behind you!" the sprite whispered and pointed with her uninjured hand.

Boggarts had followed her. Now, seeing a single wounded seelie Fae and a Normal alone in the dark, they moved in. They would not show themselves so openly to a human if they expected that human to live until morning.

Pete whirled around to face them, his back to the van with the wounded sprite laid out like a vivid hood ornament. He put his body between her and her attackers.

Their cruel laughter surrounded the injured sprite and her would-be rescuer. "Silly little fairy doesn't know enough to stay out of the road." "Bugs on the windshield can be so annoying." "We may have to eat her with a squeegee, heh heh." "We'll use her blood to spice his meat."

"I don't think you want to do anything rash here, boys," Pete warned them as his hand slipped under his jacket. He pulled a pistol as the unseelie Fae closed in.

A laughing boggart leapt at him.

As he sidestepped the hairy beast, Pete pulled the trigger on the handgun.

Bullets don't usually affect the Fae like they do humans. Since most bullets are made of lead, not iron, the Fae tend to shake them off like stinging insects.

Just under Siobhan's nose, the boggart smashed into the front of the van. A look of stunned surprise froze on its hairy face as it died.

Naturally, a Celtic wolf would have his weapon loaded with ammunition effective against unseelie Fae.

The dead body shifted to its equally unwashed and hairy human form once it hit the ground.

As the wicked, pointed smiles on the other three boggarts faded into confusion, Pete shifted to his larger demi-wolf form. He growled and showed them his teeth.

The boggarts vanished into the forest.

Pete waited a few moments to be certain they were gone before shifting back to human form. He turned to the wounded sprite, pistol still in his no-longer-furry hand.

"I want one of those," Siobhan said, pointing to the gun.

Pete grinned and holstered the pistol under his arm. "I'll see what I can do, but let's get you taken care of first."

Siobhan seemed about to answer, but her remaining eye rolled back in her head and she went limp on the sheet steel.

Liliana bit her lip. Siobhan's injuries were terrible.

How had the little sprite not died?

Her fourth eyes refocused as she closed the closet door and walked back to her business space. She was so focused on her fourth eyes, she trailed a hand along the wall to guide herself, unwilling to give even a tiny bit of attention to her first eyes. She could have divided her attention a bit more to see her immediate surroundings, but she didn't need any eyes at all to find her way around in her own house.

Pete pounded on a big carved wooden door until a familiar man wearing a white lab coat and fuzzy slippers answered it. In his human form, Doctor Nudd seemed to be made of long gangly elbows and knees. Liliana was not fooled by the grumpy, absent-minded air of the goblin. She had sparred too many times with the fiercer form hidden beneath.

Pete led the unseelie Fae doctor to the back of his van and opened the doors to reveal the badly injured sprite laid out on the couch.

"Absolutely not," Doctor Nudd said, backing up from the van, hands up as if to ward off something dangerous. "If the Goblin King ever got word I healed a seelie Fae, he'd have me skinned alive and slow roasted."

Liliana knew Doctor Nudd wasn't speaking figuratively. The Goblin King generally ate anyone who displeased him, and he hated the seelie sunshine Fae.

"There's no Goblin King here, Doc. You came to America to escape all the partisan politics in Britain and Europe. What was the point if you were just going to bring it with you?"

"You don't understand. I can heal humans, I can heal unseelie Fae, and beast-kin are generally considered neutral, with the exception of your own species. But if I heal a seelie Fae, it's aiding the enemy."

"But you've always taken care of me, and I'm supposedly the enemy, too, aren't I?"

Doctor Nudd sighed. "I've never regretted helping you find your way, my boy. You've made me proud. But I'm not willing to take that level of risk for a sprite I don't even know."

Pete grabbed Doctor Nudd's nightshirt in both hands. "You have to help her. She'll die if you don't. And it's my fault."

"You did this to her?" Doctor Nudd deepened the wrinkles on

his craggy forehead. "What could a flower sprite have possibly done to you to make you beat her like this?"

"I didn't beat her. I hit her with my van. I couldn't stop in time." He swallowed, and those clear blue eyes shone bright in the moonlight. "If she dies, I'll never forgive myself."

Siobhan opened one large violet eye and glared at the two men. "Either fix me up or leave me to die in peace. I've got a headache the size of a mountain and you two arguing is not helping."

"You would accept aid from an unseelie Fae?" Doctor Nudd said, disbelief in his voice.

"Oh, no, I'll be taking one of my many other options instead." Even badly injured, Siobhan's sarcasm was in full working order. Even Liliana could tell she meant the opposite of what she said.

Doctor Nudd ran his hands nervously through his already disheveled brown hair, making it stick out in a few new directions. He looked around at the woods as if spies watched, waiting to catch him aiding a Fae from the wrong court.

Liliana looked as well, just to be sure, but no human or Other had witnessed the clandestine meeting.

"I don't know about this," Doctor Nudd grumbled. "I am disinclined to do things that might get me executed, even if I'm not likely to get caught doing them. It's one of the reasons I've lived as long as I have."

"If it helps, I'll owe you a favor," Siobhan said with a tired sigh.

Doctor Nudd's bushy eyebrows crawled up his brown forehead. "A favor! Well, ..." He scratched his stubbly chin. "If anyone questioned me, I could say I was bribed." Every Other knew a favor from a Fae could be incredibly valuable, even from a simple flower sprite.

"I knew I could count on you!" Pete hugged Doctor Nudd swiftly. He scooped the sprite up in his arms, but her wings still dragged on the ground.

A high-pitched groan came from her as her broken wing and shattered arm got jostled. Through clenched teeth, Siobhan said, "A werewolf and a goblin. If any of my people saw me now, they'd think I was about to get cooked."

Doctor Nudd steadied her injured wing with one of his long arms. Pete held her mangled arm against his chest as gently as he could as they took her into Doctor Nudd's house to the part that was used for his business of healing.

Nudd gathered instruments as Pete laid the injured Fae on an examining table in a small room.

"You're not, are you? Planning to cook me, I mean?" the little sprite asked, not sounding overly concerned. She seemed only partially aware they had moved her to a new location. "I'm too tired to care much either way, so you might as well tell me."

Pete grinned at her and held her small uninjured hand. "Nah, there's not enough meat on you to be worth bothering with."

Siobhan groaned again. "Size jokes. Marvelous." But her lips twisted in a faint smile.

"What were you doing out in unseelie territory alone?" Pete asked her.

Her smile disappeared. "Banished. Thanks for reminding me," Siobhan gritted out. "And how was your day?"

"Kinda sucked." Pete gave her a wink, while Dr. Nudd examined the little sprite. "Crazy fairy splatted on my van and a boggart tried to eat me."

"Hey, none of that fairy rubbish, or I'll bleed on you."

Pete raised his hand in mock surrender. "Got it. Crazy, but not a fairy."

Liliana couldn't help but smile. Some things had not changed.

She paced around the circular table in her workspace with no goal in mind except a need to do something, and a conflicting need not to go anywhere so she wouldn't get lost in time and miss her favorite client's appointment.

But, where did Siobhan get the strange eye that sees in the dark?

Liliana's fourth eyes re-focused on a later time. Another man stepped up to the door of the small room, stripping off surgical gloves coated in blood.

She recognized him, Andrew Periclum, the king of the North Carolina lion pride.

"I've completed the cybernetic leg implantation, Nudd." The solidly built man with the military short haircut, olive skin, and a camo uniform stepped on a lever at the bottom of a recycler. The lid opened, and he dropped the gloves in. "I'll need you to do your ..." He waved his hands around with a disgusted look on his face. "Glowy hand waving thing."

"In a moment," Doctor Nudd said without looking up from his patient. "We have a bit of an emergency on our hands."

The man stepped forward and looked down at Siobhan with a sneer.

"Really. You're healing a seelie Fae?"

"She offered me a favor," Doctor Nudd said with a sheepish shrug.

"Let me know when you're done, then." Doctor Periclum leaned against the door jamb and crossed his arms.

Doctor Nudd held his hands over the sprite's head for a few moments. A soft green glow flowed out from his big hands into the little sprite and the scrapes on Siobhan's forehead faded to nothing, as if a week's healing had happened in a few seconds. Her broken cheekbone straightened, so the side of her face didn't look smashed in. "I think she'll be all right, but I can't do anything about her eye. There's too much damage." He looked up at Andrew Periclum. "Can you do something for her?"

"You think she'll give me a favor, too?"

"I'll pay you, Doctor Periclum," Pete volunteered. "This is my fault. I hit her with my van."

The lion-kin cyberneticist looked down at Siobhan's damaged eye and arm. "Hmm. I've never tried to miniaturize the mechanism of a cybernetic arm that small, and it would have to include expansion tech for when she changes form." He seemed to be talking to himself as much as to the other two men. "The eye wouldn't change size, much, but hooking an eye into the proper neural pathways is always tricky, and I've never studied the distinct neurology of a flower sprite in person." Andrew Periclum's voice gained excitement and interest as he spoke.

Several soft musical chimes rang out.

Andrew Periclum opened Siobhan's uninjured eye with a thumb on her eyelid. "Even the color is unusual. This will be quite a challenge." He waved a hand vaguely at Pete. "Never mind about money. This is worth my time, and Colonel Bennet's unit will pay for the cybernetics."

None of the three men responded to the chime sound. After a moment, Liliana heard someone knocking at Doctor Nudd's door. They continued to work at aiding the injured sprite without any sign they heard it.

Liliana cocked her head to one side, wondering where the sounds came from and why Pete, Doctor Nudd, and Andrew Periclum did not respond to them. Experimentally, she closed her fourth eyes, losing sight of them. She looked around her workspace with her first, human eyes. Everything seemed as it should.

Her clocks finished chiming 12:00 and went back to peaceful ticking.

So Andrew Periclum, the king of the North Carolina lion pride, was the one that helped Siobhan. Liliana hadn't even known he was a doctor, much less an expert in the modern miracle of cybernetics which could replace lost limbs with robotic parts indistinguishable from the original.

The knocking sound came again.

Oh! My client!

CHAPTER 9

OF SOUP AND SWORDS

LILIANA OPENED THE DOOR AND WELCOMED JANICE Willoughby inside with her usual flourish of arm, dramatically enhanced by the colorful scarves she used for fabric to make her clothes. Her lips curved without thought in a smile as she looked at Janice Willoughby's practical tennis shoes. The rabbit-kin had five active children ranging in ages from three to twelve. She needed comfortable shoes to keep up with them.

"Hi, Madame Anna," Janice greeted her cheerfully and walked in. "You're looking well. Scrapes from fighting Spearfinger all healed?"

"Yes. I am well. Thank you." The spider seer sat in her chair on the correct side of the round table with the crystal ball in the center.

Janice Willoughby sat in one of the three chairs on the other side of the table without prompting and dropped her purse in another.

In the memorized singsong voice, Liliana recited her usual beginning for a customer visit. "Madame Anna sees all. Pay me what you feel is fair for truth that cannot be seen by other eyes. I see what is, what has been, and what might be. Ask and the truth shall be yours."

"You know what I want to ask about, so just go ahead and do

your thing and tell me what's what." Janice waved her hands toward Liliana in a shooing motion.

Ever since Liliana told Janice Willoughby about fighting widow spiders with Pete and nearly dying, she had seen no reason to conceal anything she did from her favorite customer. In fact, she had found it very pleasant to have someone to talk with about her recently far more interesting life.

"Your husband is still safe," the spider seer told Janice immediately. "Pete will protect him, but it still seems very likely that Pete and Doctor Nudd will die. I have considered stealing the sword for safekeeping and giving it back to him at the right time, but that does not seem to end well. If Princess Aurore gets the sword..." Liliana carefully did not open her fourth eyes with that thought in mind. She already had nightmares about the widespread death and destruction that would sweep across Europe. "Pete is a good man. I think he would rather die than have that happen."

"I talked to my Lou about this magic sword business, and he offered to have Pete give it to him for safekeeping until it's needed. Since the red wolf and the goblin doctor will need it to protect Lou, that seemed like it might be a good idea?" Janice Willoughby leaned forward, looking into the crystal ball, as if she could see the change in future paths herself.

"That is a very brave offer," Liliana said. She opened her fourth eyes and looked into the crystal prop to see if this plan would save Pete and Doctor Nudd, assuming he lived that long. It looked like it would, yes. She flinched hard a moment later and shut her eyes. Seeing ugly deaths had become part of her daily routine since allying herself with Pete.

While such visions no longer sent her into shivering, rocking-in-the-corner fits, Liliana still did not enjoy seeing Janice's husband ripped to shreds by werewolves. "Um. No. That is not a good plan. The Wolfhounds are only after your husband because they believe he knows something about the sword. If he actually has the sword, they will kill him and take it before Pete can get there to help."

Janice Willoughby's already fair complexion paled. She covered her mouth with her hand. "I didn't realize. We're trying to figure out how to save Ben's man and your goblin friend. It didn't occur to me that if we change the wrong thing, it could get my Lou killed."

"It is always easier to make things worse than it is to make things better," Liliana warned her client. "The more the future is altered, the more likely something will become worse, and I will not see it. That is why I always advise customers to make the smallest change that will help."

The rabbit-kin reached across the table to pat the back of Liliana's hand. "I'm glad you're looking out for us, Madame Anna."

Liliana looked down at the pale hand resting on top of her dark olive, smaller one, uncertain how she should react. She felt her cheeks warming. It was a lot like when Pete told her he trusted her. She felt kind of good, but also kind of afraid. Janice trusted Liliana to keep her husband, Lou, safe. What if the spider seer made a mistake?

"All the Others in Fayetteville know that we're lucky to have you watching out for us." Janice's hand squeezed hers briefly, then withdrew back to the other side of the table.

The uncomfortable feeling turned briefly to a jolt of sheer terror.

Every Other in Fayetteville trusts me to keep them safe?

Liliana fiddled absently with the long ends of her sleeves, running them between her fingers, trying to calm down. If she made the wrong decision about the prince, if she made the wrong decision about Pete, about Doctor Nudd, every Other in Fayetteville would suffer, and it would be her fault.

Liliana swallowed. "You should stay for lunch. I made mushroom soup. You should stay for lunch."

Janice Willoughby accepted her invitation and chatted all through lunch about her children, her husband, and the best ways to flavor mushroom soup without meat.

Glad that mundane discussions had side-tracked the rabbit-kin, Liliana let her chatter, listening with only part of her mind. No matter what Pete did with the sword, or who he gave it to, she saw the same outcome for him and Doctor Nudd. They would not have it when Princess Aurore's pet assassins came looking for it again.

They needed that sword. Even if Doctor Nudd survived to that point to help Pete, they would both die without Fraegarthach.

Depending on what Pete did with the sword, there was every possibility that others would die as well. The soup and the company were both nice, but seeing her friends and many other people die horrible, but slightly different, deaths as she considered various options spoiled her appetite.

" ...and Ben took that bully aside. He told that boy he'd be happy to give him after-school tutorials in non-aggressive conflict resolution that happened to be at the same time as basketball practice if he couldn't think of a politer way to ask for his turn on the swings. My Sam about laughed himself sick telling me about it."

"Ben Harper? Pete's beloved?" Liliana got an odd twinge from the part of her brain that dealt with her fourth eyes. Something about Ben Harper.

Janice nodded as she picked up the bowls and spoons and put them in the sink since Liliana's room-bot was broken. "Ben's so good with the kids. Sam just adores him. He's had trouble in the past with teachers treating him like he's a bad kid, just because he has so much trouble sitting still in class. I hope your red wolf friend knows what a prize that man is."

"Pete loves Ben Harper very much. I would like to meet him." The twinge got stronger. She opened her fourth eyes again and saw an image of the teacher hiding Fraegarthach under the picnic table in his backyard. She also saw a flash of Pete wielding the ancient sword against the assassins and winning.

Oh. That might be it.

Liliana needed time and quiet to search the paths of the future to see if this would work, though. She couldn't afford to miss anything. She interrupted the rabbit-kin in mid-sentence. She wasn't actually sure what Janice had been saying, but it didn't matter. "You have to go home now, Mrs. Willoughby."

"Oh, I didn't realize it was so late. Is your next appointment coming soon?"

"No, not for one hour and thirty-six minutes." Liliana opened the back door. "Go home now, please."

"Did I do something to upset you, Madame Anna?" The rabbit-kin bit her lower lip.

"I am not upset. I am glad you stayed for lunch. I enjoy your company. Go home now, please." She was tempted to push on the rabbit-kin to get her to go out the door faster. This was the most promising path she had seen. Quiet concentration was what she desperately needed, and Janice Willoughby was not good at quiet.

"Um, okay, then." Janice grabbed her purse and stepped out the door. On the porch, she turned around. "See you next..."

Liliana closed the door.

"...week," Janice's voice said distantly through the door.

There were so many ways that this could go wrong. So many people who could die if Liliana changed the wrong thing. She looked again and again at every other person she could think of that had been harmed in the other paths she had considered. She explored some variations on the theme and realized that no one could know where the sword had gone, not even Pete. But if that condition was met, and she could save Doctor Nudd from his more immediate death, then everyone lived. Except the Wolfhound assassins.

That was it.

Ben Harper was the key.

Now, all Liliana had to do was convince an intelligent Normal to secretly hand over his beloved boyfriend's most treasured possession to a stranger.

Liliana sighed and closed all her eyes. It would be a lot easier if she just had to kill someone.

CHAPTER 10

MAN OF SCIENCE

PETE AND SERGEANT GIOVANNI FROM THE CRIMINAL Investigation Division of Fort Liberty were out investigating the murders of the two soldiers who had been shot execution style and buried in shallow graves in the forest. If not for Liliana's vision, they probably never would have been found.

Since Pete was out hunting a killer with the Sergeant and the Detective, Ben Harper was home by himself that evening. Liliana thought it would be the best time to pay him a social visit and try to convince the teacher that he should give her Pete's sword.

Dual feelings of familiarity and strangeness gripped the spider-kin as she walked past the Willoughby's house. Janice Willoughby had come to her once a week for advice and gossip since before the rabbit-kin had finished her first two years of college. Back then, Janice was a young single girl, wondering what her future might hold.

There was a bicycle on the Willoughby's front porch that Liliana knew belonged to Janice's oldest girl, Sally, named after Janice's grandmother. The spider seer had seen Janice's oldest boy, Louie, named for his father, mowing the neatly trimmed lush green grass. She had seen Janice's husband, Lou, tinkering with their SUV in the driveway. Liliana knew this house and everyone who lived in it, almost as well as she knew her own home. Yet, in all the years she had known Janice, she had never physically been at her house with the exception of one very strange night when the Willoughby's peaceful old oak tree had become a weapon of death.

So much of the things Liliana thought of as her life were really just things she had seen. Janice's days were filled with her beloved husband, her five active children, her home, her friends, PTA meetings, bake sales, all the little acts that added up to a real life. Liliana had watched over everyone else's life for so long, she had maybe forgotten to live her own for a while.

Pete and Ben Harper's house was right next door to the Willoughby's. She knew the layout of the house, knew that Pete didn't have a back porch, but in the backyard was a gazebo that Ben liked to sit in and grade his students' classwork when the weather was nice. Pete was her closest friend, yet the spider-kin had never physically been to his house, either. And she had never met the man who was more important to Pete than his own life.

She felt her feet dragging as she approached Pete's house. Social interaction was always difficult, complicated, and often awkward. Communication with a Normal, where she could not use any but her human eyes, would be even harder. Liliana had avoided social interaction of any kind as much as possible, to the point where life had become largely something she watched from a distance. If her father had still been alive, he would have admonished her years ago not to let fear control her. Cowardice was not something Simon of Nemea would have tolerated.

"I am sorry, Pater," Liliana said softly, as her fourth eyes let her look back in time at her tall, handsome father with his shaggy mane of curly, black hair and his face set in a scowl of disapproval. "I did not realize I was letting fear rule my life. But I am doing better now."

She lifted her chin, walked boldly to Pete's front door, and knocked firmly.

And waited.

No one came.

Liliana peeked quickly with her fourth eyes to see where Ben Harper was.

Oh.

The late afternoon was lovely and sunny. She should have gone to the gazebo first.

Liliana stepped up on the railing of Pete's front porch, jumped up, caught the edge of the roof, and pulled herself up.

Pete should have someone look at his roof soon and trim the big elm tree in his backyard. Some of the shingles over the kitchen looked rubbed half off by a large limb. It might cause a leak. She would tell Pete the next time she saw him.

The spider-kin walked onto the tree limb, followed it to the center of the tree, and switched to another limb that shaded the hexagonal gazebo made of cedar wood by the scent of it. She hopped lightly out of the tree and onto the roof of the small structure. Careful not to disturb the wisteria vines that were already starting to bud, she climbed down one of the support poles.

Ben Harper was staring at her with his mouth open as she dropped to the grass and dusted off a few leaves that had gotten caught in her skirt. A tablet computer lay on the picnic table in front of the blond teacher. He held a stylus in his hand, still hovering over the screen.

Liliana thought of her father always urging her to face the world with courage and said, "Hello, Mister Harper," with a confidence she didn't feel.

"Um, hello," the teacher said. "Who are you?"

"I am Liliana. I am Pete's friend."

"I don't think Pete ever mentioned having a friend named Liliana." He shifted the stylus around in his hand. He wore a slight smile as well as a confused expression, as if wondering if this were a joke of some sort.

"Pete calls me Lilly. All my friends call me Lilly. I have not met you before, but you can call me Lilly. I hope that we will become friends because Pete loves you and I love Pete. He is my closest friend." Despite the spider-kin's determination to face this social interaction with courage, she found herself looking down at her sleeves while she talked and pulling the long, trailing brightly colored fabric through her fingers. When she realized what she was doing, she dropped the sleeves quickly and put her hands behind her back.

"Oh, Lilly! Right, Pete said you've been coaching him in martial arts, and you helped him with the serial killers in Raleigh. He said he might not have made it out of there without your help. I thought you'd be bigger." Ben Harper's smile widened to something far more welcoming.

Liliana felt her cheeks heating. She clenched her hands together behind her to keep from messing with her sleeves again. "He might not have been in danger, Mr. Harper, if I had not told him to talk to the..." she hesitated. She had almost said "widow spider," but caught herself barely in time. Ben Harper did not know about Others. Most of Liliana's clients were Others or Normals who were somewhat in the know. She had not had a long conversation with an ordinary human who knew nothing of the hidden peoples in some time. "... the woman who owned the club in Raleigh."

"You helped him find the killers and come home to me alive. I'll always owe you for that. And call me Ben. My students are about the only ones who call me Mr. Harper. What brings you here?" He gestured at the vine-covered gazebo. "Pete's not home right now if you came to talk to him."

"No, Ben. Pete is hunting another serial killer with Detective Shonda Jackson, Sergeant Zoe Giovanni, and Lieutenant Runningwolf. I came to talk to you."

Ben Harper's smiling mouth did a funny sideways twist. "Most people come to the front door."

"I knocked, but you didn't answer. I knew you were in the gazebo. You like to grade homework here when the weather is nice. The weather is very nice today." Liliana started to feel a little less nervous. Pete's beloved was not hard to talk to.

"Um, yes, it's a lovely day. So Pete told you that I grade schoolwork out here?"

"No. I just knew." Liliana could not tell Ben Harper that she was spider-kin, but her big wooden sign was on a major street in Fayetteville. "I am also known as Madame Anna of Anna Sees All. I am a seer."

The human's smile changed again. Ben Harper's face seemed to be made for smiling. He had a wide variety of different kinds of smile. "A seer, huh? What have you seen about me, besides where I like to sit to grade homework?"

"Pete is going to ask you to marry him. But you will say no. It will make him very sad. And you should give me his sword. If you don't, someone will steal it and Pete will die."

Ben's smile did some very strange things, first widening into delight, then tilting wryly, then fading into confusion. Liliana had never met anyone who seemed to express nearly every emotion with a smile.

"Uh." He set the stylus down on the table. "That's um. Pete's going to ask me to marry him?"

"He has a ring. He has just been waiting for a good time. There has not been a good time lately because so many people have been dying. Pete and Sergeant Giovanni have to help Detective Jackson, so Pete has been busy and distracted. He wants to take you somewhere nice and ask."

"Pete told you all that?" Ben asked, his smile turning ironic.

"Pete did not tell me any of that. I am a seer. I have wondered why you will tell him no, though. Pete is beautiful and smart and fierce and loves you. Why will you not choose him for your mate when he has chosen you?"

Ben's smile seemed a little teasing, and he looked around as if someone else might be hiding behind the big elm tree or in the decorative hydrangeas by the fence. "Why is Pete so sure I'll tell him no that he sent you to talk to me? Maybe I'll say yes."

Liliana sighed. Once again, she was completely failing at communication. She sat down at the picnic table and reached across it to touch Ben's hand. Sometimes people paid more attention if you touched them. "Pete thinks you will say yes. Pete doesn't know I am here." She looked up directly into Ben's dark brown eyes for as long as she could stand it. "I came because I need you to give me Pete's sword so it will not be stolen, and Pete will not die. I just wondered why you did not want him for your husband."

The smile faded from the teacher's face. "You're serious. Pete didn't send you?"

"Pete doesn't know I am here, and you must not tell him. The paths of the future where he finds out and comes to me to ask about it are bad ones. You must not tell him."

"The paths of the future, right." Ben Harper smiled again, but the smile bothered Liliana. It reminded her of the people who spoke to her very slowly. "Look, Miss Lilly, I'm not one of your customers. You don't have to put on an act for me."

Liliana frowned and fought to remain calm against rising anger. "No. You are not a customer. You are my best friend's beloved, who will reject him and break his heart. And if you refuse to give me his sword, you will get him killed too."

"I'm not the one who sent him straight into a club full of armed serial killers," Ben Harper pointed out sharply, his smile vanishing.

Liliana blinked her human eyes and pulled her hands back into her lap. She ran the bright silken sleeves of her blouse through her fingers. It didn't help. He was right. She blinked again and a tear ran down her face. "I did not mean to nearly get Pete killed."

The spider-kin got up abruptly. This was not working. Ben would not give her Pete's sword. Ben did not like her.

"Whoa. Whoa. Wait a minute."

Liliana ignored him and climbed back up the gazebo support pole, still blinking tears from her human eyes.

"Lilly, please, stop a minute. You said something about Pete dying?"

Liliana stopped when she reached the gazebo roof. Ben was right. The spider-kin could not just give up and leave. Pete's life would be forfeit. "You believe I am a charlatan who puts on an act. You do not believe that I can see the future, so why would you care what I have seen?" Liliana sat down on the peak of the gazebo roof and wiped her human eyes.

She always wondered why only her human eyes wept. She had seen Stella's spider eyes weep when she lost her beloved, so it was not the same with all spider-kin. Only her kind. Or at least, only her. There were so few spider seers left, she didn't really know.

She couldn't remember ever seeing either her older sister Isabella, or her first mother, Solifu, cry. Liliana didn't remember crying much herself over the last few decades. Yet lately, Liliana seemed to be doing it a lot. Her life was no longer a bland nothing with every day the same as every other day. It had lovely high points, but it also had moments like this when she wondered why she'd ever left her house.

Ben stepped out onto his back lawn and backed up until he could see where Liliana sat. "I teach science, not fantasy." He shrugged and smiled apologetically. "Fortune tellers are always charlatans. I don't believe anyone can see the future. It's nothing against you personally."

The spider-kin pulled her knees up to her chest and wrapped her arms around them. "You will say no to Pete when he asks you to be his for life. I have seen this. Am I wrong?"

Ben looked down at the grass. "Maybe not."

"Pete's soul is shining and good. He is the bravest man I have known since my father died. Why will you reject him?"

"Is this some really weird version of a shovel speech?"

Liliana tilted her head to one side. "What is a shovel speech?"

"You know, 'I have a shovel, and if you break his heart, I'll kill you and bury the body where no one will find it.' That speech."

"That is something that people do?" Liliana asked, shocked.

"Why do I get the feeling I'm talking to one of my fifth graders?" Ben said, softly.

Liliana did not think Ben meant for her to hear that, so she pretended she hadn't.

"In general, people don't actually kill each other over hurting a close friend or relative, but the threat is intended to make it clear how important that person is to you, and that you won't tolerate them being treated badly," Ben explained.

Liliana thought about that. "I would not kill you for breaking Pete's heart."

Ben grinned at her. "That's good to know."

"I might break your bones, or threaten to cut off a limb or something, but I do not think I would kill you."

Ben laughed. "That is definitely a shovel speech." His smile softened. "You must love Pete a lot."

Liliana swallowed and hugged her knees tighter. "If he loved me like he loves you, and he asked me to be his for life, I would say yes."

"Hence your confusion as to why I might say no." Ben sighed. "Come down and I'll make coffee, and we'll have this conversation where it won't give me a crick in my neck." The teacher picked up his tablet and stylus from the picnic table and went into the house.

Liliana climbed down and followed him. "I do not like coffee, but I like tea."

"I've got some Earl Grey around here somewhere." They said nothing more about Pete while Ben prepared a cup of tea and one of coffee, only exchanging a few words about sugar and cream.

Once they were inside and settled on the soft living room couch with their warm drinks, Ben spoke again. "Pete and I met in grad school, both pursuing our doctorates in biochemistry. Back then, if he'd asked me to marry him, I would have said yes without hesitation. Now that he works for the military, he keeps a lot of his life to himself. Sometimes I think there are more things I don't know about Pete than things I do."

Pete could not tell his beloved about fighting widow spiders or the empty pain a wolf-kin felt when he had no pack. He could not tell Ben Harper about two of his closest friends, the oak goblin and the wood sprite, or much about Liliana, the spider seer. As long as Ben Harper believed only in science and refused to even admit the possibility of more, he would never be able to share in much of Pete's life.

Ben's hesitation made a little more sense now.

There wasn't much Liliana could do to help, though. Normals had been known to go insane when suddenly confronted with the truth of the world, or more often, they simply found "logical explanations" for the stranger things they experienced and insisted on the insanity of those who saw the truth.

She sipped her tea and wished she could open a few more eyes to look for ways to help without possibly sending Pete's beloved into hysterics.

Ben set his cup down on the coffee table, and his smile turned bitter. "You fought with him against those killers. You know what he's doing on a daily basis. He didn't even tell me why he was going to be late tonight. You probably know him better than I do."

This man loved Pete but could never completely know his mate until he first accepted that the world was not how he had always believed it to be. Her heart hurt for Ben. "When I am sad, sometimes, Pete hugs me. When Pete is sad, he wants you to hug him. I have fought at his side, but when the battle ends, it is you that he comes home to."

The smile the teacher gave her conveyed both sadness and gratitude. Ben Harper's smiles said more than his words. "So what's this about his sword?" the teacher asked.

"Assassins are going to target Janice's husband because they believe he has information they want."

"Wait, are you talking about Janice Willoughby? Her husband, Lou, the mechanic?"

"Yes. Janice is my best customer. I warned her about the assassins, but I promised her that when danger came, Pete would protect Lou."

"Of course he would."

"Yes, but without his sword, the assassins will kill him instead, and Doctor Nudd, too, since he will try to help Pete protect Lou Willoughby, assuming he survives that long."

"Okay, that all sounds plausible, although I'm not sure why assassins would be after Lou, or why Pete would need his sword when he has his gun and his knives."

"His gun and knives will not work. He must have the sword, or he will die."

"So why won't he have it?"

"Someone will steal it very soon."

"Who?"

Liliana considered. She knew who would steal the sword, the water wizard, William Eliot, but it was a secret, and telling would put Alexander Bennet in a bad light with Pete. "It doesn't matter who will steal it." Ben did not believe that she could see the future and was just humoring her, so if she told him, he probably would not believe her anyway. "What is important is that you must give me the sword to keep it safe, so that I can make sure Pete has it when he needs it. And also, you must not tell Pete, or anyone else."

"What am I supposed to say if Pete asks me where his sword went? His mother gave him that sword."

"I will take the sword. If anyone asks, tell them the sword was stolen. I will steal it."

"But you'll give it back?" Ben asked.

Liliana nodded. "I'll give it to Pete when he needs it most."

The teacher shook his head and pinched the bridge of his nose. "This all assumes that you can actually see the future. You really believe that you can, don't you?"

"I am not a charlatan. I see what other people cannot. I saw that you would refuse Pete's proposal."

"Okay. You're sincere, obviously very intuitive, and Pete doesn't think you're crazy, but I'm still not comfortable handing over a family heirloom without telling Pete, based on some dream or feeling you had."

Liliana tried to consider what she had said from a normal human's point of view and could not see any way to convince Ben Harper.

Pete would die if she could not. She knew that Ben Harper would be as heartbroken as Liliana would be when that happened, if not more so.

Oh. That is the important thing.

"Pete will die if I do not do this."

Ben's smile was again the condescending smile of an older person amused by the naivete of someone younger. "But I don't believe that's true, Lilly. I understand that you believe it, but..." he shrugged.

"You are a man of science. There are two possible outcomes here. Either I am wrong and Pete will be fine, or I am right and Pete will die if I don't take the sword. If you do not give me the sword, you are betting Pete's life that I could not possibly be right."

Ben's condescending smile gained an edge of fear.

"As an experiment, permit me to steal the sword. If nothing happens, then I will return it in one year and admit that I was wrong, and that I cannot see the future. Pete will have his sword back, and your hypothesis will be proven. No harm will come to anyone."

"And if you're right?"

"Then I will give Pete the sword when he needs it, and he will not die."

Ben drained his cup, set it down on the coffee table, and stood. "He keeps the sword under the bed when it's not in his van. I'll pull it out this evening, and 'accidentally' leave it in the gazebo under the picnic table." He winked at her. "It would be a shame if it got stolen."

Liliana smiled and finished her tea.

CHAPTER 11

THE CYBER-FAE AND THE ROOM-BOT

LILIANA PRACTICED WITH PETE, SIOBHAN, AND DOCTOR Nudd every day that they could spare the time. Pete's schedule was as busy as Doctor Nudd's, between his work in the biochem lab on base and spending valuable time with his beloved teacher, not to mention trying to track down a new murderer. They had all stopped Spearfinger just in time for a new killer to start leaving pieces of his victims torn limb from limb hanging from tree branches. Detective Jackson had not wasted any time bringing in Pete and Sergeant Giovanni since it was clear no Normal had done that. But they had not yet discovered who the culprit was.

And there had been no new leads as to who might have killed the two women found buried in the forest.

Doctor Nudd's medical practice, which was almost entirely made up of beast-kin and unseelie Fae, often meant he kept odd hours, or had to cancel suddenly.

One day, a few weeks after they had all begun to practice together, Nudd called Liliana to let her know he could not make it to practice. Pete had already told her that he and Ben had a date, so he would not make it either.

Liliana called Siobhan. Instead of meeting in the woods as they usually did, she invited the fuchsia sprite to come to her house.

They could practice in the garage, which the spider-kin had long before converted to something like a gym since she didn't have a car. With gym mats on the floor and bars, ropes, and obstacles built into the open attic space above, it lent itself well to both swordplay and unarmed combat practice.

They started with swords. Without the two men, who were relative swordplay novices, the spider and the sprite honed each other's skills to the next level. Siobhan wielded her long slim blade like an artist wielded a brush. It had been a long time since Liliana found someone to cross swords with who truly challenged her, and even had some interesting new tricks to teach her.

The spider found herself smiling and laughing out loud sometimes as they sparred. The sprite grinned back at her with a glint of mischief and battle joy. Liliana was more agile, and accustomed to the odd configuration of her two-story garage practice area, but not as skilled with a blade as her opponent.

Siobhan could fly when she needed to, giving her another edge that countered some of Liliana's acrobatic abilities.

Liliana had forgotten how much fun combat practice could be with a well-matched partner.

After an hour or two of delightful fencing involving both of them dancing on beams and somersaulting through obstacles to put an Errol Flynn movie to shame, Liliana coached Siobhan painfully in unarmed combat for another hour. The sprite was not strong, but she was small, clever, and quick. Liliana did her best to focus on techniques that would lend themselves to such strengths. She wasn't certain how much her training would truly help the small warrior. Siobhan was worlds more formidable with her weapons than she was without them, but Liliana had promised to teach her. Liliana kept her promises.

When they were both exhausted, Liliana invited the Fae into the personal part of her home with some trepidation. She did not know Siobhan as well as she knew Janice Willoughby, who was the only other person she had invited into her house for a social visit this century. But she did not think it would be proper to send the exhausted, sweaty sprite home without offering her a chance to rest first.

"I hope you do not mind tea with honey. I do not have any beer, like Dr. Nudd has." Liliana handed the tired sprite a tall glass of iced sweet tea she'd made in the sun that afternoon.

"Cheers." Siobhan flopped on Liliana's second-hand, overstuffed couch and gulped down tea with enthusiasm. "You're a woman after my own heart, spider girl."

Liliana sipped gratefully at her glass of cold tea. It was exactly what her tired body needed. Her muscles had a pleasant, warm ache to them. A smile played around her lips. She couldn't remember the last time she had enjoyed herself that much. "You should come and practice with me more often."

Siobhan chuckled. "Maybe I should. You certainly keep me on my toes." Her face clouded for a moment, losing its tired good cheer. "Hey, about sending Pete after you ..."

The spider-kin nodded. "I considered killing you for that."

"I'd have considered killing anyone who put a red wolf on my trail too." Siobhan shrugged, clearly not concerned.

"I fit the description he gave you of the killer, and I am spider-kin. If you did not know the difference between a widow spider and a spider seer, then it made sense." In her place, with the knowledge that Siobhan had, she might have given Pete the same advice.

Even exhausted, the sprite did not seem capable of sitting still for long. Siobhan's nimble hands turned the now-empty tea glass round and round.

In the quiet of her home, along with the usual ticking of her clocks, Liliana noticed a tiny, soft whirring sound that she couldn't place. She looked around her house curiously with her human eyes, seeking the odd whisper of sound. She considered opening more eyes, but her spider eyes made Siobhan uncomfortable, and she didn't wish to disturb her guest.

"Your bot is banjaxed," Siobhan commented. She gestured at the forlorn room-bot in the corner, one of its telescoping arms permanently bent at an angle it was never meant to reach.

Liliana missed the convenience of the little bot, but she never could have afforded it if it hadn't been a gift. The price of repairing it was prohibitively high. Without it, her wood floors and the knickknacks on her shelves were often dusty, and she had to do her own dishes and laundry. "I used it to slow Pete down, so I could escape the day he came to kill me."

"My fault then." Siobhan dragged the bot over to the middle of Liliana's bright, hand-woven living room rug. One of its wheels refused to turn, so the sprite tilted the bot onto its other two. She pressed a spot on her left arm and a panel opened in her pale, freckly skin.

Liliana blinked and opened her second eyes to look at the sprite's arm while Siobhan's attention was focused on the bot. The arm was colder than the rest of her from the shoulder down, and there were struts of some cold material extending into her body, as a replacement for her collarbone and shoulder blade. "Your arm is not flesh!" Her second eyes told her that the sprite's left eye was also artificial.

So that was how she saw Liliana on the night they fought.

As Siobhan's arm moved, the servos inside made the faint whirring sound that Liliana noticed earlier.

Siobhan grinned, held up a tiny Phillips-head screwdriver, and showed the hollow storage space built into her forearm. "Tools wherever I go without lugging a toolbox."

That must be where the sprite kept that little two-shot pistol she always seemed to have, hidden somewhere in her artificial arm like the tools.

Siobhan used the tiny screwdriver to open an access panel on the bot. As she touched circuitry, the broken arm flopped. "Hmm."

Liliana remembered her vision with Andrew Periclum talking about the challenges of cybernetics on a flower sprite. He must have figured out a way. "How is that possible? You change size when you shift form."

The sprite shifted quickly to her smaller, demi-plant form. Her body lost two feet of height and most of its mass. Brilliant violet and fuchsia dragonfly style wings sprouted wide to nearly brush the walls of the small living room. Her arm telescoped down smaller, in a manner not unlike the bot's arms.

"Doctor Periclum said that making the eye adjust size and color was a lot harder, even though my eyes don't change size as much as my arm."

Liliana noted with interest how large Siobhan's demi-plant form's bright violet eyes were in proportion to her petal pink, heart-shaped face. Her miniature form looked delicate and exceptionally cute. Adorable even. The spider-kin might not be skilled at social interaction, but even she knew better than to speak that thought aloud to the fierce sprite.

Siobhan switched back to her larger human form to wrestle the bot onto its side. Her wings withdrew into her body like a flower blooming in reverse. The cropped heavy metal band T-shirt she wore had slits cut into the back, just like her jacket, to allow the wings to come and go unimpeded. "I can't take plant form without losing the arm and the eye, but I haven't done that in over a century anyway. There's too much of a chance I wouldn't wake up."

"Andrew Periclum made your cybernetics?"

"Yeah, Doc Periclum's the cyber specialist at Fort Liberty. He's the only one in the world who specializes in cybernetics that change size and shape for Others." The sprite didn't look up from where she had parts of the room-bot spread all over Liliana's rug. "He did me up after I got hit by a van. He usually deals with soldiers after they get body parts blown off. He said his work on me was 'a miracle of miniaturization.'" Her freckled nose wrinkled adorably as she used her tiny tools on the bot's damaged telescoping joint.

"It does seem quite extraordinary. I did not know that technology was so advanced. I also did not know the king of the North Carolina lion-kin pride had such skill until recently."

"He's king of the pride? So people actually do bow and scrape around the doc on a regular basis," Siobhan said. "That explains a lot."

"It is considered polite to bow or curtsey to the king of lions, yes. He is the informal leader of all beast-kin in his pride's territory, and all lions, hyenas, and jackals serve him directly." Liliana tilted her head and considered the sour expression on her guest's face. "Why do you dislike Andrew Periclum?"

The flower sprite glanced up with a wry expression. "That obvious, huh?"

"I would have expected you to speak of the man who gave back your limb and sight with admiration or gratitude."

"You sound like him. His majesty, the almighty Doctor Periclum. I should bow at his feet for lowering himself to bestow his brilliance on a mere lesser Fae." She snorted. "Arrogant git. Nudd saved my life, even though he was afraid it might cost him his, and he's never even called in the favor I owe him."

Liliana shivered suddenly as the part of her mind that handled her fourth eyes prodded her. With the sprite's attention back on her work, the seer risked opening her fourth eyes for a moment. "Doctor Nudd will die very soon unless..." Possibilities flickered into being as she considered the favor the sprite owed the goblin.

Siobhan stared at her, mouth open, tools forgotten in her hands.

Quickly, Liliana closed her fourth eyes. People seemed to look at her with their mouths open a lot. "Apologies. I know my eyes disturb you."

Siobhan scoffed. "Not nearly as much as hearing that my best friend is going to die disturbs me." Her cupid's bow lips tightened into a thin line, and her blue, human-form eyes narrowed dangerously.

"I am very sorry." Liliana had made her guest upset. She thought she was doing so well at social interaction. Now, she'd committed a serious faux pas that might cost her a valuable ally. "I did not mean to offend."

The sprite made a sour face and waved that away with her cybernetic arm. "Spill, spider girl. Nudd's going to die unless what?"

"I am not certain. Death is difficult to see around. I have only seen a badger-kin with a needle in his arm near the doctor when he dies. I think it is Lieutenant Runningwolf since he is the only badger-kin I know, but I have not seen his demi form. I know that if Doctor Nudd removes the needle from the badger, he will gain time. He will live a few minutes longer, but he will still die. But when you mentioned that you owe Doctor Nudd a favor..."

"You got some kind of spooky spider eyes intuition that I might be able to save Nudd by paying back my favor?"

Liliana tilted her head to one side. "That is reasonably accurate, yes."

"Huh." The sprite went back to reassembling the bot, hands working while her mind appeared to be considering what Liliana said.

Taking the sprite's comments as permission to use her fourth eyes, the spider-kin opened them again and searched. With Siobhan's favor to focus on, she could see a few more of the events surrounding the goblin healer's death. Some of her visions now included the fierce little sprite's death as well, or instead of the goblin. "If you choose to try to save him, it may cost your life in his place, or you may die together."

The sprite finished putting the access panel back on the room-bot. She didn't look up while she turned the bot on and ran it through its test sequence. "I'd have been dead ten years ago without him."

"Your life is your own. You do not owe it to anyone, especially not an unseelie Fae." Siobhan had called Doctor Nudd her best friend, but most would consider a goblin and a sprite to be mortal enemies by their very nature.

Siobhan lifted her chin. "Right, my life's mine, yeah. And I get to decide who I would trade it for." Liliana did not need to open her third eyes to perceive the smoldering heat of old anger. "Nobody, especially no court, can tell me who my friends are."

Liliana made a mental leap that for once wasn't in a random direction. "The leaders of your people banished you."

Siobhan looked at her, and her human blue eyes were filled with pain and old anger. "Yeah. And executed my friend. She was an unseelie mistletoe sprite. Never hurt a soul in her life. She told the best jokes."

Liliana leaned forward and squeezed Siobhan's shoulder. "I am sorry for your loss. It is very hard to lose a friend."

The sprite smiled at her oddly, large eyes shiny. "You're the only person who's ever said that, you know? Most people assume we couldn't have been very close." She turned the bot on, put her empty tea glass in its bin, and stood up. "Time to go."

Liliana pretended not to notice as Siobhan surreptitiously wiped her eyes with her back turned.

While the room-bot busied itself washing their tea glasses inside, Liliana walked Siobhan out the back door to the customized Harley Davidson Spirit in the driveway. The weather had been mild lately, hinting at the beginning of spring. The sky was clear and studded with bright stars.

"I have been wondering," Liliana said. "How did you arrive in time to save Pete and I from the widow spiders? Doctor Nudd said he couldn't get there from Fayetteville in time to help."

"I was at a bar called Locked and Loaded in Raleigh with a couple of the Other soldiers from Liberty. It's just a few blocks away from the Mirror Club. I was worried about them with all the deaths and disappearances. When I heard them talking about going to the city to go carousing, I decided to tag along. So I was already close by when Nudd called."

"Do you often protect the soldiers?"

Siobhan shrugged, kicked a toe at a clump of grass, and her pale human cheeks shaded pink, nearly as bright as her demi-plant form's wings. "Those kids need someone to make sure they make it back to base in one piece."

"Where did you get such a powerful gun on such short notice?"

Siobhan grinned, reached into her motorcycle saddlebags, and pulled out the machine pistol Liliana remembered, stroking it like a beloved pet. "I carry this baby with me everywhere, except on base."

Her expression turned sour. "The gate guards make me leave it behind."

"Do you go on base a lot?"

"I do some work making weapons and ammo that are effective against bullet-resistant Others. They're pretty hush hush about what they want them for."

One of Liliana's preferred strategies for social interaction when she was younger had been to get people to talk about the things that interested them. She remembered that it worked well for her then and went with it now. "I did not know that weapons of such power came in such a small size. Did you modify it?"

"A little, but not for size. It started out as a fully automatic pistol with a long barrel." She ran a small finger along the barrel to show its length. "This model is designed to be easy to add on to. See the picatinny rail. I attached the forward grip to help me deal with the kick and an extended magazine, so I don't run out of ammo." She pointed to the section on the front that had a thick, short second barrel and trigger. "The grenade launcher is my latest addition. The kick-back is brutal, and I can only get stun grenades, but there's just something so class about having a grenade launcher my size. The base model is a Kel-Tec PLR sixty...you really don't care, do you?" Siobhan looked up at her with narrowed eyes.

Liliana's cheeks flushed. The perceptive sprite had caught on to her strategy. "I know very little about guns, but I can respect any weapon wielded with courage and precision."

Siobhan punched Liliana on the upper arm with a grin. "Nice save."

Liliana rubbed her arm, wondering why the little sprite considered bruising her shoulder to be a gesture of affection.

Siobhan put the machine gun back in the saddlebag of her custom bike, mounted, and started it up. The quiet hum of the electric motor was completely drowned out by the blast of thumping base and screaming guitars that were probably supposed to be music.

"Later, Lilly," Siobhan shouted, waved, and popped a slight wheelie as she accelerated onto the street.

As the pounding music faded away, Liliana smiled to herself. Siobhan called her Lilly, like Pete did. She liked that her friends called her by a different name from her clients.

Her friends.

She'd been alone for so long, then Pete was her only real friend for a while with the rest just allies or acquaintances. But Siobhan called her Lilly, and Doctor Nudd said they were friends, and Janice had lunch in her house. She didn't just have one friend anymore.

Liliana had friends.

Since she left the circus, she had lived without friends. The life had been chaotic, but the camaraderie of circus folk ran deep. She hadn't realized that she missed it, just as she hadn't realized how much she missed flying on the trapeze or sparring with a worthy opponent.

She spun in a circle on her little patch of grass, letting her skirt swirl around her legs. Ignoring the risk of being seen, she opened her second eyes just so she could see all the brilliant colors of the stars. Her life had changed a great deal since the day a Celtic wolf walked into her shop and accused her of murder. It was almost as if she had been asleep for years. Her new friends woke her up and dragged her out into the light of the stars. Her friends reminded her to live, not just exist.

Friends made her life so much better. She shuddered at the thought of how much more barren her life would be when, after she had friends for a short time, she lost them all.

What she said to Siobhan was very true. It was hard to lose a friend.

She stood still in her yard, six eyes on the sky, two looking into the past, and swore an oath to herself and to her dead parents. "I won't lose them like I lost you, Pater, Mut, Mamãe. I won't go back to being alone."

CHAPTER 12

TIME AND PATIENCE

LILIANA SWUNG AND FLEW FROM BAR TO BAR AND ROPE to rope in the space originally designed for a two-car garage and attic storage. Some decades back, she had removed the ceiling drywall, revealing the large attic under her high roof. She'd hung inch-wide metal bars and strong ropes from various parts of the house superstructure. It was the same space that she and Siobhan practiced combat in, but Liliana practiced in it for a different reason when Siobhan was not there.

Trapeze and high wire had been two of her favorite performances back when she was in the circus. It took focus and full attention, like combat. So now, she danced along the ropes and swung from one to another, watching where her hands and feet would land with her two human eyes, and watching other times, places, and people with her fourth eyes.

At least, eventually, she hoped to be able to do that. If she practiced a lot.

She had nearly died the first time she tried fighting with her fourth eyes open against Siobhan. Her first mother had been able to see blows coming both in the present and in the future. It made her incredibly formidable in combat. But Solifu did not live long enough to teach her young daughter the trick of splitting her consciousness that completely.

Even her older sister, Isabella, could only open her fourth eyes for a few seconds at a time during combat without risking distraction and death, and she was two hundred years older than Liliana.

Whenever Liliana became too accustomed to the placement of the ropes and bars, so that she didn't need her human vision to find them, she would move them to a new configuration. Sometimes, she practiced at night with the lights off and used her second and fourth eyes. Over the last few months, she had been getting a tiny bit better at splitting her consciousness, but her fourth eyes could still distract her at crucial moments.

An image of the handsome Fae colonel, a moment when he smiled at her while wearing his shimmering demi-stone form, appeared in her wandering fourth vision. The smile had not been cold. It was warm and amused when she told him out of nowhere that she liked Pete.

She jumped for a swinging bar. And missed.

Again.

The momentary distraction at the wrong moment was all it took to make her fall.

She landed reasonably well on the gym mats covering the concrete garage floor. The spider-kin rolled to absorb the force of the impact. Physically, she was not injured, but everything in her ordered, internal world felt like it was slipping out of her control.

Liliana pounded her fists into the rubber mats under her. "Aaaaaaagh!"

She had not found a way to save Doctor Nudd.

Even with his sword, Pete would not survive the coming attack from the Wolfhound assassins without his mentor fighting beside him. Siobhan might be able to save Doctor Nudd, but Liliana did not wish to trade the life of one friend for another.

Without Nudd and Pete, Fayetteville would rapidly become a deadly place to be, for many Others and Normal humans as well.

Plus, she had begun to feel like even the ticking of her clocks was oppressive, counting down the narrowing gap before her blood fire time. It was a few years ahead, so it shouldn't have been weighing on her so much, but it seemed that every little thing reminded her that she had no mate and that was likely to continue to be the state of things until her biology drove her mad.

The day before, she'd snapped at one of her customers who asked her a particularly silly question. All the future, all the past, and all the world were within her range of vision, and people asked her if sweaters would go on sale after Memorial Day.

Sweaters always go on sale after Memorial Day.

Liliana cancelled her appointments for the rest of the week. She couldn't afford to alienate the people who counted on her. She had to get her life back in proper order and make sure that her friends didn't die.

Someone knocked on Liliana's door. Not the public door to her business that people knocked on normally, but the door to her home.

The spider seer glanced through the door with her fourth eyes to see who it was. It was Pete. She had been expecting him sometime soon.

Pete had never come to visit at her house before, except the one time when he came to accuse her of murder. Usually, they met for combat practice in the forest near Doctor Nudd's house, for music and alcoholic beverages at Doctor Nudd's house, or for hot drinks and talking at the Starbucks down the street.

Today, Pete had called Dr. Nudd and said he was busy and would not come to the forest to train.

In truth, Pete had been no more busy today than any other day. That wasn't why Pete cancelled combat practice.

Pete was sad.

Liliana opened her door and left it open for him while she went into the kitchen to get him a beer.

The week before, she bought the kind of beer that the wolf-kin and the oak goblin healer both liked. Her fourth eyes told her that they would both come visit her soon. Siobhan would also visit, but she often visited her for sword practice in the garage these days. She enjoyed dark, bitter craft beers and sweet fruit juice as well as honey-sweetened tea. Cherry cider was her favorite. The Fae Colonel preferred wine, or aged scotch when he wanted something stronger.

Liliana had not foreseen for certain that the prince would visit her, but it was a possibility. In case he did, she had his favorite wine. It was extravagantly expensive, and she did not really expect him. The bottle sat in her pantry, tilted down to keep the cork wet, nonetheless.

She sighed and rolled her human eyes.

She was thinking about him again.

Stop it, already. Pete needs your attention.

The spider-kin handed her dearest friend a beer and sat down on her comfortable, overstuffed, second-hand couch, avoiding the spot with the spring that was starting to work its way through. She was really getting the hang of this social visiting thing.

Pete followed her into the house and closed the door behind himself. "Um, hi, Lilly." He sat down in the armchair next to the couch, perching on the edge rather than settling in comfortably. Clearly, something was bothering him, but he seemed nervous about asking. He picked at the label on the beer bottle between his hands instead of drinking it.

Liliana looked into him with her third eyes. She nodded as if he had spoken.

"Ben loves you," Liliana told him, remembering the softness in the teacher's voice when he talked about Pete. And the sadness at how little he knew about Pete's current life.

The spider seer would never admit, but she sometimes watched the two of them together. It was a little like watching a romance movie starring people she knew. It made her feel warm, happy for them, and more than a little envious.

The contrast between Pete with Ben, and William Eliot with Sergeant Giovanni made her slightly nauseous. Eliot's cold manipulation of the passionate sergeant's nature made Liliana angry on her behalf. Sergeant Giovanni had a tendency to give her heart foolishly, but she always gave it generously.

She was one that loved not wisely, but too well.

Hopefully, things would work out better for her than they had for Othello and Desdemona.

Pete smiled, but his normally radiant smile showed more sadness than joy. "I guess you know why I came." Pete had finally asked Ben to marry him, but as the spider seer knew he would, Ben said, "No."

She could have warned Pete, but telling the wolf-kin ahead of time would not have helped.

"You don't know how to tell Ben that you're wolf-kin without him thinking you're insane, or he is. And Ben won't marry you because he knows that you're hiding much of yourself, and fears that he doesn't fully know you."

"Yeah. That's pretty much it in a nutshell." He transformed just his hand and popped the beer top off the bottle with a claw. He took a swallow and set the bottle down on a crocheted coaster on Liliana's little handmade folding end table.

The spider-kin nodded. She knew why he came. Her best friend wanted advice on his love life.

She also knew that when it came to love, her advice was nearly useless. She had seen love. She recognized it in others. But Liliana had never been in love.

There had been lovers, of course. But that was a thing of the body, usually initiated by men. Women had approached her a few times as well, but she did not find them as physically fascinating. With men, she found sex enjoyable as long as they had good reasons for wanting her. With some lovers, she had felt friendship or affection. With most, though, she had simply felt attraction, and it had worn off quickly when she realized they wanted something from her, such as her venom, her sight, or her body.

Spider seer venom in particular was a powerful temptation. If they knew about her nature, lovers sought her out for the near immortality her venom could offer. They didn't want *her*, just her venom. A few didn't know about spider seers and sought her for her own qualities, but when they found out, they often became obsessed with the lure of immortality.

Liliana did not want anyone to stay with her only for the benefits of her venom. With her first blood fire time coming in less than four years, she needed to find a relationship with more depth. She needed to find something real like Ben and Pete had.

"So?" Pete asked. "What can you tell me?"

Liliana did not have to look again. She had already looked and looked for an answer. No outcome had appeared where Pete explained to Ben what a wolf-kin was, and that he was one, that had not ended badly. The only way Ben would accept Pete's Other nature would be if he found out on his own.

"I am very sorry, Pete." She reached across to the chair arm and touched the back of his hand. "There is nothing you can do. You must give him time." Eventually, all the odd things that happened in Fayetteville would coalesce in Ben's mind. It might happen suddenly, like if an Other exposed their inhuman form to him, or it might happen gradually, as lots of little indications of Other activity, and Pete's Other nature added up. "Some aspects of the world are not as he was taught them. One day, he may figure that out for himself." The middle school science teacher had already noticed a few unusual things about some of his students, like Janice's children. "Perhaps then, if you are careful, you can gently ease him into our hidden world. But you must be patient."

None of the good outcomes were close in time. There were a hundred outcomes that Liliana had seen that were varying levels of awful. In some possible paths, either Pete or Ben died. In others, they ended up hating each other. The spider seer had seen a lot of future paths that involved restraining orders.

One particular path caught Liliana's attention. In that one possible future, Ben shattered Pete's heart. The wolf-kin came to his pretty friend, Liliana, for comfort and eventually, Pete became hers.

At first, Liliana had been intrigued and excited by the existence of that future. She adored the handsome wolf-kin but knew his loyal heart would never betray his beloved Ben. For a time, she considered advising Pete toward the path that would lead him first to heartbreak and then to her arms. Pete would be the one to be with her when the blood fire time came.

Liliana opened her fourth eyes and looked at that flicker of possible future one last time where Pete held her in his arms and kissed her as a lover does. She knew what to do to send him down that path. She considered it one last time. It was still a possibility.

But even considering it was an act of incredible selfishness. She ran the trailing ends of the brightly colored silk scarves that made up her skirt between her fingers. A wash of shame filled her. She wanted what Pete and Ben had, but she was not willing to see her favorite wolf badly hurt to get it.

And in the end, she knew that Pete was fundamentally a different kind of person from her. They were not an ideal match long term. He would lose his chance for a life of joy, and she would gain only a few years of happiness before they parted ways.

"I will speak to Janice Willoughby. Perhaps we can find a way to help Ben accept Others. But you must be patient. It will take time." As Liliana watched, that flickering possibility that Pete might one day be hers vanished forever. She let it go with only a trace of regret.

She wanted Pete happy far more than she wanted him for herself.

"Time and patience, huh?" Pete sighed. "That's all you've got for me?"

"For you, yes."

Pete raised his pale brows at her. "What do you mean, for me?"

"Sergeant Giovanni did not take my advice. She has fallen in love with the man with the silver rose."

"Eliot," Pete said. "Something about that guy just doesn't smell right. It's not just you, Lilly. She didn't listen when I warned her away from him either. Zoe's never had the best sense when it comes to men."

"William Eliot is a powerful wizard from an old family. There is both human and Sidhe royalty in his bloodline. She must not wear the locket."

"Um, what?"

"He will give her a locket. Steal it from her if you have to and empty the contents under running water. It will have no effect on you. Most of the wizard's magics will not affect you as long as you stay away from large bodies of water."

"You want me to take jewelry away from Zoe? What are you trying to do, get me killed?"

Liliana tilted her head to one side, confused. "That is not what I intend at all."

Pete chuckled. "I know, Lilly. Just a joke."

Liliana blinked. *How is that funny?* She gave up after a moment. "The wizard does not want Sergeant Giovanni. He desires another. But the locket is spelled to bind her to him. She will do anything he asks. When he is done using her, he will spurn her, and she will kill herself."

The wolf-kin's lips tightened into a thin line. "No way I'm going to let that happen." His face turned thoughtful. "Why would he do that to Zoe? What is it he wants?"

"He wants her to steal your sword for him."

"My sword? The one my mother gave me? It's gone already. Someone stole it a few days ago. Do you think that's what happened to it?"

"He did not steal it, nor did Sergeant Giovanni, but they would have if you still had it. Your sword will return to you when you need it."

Pete chuckled. "Sounds like something a sword in a legend would do."

Liliana blinked her human eyes at him for a few moments. "You really had no idea what you held, did you?"

"It's nice, well-balanced, and really old, but seriously, it's just a piece of metal. Not worth killing anyone over."

"It is Fraegarthoch, the Retaliator, an ancient sword of Fae, from the time long before Rome when the Sidhe ruled as gods in

Ireland and Iceland. If a land-bonded Sidhe Fae held that sword, every sleeping Fae in a hundred-mile radius would wake up at once. The rule of science would begin to fade from that point outward, and the rule of magic would return. The world as we know it would end."

Pete looked at her for a long moment. "Right. That would be bad." He ran his hand through his thick red hair. He gulped down about half the bottle of beer. "Maybe I should have destroyed it," Pete said hesitantly. "Melted it down or shattered it?" He clearly did not wish to break the gift his long dead mother left him.

"You cannot. Fraegarthoch is virtually indestructible. It would take incredibly powerful magic to destroy it, and probably heat on the level of the heart of a volcano."

"Wonderful." Pete rolled his eyes and downed another big gulp of beer. "Well, at least we don't have any Sidhe royalty on this continent. North America is probably the safest place for something like that to be."

"There is a Sidhe prince in Fayetteville. Also, his sister, Aurore, the daughter of Titania, the unseelie Queen of Air and Darkness, knows that you have the Retaliator. She sent an assassin protected by magic to kill you and steal the sword, but the prince killed the assassin to keep you safe."

"Wait, an unseelie Sidhe prince killed someone to protect me?"

"Yes. I don't believe he knows yet what sword you hold, only that his sister wants your sword badly enough to kill for it."

"Who is this guy? Why didn't I know about this?"

"He does not want you to know who he is."

"Why not? I mean, sounds like he saved my life?"

"He is unseelie. You are a Celtic wolf. He does not wish to be your enemy."

Pete rolled his blue eyes. "Doc Nudd is unseelie. Some of the Others I work with at Liberty are unseelie. You know none of that matters to me."

Liliana smiled at her hands. "I know. He does not. Although perhaps he is beginning to understand."

"You should introduce me to this prince."

"I think that would be a bad idea. If he holds your sword, the world order could be shattered and reality re-written."

"Fair point. You don't introduce Frodo to Sauron at a cocktail party and casually mention he has a cool ring."

Liliana chuckled. She took a moment to enjoy the literary parallels. "Does that make me Galadriel?" she asked him, grinning at his black combat boots on her brightly colored hand-woven rug.

"I think you might be Galadriel and Eowyn in one body, with a dash of Gandalf thrown in."

Pete's view of Liliana always pleased her.

She would see him happy. There must be a way to make that happen. "I like your Ben. He will be kidnapped soon by an adhene, but do not worry. They kidnap people sometimes when they find them pretty. They are not evil, just lonely and not skilled at social interactions. You must not fight the adhene."

"Lilly, if someone kidnaps Ben, I'm going after them."

"The adhene are very powerful seelie Fae. She will crush you if you fight her, but if you do nothing, Ben will slap the adhene when she tries to kiss him without permission. Siobhan will scold her. The adhene will be embarrassed, and her feelings will be hurt, but she will release Ben unharmed after only two days."

"Two days? I'm not going to do nothing if someone kidnaps Ben and keeps him for two days."

Liliana sighed. The trouble with knowing the best advice was also knowing that people often did not follow it. This could either be a minor thing that happened, a strange anecdote for Ben and Pete to laugh about, or Pete could get himself killed by trying to be the rescuing hero. "When I told you we had to wait to rescue Sergeant Giovanni from the widow spiders, you trusted me."

"Yeah. And you were right, every step of the way. And I know, I should have shot the stone woman in the hand when you told me to." He drank the rest of his beer and sighed. "All right, Lilly. When is this going to happen?"

She tilted her head to one side. "I am uncertain." Her visions jumbled and shifted, mixed in with images of the prince's murder. "A few months. A lot will be happening at the time. You will return home and find an enemy there instead of your beloved. Defeat the enemy, but do not search for Ben. Ask Siobhan to do it, instead."

Liliana glanced into Sergeant Giovanni's future and was delighted to see that Pete would follow her advice despite his misgivings. Sergeant Giovanni would survive, be disillusioned with the wizard, and continue to be her normal, competent, cynical self.

The day the adhene would take Ben was less certain. Too many different paths intersected on that day for her to see for sure, but she did get a momentary glimpse of Pete talking to Siobhan about finding Ben for him.

Pete chuckled. "Ben will slap a powerful Fae, huh?"

"He is a good match for you." Liliana reached across and patted Pete's arm. "Be patient. Give him time." The fates of Janice Willoughby and Ben Harper were becoming more intertwined every day as their friendship deepened. "Janice and Lou Willoughby and their children might be able to help ease Ben's transition into the world of Others. I will speak to Janice about the best way to gently introduce him to the hidden peoples."

Pete wrinkled his freckled nose. "Being patient sucks, but I've never gone wrong trusting you." He got up and went to her fridge to get himself another beer. "What about you?"

"What about me?"

"I asked for advice on my love life. How is yours?"

An image of Colonel Alexander Bennet flashed in Liliana's mind. Again.

Liliana sighed. "I don't really have a love life."

"Why not? You're pretty and available, and I know you need to find a life partner soon. What's holding you back, Lilly?" Pete settled back comfortably into the armchair. He seemed far more relaxed now that the tables were turned, and Liliana's love life was under scrutiny.

"I'm good at fighting. I'm good at seeing. I'm not very good with relationships. I only get kissed by men who do not love me."

Rather than the brotherly kisses Pete often gave her, she thought of the feel of Alexander Bennet's warm lips on her fingers. What would those lips feel like on hers? Warmth flushed her skin at the thought.

Pete laughed at her. Everyone laughed at her. For some reason, it didn't bother her as much when Pete did it. "That's not really that unusual, you know."

Liliana tilted her head to the side. The wolf-kin knew a lot more about love than she did, despite his young age. It might be her turn to take some advice, rather than giving it.

Pete said, "Love at first sight, or even first kiss, isn't really how it usually works. Love takes time to build."

The spider seer turned that over in the various segments of her mind. Alexander Bennet was attracted to her. And while William Eliot was not a man she would have chosen, she could accept him if he made Alexander happy. Alexander obviously cared for him. Perhaps if she knew him better, she would, too. Maybe if she took her own advice and gave the relationships time and patience.

Considering possibilities allowed her to look at more images of the Sidhe prince at various points in time.

He really is very nice to look at.

Pete stayed, sipping his beer for a while. When he finished it, he stood up and leaned down to give Liliana a peck on the check. "I'm going to head out now, Lilly."

"I'm glad you came, Pete. Come and visit me again any time you wish."

"I will." Pete smiled at her and left.

CHAPTER 13

KING OF LIONS

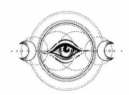

TODAY WAS THE DAY THAT DOCTOR NUDD WOULD DIE.

Liliana had a lot to do.

She had determined that, while her own presence would not save Doctor Nudd, the highest probability of his survival involved her being physically present to aid him at the crucial moment.

Her main problem was that Doctor Nudd's death would occur on base at Fort Liberty. For a person who didn't officially exist, and wanted to keep it that way, walking onto an Army base was not a simple thing.

There was an added complication. She had already foreseen that Alexander Bennet would be in considerable danger today. While he had been unwilling to trade access to the base for her help, she felt she had to help anyway.

Ignoring visions that insisted the Sidhe prince who protected Pete and whose lips sent thrills from her fingers all the way to her toes would be badly injured or possibly killed when she could prevent it—that was not something Liliana could do.

She tried looking ahead in the day to see if there was a time when any one of the other people who would be involved in Doctor Nudd's death went off base. Pete would be off base for a time, but he would arrive too late to save Doctor Nudd. Perhaps she could find someone else who could get her on base sooner, while still allowing her time to help Alexander Bennet.

She was in luck.

Doctor Periclum would travel to a nice restaurant in downtown Fayetteville for dinner. A violent spring storm had moved in. As it was pouring rain with a possibility of hail predicted, he would opt to park his large, sleek car in a parking garage.

She could speak to Andrew Periclum when he finished his dinner meeting. A pride member had arranged the meeting to provide the king of lions with a large amount of transferable pay cards. Liliana did not know why the jackal-kin did that, but pride business was not her concern. She hoped to convince the king of lions to smuggle her onto the base.

Liliana found a comfortable out-of-the-way spot in the concrete roof structure of the parking garage near where the lion-kin's car was charging and waited. She had seen that Andrew Periclum would come out of the restaurant and return directly to base.

As a lion-kin's daughter, she was technically a pride child, even though she was not a lion, jackal, or hyena herself. A good pride-king would nonetheless give her aid in return for the loyalty she had pledged to him.

She wasn't sure if the lion-kin cyberneticist who built Siobhan's eye and arm even remembered that Liliana was a pride-child, but she could remind him. If he did her this favor, it would obligate her to give the pride aid in some way at a later date, much like an exchange of favors among the Fae. She would accept that obligation if it helped her to save her favorite goblin and her favorite sprite.

If the king of lions was not willing to smuggle her onto the base, then she considered possibly hiding in his trunk. The large black vehicle was equipped with modern magnetic shielding designed to protect from many projectile and energy weapons. It would also keep the base's entrance scanner from detecting her as long as it was on, and unlike most base visitors, Andrew Periclum routinely left his on.

The puzzle was, how could she either convince the king of lions to help her or get into his trunk without his knowing. If the first tactic failed, she would probably lose any possibility of trying the second tactic.

When she looked more closely at the car, she saw something unexpected. The car was occupied. Apparently, someone was waiting to drive Doctor Periclum back to the base: a muscular lion-kin with three slash scars on his face that looked like claw marks. She remembered him as the man who had been Andrew Periclum's second during the pride succession challenge. He had filled out with even more muscle over the years, and the scars pulled his lip in a way that gave him a permanent sneer. It made him look very fierce.

Well, then. The trunk was not an option. She would have to convince the doctor to let her ride with him and his driver. She looked ahead in time, with the idea of asking for that favor firmly in mind. If she did not see a likelihood of success, then she would have to abandon her plan and find another way.

The spider-kin watched as Colonel Alexander Bennet's urban camouflage-painted car with big, knobby, all-terrain tires parked directly under her perch in the roof structure. She had seen that this was the location of his danger and hoped to have time to save him, then ask the pride-king for a favor.

She looked forward in time to see why the prince had come.

Oh. Hmm.

Liliana sighed. She would have to change her plan. The king of lions would not be granting her any favors. The Colonel's plans completely negated hers.

She should simply leave while there was time and find another way onto the base, but that would leave Alexander Bennet to an unpleasant fate. The probability of his death was low, but the probability of serious injury was high.

She sighed and shimmied down her safety line onto the broad flat hood of Colonel Bennet's car. She had left a few lines dangling from convenient alcoves in the concrete ceiling structure here and there.

The prince had been getting out of his car when she dropped onto it.

He dropped his hand to his sidearm, unsnapped it, drew it, and pointed it at her, nearly as fast as an old west gunfighter. It was drawn and pointed before his face showed recognition. "Liliana!"

She nodded to him and sat cross-legged on the hood of his huge car with the big tires, putting herself close to eye level with him.

"Why are you here?" the prince asked, lowering his gun to his side.

"I also came to speak to Andrew Periclum. I was going to ask the same favor of him that I already asked of you, but because of what you will do, I will not get the chance."

"I'm sorry?" he said, as if it were a question.

Maybe he was asking her if he should be sorry for forcing her to alter plans? She shrugged. "You believe that Andrew Periclum has defied you, broken his word, and harmed your soldiers. You should not be sorry." She felt her lips tighten in contempt. "A pride-king's word is law. If Andrew Periclum has given his word to you and broken it, then he is an unworthy pride king. Your mission here is an honorable one."

The prince raised both brows at her, one wrinkling smooth dark skin, the other mottled scar tissue. "Honor is a word I hear used a lot. You say it as if it means something to you."

"My parents raised me to respect honorable people, even if they are enemies."

"Are we enemies now?" he asked, hand tensing around the gun at his side. It wasn't pointed at her, but the threat was clear.

Liliana looked at him directly with her human eyes for a second, then back down at her hands in her lap. "I still have not decided."

His eyebrows went up again. They were the most expressive part of his otherwise stoic face. "I expected you to say no, whether it was true or not."

"I always speak the truth. If we become enemies, I will tell you." She shrugged. "Or I will simply kill you, but I will never tell you that I am an ally if I am not."

His full lips twitched at the corner, the faintest shadow of a smile. "I'm not used to that much honesty."

"Andrew Periclum will enter this building in six minutes. You should stand there before he comes, so he will not see you." She pointed to a concrete roof support pillar that would hide the prince's presence from the pride-king until he came close.

Liliana hopped down off the car and walked with him to the concealment. The top of her head barely came up to his broad chest. He towered more than a foot over her, something that struck her every time she faced him up close. "Today is the day I spoke of before, when you are highly likely to be injured or possibly killed. I will offer you the same bargain again. If you will get me onto your military base unnoticed, I will make certain that you leave this building unharmed."

"My answer is the same."

Liliana sighed and nodded. She would have been surprised if he changed his mind.

Andrew Periclum's footsteps echoed in the concrete parking structure.

Liliana shook her head in disgust. The king of lions moved with the stealth of a hippopotamus. Her father would have been appalled.

The prince turned to watch him.

Liliana scrambled up a line and into a convenient alcove, not wanting Andrew Periclum to see her with the prince. Even if he was an unworthy king, still, Andrew Periclum was her king. And the Fae prince was not planning on being polite to him.

Alexander Bennet turned to look where she had been and seemed unsurprised that the space she previously occupied was now empty. He flashed a delighted grin at the empty concrete of the parking garage.

Andrew Periclum passed the concrete pillar.

Liliana turned her attention, and the focus of all eight of her eyes, to the two men below. While she watched, she prepared a line of silk with a large loop on the end.

With his wide-barreled pistol held casually down by his leg, the tall Fae prince stepped in front of the king of lions.

The lion-kin doctor stopped barely in time to avoid colliding with the prince's chest. The pride-king stood above average height and was in excellent physical condition, yet Colonel Alexander Bennet still towered over him.

"Oh, hello, Colonel," Andrew Periclum said. He put his hands casually behind him and stepped his feet apart into something like a military parade rest posture. With her fourth eyes, she saw one hand touch his wrist phone, activating it in some way.

"You gave me your word that your experiments wouldn't do any harm to my people," the prince said.

Andrew Periclum shrugged. "As far as I know, they haven't."

Liliana blinked her third eyes. They told her that his words were, without doubt, a lie. Yet nothing in the lion-kin's face or posture revealed the lie. For a beast-kin leader whose trusted word was the source of his power, Andrew Periclum was far too skilled at lying.

"Then why have eight of the twelve soldiers on your list disappeared and later turned up dead? Two more went missing this week."

Andrew Periclum shook his head and waved a hand dismissively "A tragedy, sure, but nothing to do with me." Another blatant lie without a flinch, Liliana noted. "Your CID attack bitch and your pet Celtic wolf have already dealt with the monsters responsible for most of those deaths, I hear. And no one knows what happened to those two women found in a shallow grave in the forest."

Muscles bunched in the prince's dark jaw. "You covered your tracks well. There's no evidence to trace this back to your doorstep, but I can see the pattern. They were all Others on my team, seasoned veterans who had cybernetics you designed. I don't know what you're doing, but these people were all under your care. I'm getting a new cyberneticist transferred in to look over your work."

Andrew Periclum snorted. "Good luck with that. I'm probably the only Other cyberneticist in the world. And not everything is your decision, Colonel. My processes are revolutionary, designed to make Others an even more powerful force." He leaned forward into the Fae prince's personal space. "My process could give this country the military edge. And Princess Aurore loves the idea of boosting Other powers with modern science."

The Fae prince's hand shot out and clenched the fabric of the military doctor's uniform faster than Liliana could blink. "You will inform the brass, and my sister, that the project was unsuccessful, and you will stop it. Now." The dark prince's deep voice sounded calm and controlled. He showed no sign of the seething rage bleeding orange around the prince's mind shields just under the mirror surface.

From her perch, Liliana could feel the concrete of her alcove tremble. She thought at first it was an echo from the thunder outside, but they were deep underground beneath multiple layers of concrete. The fury of the storm outside didn't penetrate here.

She placed a hand on the gritty artificial stone, head cocked to one side. The subtle tremor was no more than a heavy truck driving through might cause, but her third eyes could see the slight shading of fire orange in the concrete itself.

The Sidhe prince was angry. Although the prince did not appear to be deliberately exerting power to affect it, this man-made cave with its steel roots sunk into the bedrock beneath the little town shared his anger.

The king of lions barked a laugh in the prince's face. "You forget that I am not in your chain of command. Neither of them, your highness." He spoke the title with a twist of sarcasm, not respect. "I will not declare my work a failure when it isn't. My reputation is on the line."

Alexander Bennet lifted the gun in his hand, bringing it up to point at the doctor's face. "I don't give a damn about your reputation, your majesty." He gave back the same sarcasm on the honorific title. "No more of my people are going to die."

The squeal of tires made both men look up. Periclum's sleek

black car, the electric engine nearly silent, barreled toward them at high speed.

In his surprise, the colonel's grip on the doctor's uniform loosened.

Andrew Periclum shoved the Fae prince hard and stepped to the side.

As Colonel Bennet stumbled into the path of the speeding car, Liliana dropped her loop of silk.

Even as he tried to jump out of the way, the spider could see that he would not clear the car's path.

She pulled with all her strength on the silk cord looped around his shoulders. It boosted the momentum of his own leap so he went farther.

Colonel Bennet lost his grip on his gun as he hit the concrete. He tucked his long legs in just as the tires of the car brushed past, leaving a black mark on his gray and faded green camouflage printed uniform pants.

The car screeched to a stop a few feet away, the king of lions got in it with a defiant wave, and the car accelerated again.

Behind the wheel, the huge lion-kin with the claw scar on his face that she had seen in her vision earlier smiled in a way that wasn't the least bit pleasant.

CHAPTER 14

NOT FAVORS

LILIANA DROPPED FROM THE ALCOVE IN THE CONCRETE ceiling.

The Fae prince eyed her warily, upper arms bound to his sides by her silk, but far from helpless.

She walked away from him to pick up his gun and walked back.

Colonel Bennet rolled up to one knee as soon as she turned her back but hadn't made it to his feet yet when she turned to face him, gun in hand.

He froze.

Liliana's feelings about this Fae prince were muddled and uncertain, but she knew that she absolutely did not want him to be afraid of her. That would severely limit her life expectancy. She closed all but her human eyes, reversed the pistol so she held it by the barrel, and extended it to him, down low, so he could take it with his currently limited reach.

As the pistol grip touched his palm, some of the tension in his shoulders eased.

Liliana popped out one of her arm blades, carefully, in a direction that was clearly not aimed at him. "I can cut the silk if you will allow me."

Colonel Bennet nodded permission.

As she cut the cord around his upper arms, she felt the warmth of his skin through the uniform. On his knees, his face was only a few inches lower than hers.

She breathed the warm, masculine scent of his skin. Her eyes traced the burn scars from his neck, up to his cheek and over to his temple where a streak of white in his short black hair led to the mangled curve of his ear—the only flaw in this otherwise flawless man.

The Japanese had a concept of *wabi*, the small imperfection that highlighted the perfection of the whole. Her brother-in-law, Rizki, taught Liliana the concept. Colonel Alexander Bennet embodied it.

After she tossed the silk away, the spider-kin flicked her wrist to sheath her blade.

A small crease formed between his brows as if she puzzled him. "I told you I wouldn't grant the favor you asked for." His melodious voice all but whispered since she stood so close. "I still won't bring you onto my base."

Liliana nodded. "I will have to find another way to protect my friends."

The spider seer thought of seelie Siobhan and the unseelie goblin the sprite called her best friend, and the dead unseelie sprite Siobhan mourned. She thought of Doctor Nudd's paternal attitude toward a Celtic wolf, the enemy of all unseelie. Fayetteville seemed to be a place where old enmities could be safely set aside.

And the second time they'd come face-to-face, the prince had plainly sworn to her that he wouldn't let those old lines define him.

Liliana wondered why, even as she held out her hand to a son of the race that had so many times ordered her kind put to death.

He looked at her slender hand for a long moment before taking it with his much larger, stronger hand.

An oddly pleasant tingle spread from his hand through her body, making her shiver. That was some very powerful chemistry.

Colonel Bennet kept hold of her hand as he got to his feet, but he didn't pull on her at all. His thumb caressed the back of her hand. "Thank you, Liliana, for aiding me with no promise of reward. Again."

The heat from his hand spread to her cheeks. She stared at his shiny black boots. "You would probably have survived."

"Probably." He chuckled softly.

"I have to go," Liliana said.

"I understand." He gave her a formal bow over the hand he held. He clearly out-ranked her socially, yet he had given her a bow appropriate for an equal—oddly out of place in America where almost no one bowed. His eyes took on a mischievous sparkle for just a moment, and he turned her hand over. He gave a lingering kiss to her palm, his lips warm and soft.

Heat fired every inch of Liliana's skin, making her heart pound like she'd just been in combat.

He looked up at her, still bent over her hand, his dark eyes sparkling with mischief, his full lips quirked at the edges.

On impulse, she moved her hand to his cheek, stroking skin, a tickle of shaving stubble, and bumpy scars. She leaned forward and brushed his lips with hers for the barest moment. As she jumped back, the feel of his lips lingering on hers, he stared at her in open surprise.

Liliana swallowed, her heart racing, and her cheeks hot, wondering why she'd done that. "I have to go," she repeated.

Alexander Bennet chuckled softly and repeated, "I understand."

Liliana turned and walked quickly, she definitely wasn't running, away.

Her friends' lives were at stake. She didn't have time to be flustered. She didn't have time to think about the searing heat of his lips on hers or the tremble in her knees.

Shaking her head to clear it, she ascended the ramp to the exit. She looked with her fourth eyes to find an available auto-cab, but they were all full of people going home to get out of the bad weather.

The spider-kin stepped out of the parking garage and started walking in the pouring rain. The wind blew her hair and her skirt in multiple directions. Lightning danced in the low clouds.

She tried to ignore the driving rain and the cold wind and explore various possible ways of getting onto the Army base to save Doctor Nudd and Siobhan. She could see that the little sprite was already on her way to the base. Liliana could not ride with her. Siobhan's motorcycle had no place to hide another person.

Lightning flashes made the slanting rain jerk in the air like an old movie shown at the wrong speed. Thunder crashed and rumbled.

Pete had gone to see Detective Jackson at the police station. His van had a secret compartment where he stored his weapons, shielded from military scanners. Hiding in there would be one way for her to get on base undetected. But Pete would not return to the base soon enough to save the goblin or the sprite.

Her teeth chattered together, disturbing her train of thought. Liliana hugged herself harder. This storm was very poorly timed. It made everything more complicated. At least the hail that kept threatening hadn't yet materialized.

A bit of ice the size of a pea stung her arm.

Hundreds of small hailstones fell all around her.

She felt an urge to stamp her foot and glare at the storm clouds and raging wind. She would have to find shelter until the hail stopped. It might get bigger. She couldn't afford an injury today.

The prince's all-terrain vehicle pulled up next to her and stopped. A field of air automatically repelled rain and hail with equal perfection over the windshield.

Alexander Bennet pushed the button that rolled the passenger side window down and looked at her from the other side of the car.

Liliana wasn't sure what she was supposed to say. She could tell him that it was raining and hailing and windy, but he already knew that. He knew where she needed to go. And he had already told her that he would not take her there. Asking him to change his mind was pointless. "Your seat cushion is getting wet."

"So are you," the Fae colonel pointed out.

Liliana looked down at herself, blinking rain out of her eyes. The velvet scarves that made up her blouse and skirt were plastered to the leotard underneath. "I am already wet."

"Then it won't matter when you sit on the wet seat cushion."

"I need to go to the base."

"I'll take you wherever you want to go. Except there."

Liliana considered that. "Okay." She opened the door, climbed up on the steel running board, and into the car with the giant tires. The heavy door shut out the wild wind and pouring rain as he pushed the button that rolled up the window.

Colonel Bennet looked at her expectantly.

He would take her anywhere except where she actually needed to go. Maybe she could affect Pete's path just enough to get him there in time? It was the only option she could see.

"Take me to the police station."

The prince turned the heater up a little higher, then told his GPS where to go as he accelerated down the road. She noted that he drove manually with his own hands on the wheel. She wondered if he didn't trust the auto-drive, or if he just disliked sitting and doing nothing while the machine navigated.

As the warmth of the heater sank into Liliana's skin, her muscles loosened. Her teeth stopped chattering. Lightning still flashed bright outside the confines of the car. It painted the scars on the prince's face in harsh contrasts, making his appearance shift abruptly from handsome man to nightmare demon. The wind whipped trees in every direction. A few small branches blew across the street in front of them.

"Why did you give me a ride?" she asked the prince.

"You did save my life."

"You would probably just have been injured. You are not that easy to kill."

His mouth quirked up on the edges. He glanced away from the storm-swept road for a moment to look at her. "I'd also like to know more about what you said. We have more time to talk."

Oh. Of course. Answers to his questions were the price for the ride.

"Who's going to die today on my base?" His voice sounded casual, calm, almost bored, but his long-fingered hands were tight on the wheel. She did not think it was because of the storm.

The Fae prince showed little of his emotions on the surface, and Liliana had been forbidden to look with her third eyes, but she strongly suspected that he was worried for his people.

Some things began to make a disturbing kind of sense to her. This Sidhe colonel had confronted the pride-king specifically because he suspected he'd done harm to his soldiers. The artificial stone around him shared his anger. Both of those things hinted at old world power and obligation. Liliana remembered that when this Sidhe prince called, not just the living tree, but the earth itself had answered him.

Sidhe were no more powerful than other Fae unless an area of land chose them. The larger and more populated the land area that chose them, the more powerful the Sidhe became.

Since the slaughter, decimation by disease, and displacement of the native tribes, the American Sidhe had faded. No land in the United States that she knew of still had a bond with the old Sidhe. Just like spider seers, North American Sidhe had been hunted, so very many of them killed, some perhaps gone to sleep in their mineral or plant forms for centuries or forever. Everyone thought them extinct now.

Liliana suspected they were no more extinct than her own kind, but kept their existence hidden for the same reason she did—to stay not extinct.

The old Sidhe might be gone, but the land remembered. For centuries, it refused to choose any outsider. No non-native Sidhe had ever been chosen by any land in North America. Those who hoped to be chosen gave up and went back to their homelands across the sea.

Yet, it seemed natural that a Sidhe who had dedicated his life to the military would have an affinity for a military location, and Fort Liberty was one of the oldest military bases in the United States.

"Did you land bond with Fort Liberty?" she asked him. It

wasn't her turn to ask a question, but that seemed like an incredibly important thing for her to know.

His gaze did not leave the storm ravaged road. He showed a total lack of reaction. "I don't know what you mean." Everyone reacted when someone asked a question, whether with confusion or curiosity, fear or irritation. People always reacted to questions.

"I don't lie to people. I don't like it when they lie to me, especially since I almost always know," Liliana said. He had old-world manners and old-world abilities. Of course, he knew what it meant to be bonded to the land.

The prince glanced down at his steering wheel for a moment, but he didn't apologize for the lie.

Liliana looked out the window at the tall pines, oaks, cedars, and elms waving wildly in the fierce wind.

By not answering, the prince had answered her question. She wondered if he was powerful enough to land bond with the entire town of Fayetteville, or even more of North Carolina. It would explain why so many Fae and beast-kin seemed drawn to this area. It might also encourage the flourishing of the Green that Liliana had noticed. More than might be explained by the general greening of the world.

Most importantly, an honorable, landed prince in Europe would feel an obligation to watch over the well-being of his people.

That left the still unanswered question of who exactly the prince considered *his*. The soldiers on base were a given. Of course the warriors who took his orders would be his to watch over. An unseelie prince would not be likely to claim a seelie sprite, even if she did supply him with custom weapons. However, an unseelie doctor who healed his soldiers would be someone a landed prince would almost certainly consider his to protect. "If I cannot get to the base, either Doctor Nudd or Siobhan will die."

"You don't know which one?" Colonel Bennet turned a corner and crossed a low section of the road. Water sloshed nearly to the top of the big wheels, but the sturdy military car plowed steadily through.

Liliana thought about Siobhan on her motorcycle. The sprite had to want to get to the base very badly to drive in this weather.

She gave one last shiver, feeling guilty but grateful for the heated vehicle. "It might be both of them, Siobhan and Doctor Nudd. The future is forged by the choices we make. Doctor Nudd will die unless Siobhan chooses to risk her life to save him. Or unless I can get to the base to save them both."

The prince's black brows pulled together, and his lips tightened, barely perceptible changes in expression that Liliana noted with interest. She would have to watch the prince closely. Many of his expressions were more subtle than other people's.

"Why would a seelie Fae sacrifice herself to protect a goblin?" His voice was still unconcerned, as if they chatted about the rainstorm. Liliana thought she detected an edge of bitterness. She wished she could open her third eyes to confirm what she suspected. She hadn't seen who treated him so badly in his younger days, but she'd seen hints that they were Fae from the day court.

Siobhan and Doctor Nudd's relationship was not something either would want the local land ruler to know about, and Liliana did not disclose other people's secrets. "Siobhan offered Doctor Nudd a favor to save her life when she was badly injured." The trading of favors was the one interaction that was considered acceptable, even across the strict social barriers of the two courts of Night and Day.

"And he's likely to call in the favor to save his own life." He nodded to himself to show understanding.

Fortunately, the prince wasn't asking a question. Liliana greatly doubted that Doctor Nudd would deliberately put Siobhan into danger to protect himself.

"Is there anything else you can tell me?"

Liliana cocked her head to one side and considered. "You confronted the pride-king because all the soldiers who died, even the ones the widow spiders killed and the two women who were shot, they were all his patients."

"Yeah. I don't know what's going on, but he's involved somehow."

"As I said, I can see lies. When you asked him if his cybernetic work had caused harm to his subjects, he said that as far as he knew, it hadn't. That was a lie."

Alexander Bennet's eyes took on a soft red glow like a burning ember of a fire, an indication of his Otherness that he would probably suppress if she were not also Other. "So his experiments *are* harmful to my soldiers. I knew it. Too many coincidences. And he's aware. But there's no evidence that he had anything directly to do with their deaths. What does an unscrupulous cyberneticist at Liberty have to do with a nest of widow spiders in Raleigh?"

"Oh," Liliana remembered something important. "When I was trying to get Pete back from the widow spiders, I watched them talking. Kristen, the young pregnant spider did not want to kill anyone. Lady Daphne told her that the doctor who sent them said they were going to die anyway. She was just making use of their bodies."

"The doctor? Did they say who?"

"They did not. But..." Liliana looked directly at Alexander Bennet for a moment, and he glanced back at her at the same time.

"Periclum," Alexander Bennet said.

"The pride-king," Liliana said at the same moment.

"Something he's doing to the soldiers must be killing them slowly," Alexander said. "And he used the widow spiders to cover his tracks."

"He might also be the one who murdered those two soldiers I found in the forest. That would explain why it seemed that they were already dead before they were shot. He might also be the one who will murder Doctor Nudd. I will look to be certain." Liliana opened her fourth eyes, focusing on the king of lions and also on Doctor Nudd's death. She saw the hand that held the sword that would end her favorite goblin's life. It belonged to Andrew Periclum in demi-lion form.

"The king of lions is the enemy." Liliana nodded. She was

somewhat startled by the knowledge, despite the logic of the conclusion. She had almost asked the murderer to give her a lift to the murder scene to prevent him from killing someone.

That might have gone badly.

A muscle in the prince's jaw jumped. "I should have killed him when I had the chance."

"You did not have the chance. His champion protected him."

"Bradley." The prince's mouth pinched as if he tasted something bad.

So that was the name of the man with the claw scars. Bradley.

He pulled up in front of the police station. "Here?"

"Yes. Thank you."

The prince shrugged. "We're even."

"You did not promise me a favor." Liliana looked at his face for a moment, confused.

His lips twitched in a tic at the edges. "You didn't promise to keep me from getting hit by a car."

They had exchanged "not favors." Again.

It was as if the two of them, with unspoken agreement, had turned the laws of Fae bargaining on their heads to become a free exchange of whatever gifts or favors the other person felt like giving.

And now they both knew the enemy they fought, even if he did not trust her enough to let her fight at his side.

Yet.

She looked back at the colorful bar of ribbons on his chest, a smile painting her lips, before getting out of the warm car and heading back into the teeth of the storm.

Chapter 15

The Spider, The Wolf, And The Detective

The driving rain soaked Liliana to the skin again in the few seconds it took to reach the front door of the police station. She ducked quickly inside as the door automatically shut. The warmth loosened some of her muscles, but the crowd tightened them right back up again.

A surprising number of people crowded into the station lobby. Many were shouting about their power being knocked out and people stealing from them while security systems were down. Some griped about wrecks caused by traffic signals failing, confusing their auto-drive programs.

Liliana wrapped her arms around herself, hugging tight, and shivering, six of her eyes firmly shut, the other two pinned on her soaked ballet shoes. People bumped into her, crowded her, shouted, and jostled. She fought hard against the urge to shut down. Too many people in too small a space could make her mind retreat inside itself where she would become unaware and time would pass without touching her.

Her favorite goblin and her favorite sprite did not have time for her to shut down.

Liliana got in a line with a bunch of other people and waited her turn. She watched a big digital clock on the wall with large red numbers out of the corners of her human eyes, as it marked the time Doctor Nudd and Siobhan had left to live.

Finally, she reached the front of the line. A policeman with a mustache that made her wonder if he might be walrus-kin sat behind a desk she could barely see over. He asked her business there.

"I need to speak to Detective Shonda Jackson," she said. "I have information related to a case." That should get her in, and while the goblin's murder was not yet a police case, it undoubtedly would be by the end of the day if she didn't manage to prevent it.

"Jackson, huh? Wait over there. I'll call her in a minute."

Liliana sat in the hard chair as instructed and watched the digital clock to know when a minute had passed. When two passed, she considered doing something, but she wasn't certain what. She had already waited in the line once for approximately fifteen minutes for the privilege of talking to the walrus man. She did not wish to do it again. The man left her waiting for another seven minutes while he dealt with others. Liliana was beginning to worry that Pete would leave before she could get to him. If that happened, one or both of her Fae friends would die.

Liliana ignored the social rule that said she must wait her turn. She was running out of time. She shoved a man three times her size with a lot of tattoos aside and took his place at the front of the line.

He gave her an aggrieved look and said, "Hey!" He had waited his turn properly.

"Sorry," she mumbled. "I need to see Detective Jackson now," she told the walrus. "Lives depend on it."

"Okay, lady, keep your shirt on."

Liliana blinked at him for a moment, confused. "I have no intention of taking my shirt off. I am already cold."

The walrus officer blinked back at her for a few seconds, then shook his head and yelled over his shoulder, "Hey, West!

A man in police uniform, who was even bigger and more muscular than the tattooed man behind her, shifted his armful of files and answered. "Yo!"

"This lady says she needs to talk to Jackson right now. Life or death."

"On it." The big police officer escorted her into the building, dropping stacks of folders on various desks as he went.

She had seen this man a time or two before in visions and in the forest after she found the grave of the two soldiers. "You are Detective Jackson's friend."

Liliana followed so closely behind the broad back of the officer, she had to be careful not to tread on the heels of his shiny black shoes. She took advantage of the shelter to open her third and fourth eyes. He was a good man, but he was fated to be murdered on the same day as the Sidhe prince.

The spider seer flinched. Why was it that every person she looked at lately was destined to die horribly and suddenly in less than a year? A frightening trend. A storm was brewing in Fayetteville, and it would hit with far more effect than the wind and thunder outside.

"I don't know if you'd say Detective Jackson and I were friends, ma'am." He ducked his head and shuffled some of the papers in his hand. "We just work together."

Liliana had seen a teenage girl with long dark hair, pale skin, and blue eyes just like the big officer's. Detective Jackson held the girl's hand while she walked into a drug rehab clinic. Liliana decided not to dispute with the man about his relationship with the detective but helping his little sister with a drug addiction problem seemed well beyond the shallow social bonds of a co-worker.

Across a wide room filled with desks and people and shouting, was the detective's desk. Detective Jackson was speaking to Pete and Sergeant Giovanni. Pete was just grabbing his jacket off the back of a chair. That was not good. Time was running out.

"Hey, Jackson!" Officer West shouted across the crowded room. "This lady needs to talk to you."

Everyone in the room turned to stare at Liliana. She wanted desperately to crawl under a desk, or better yet, into the roof rafters behind the suspended ceiling. She hugged herself tightly, stared at her toes, and fiddled with her soggy sleeves. She wondered if this was how her eyes made Siobhan feel, like an amoeba under one of Doctor Nudd's microscopes.

I must not shut down. I must not shut down.

But it was too much.

"Lilly, what's going on? What are you doing here?" Pete's voice spoke right beside her. He was on the other side of the room a moment ago. She had lost some time. Probably not very much. Hopefully, not too much.

Officer West had one of his heavy arms around her shoulders. She shivered away from him. She didn't know him. People shouldn't touch people they don't know without permission.

She looked up and around quickly with just her human eyes, but it was still overwhelming. Too many people. A lot of them were still staring at her. Only Detective Jackson, Sergeant Giovanni, and Pete were familiar faces. The rest were strangers.

So many strangers.

"Hey, if it isn't Anna Sees All," Sergeant Giovanni said. "Seen anything interesting in your crystal ball lately?"

Liliana hid her face in Pete's chest. "Get me out of here, Pete," she whispered.

"Sure, Lilly." His wiry arm replaced Officer West's meaty arm. It helped. "I've got you." Pete nodded thanks to the big man, and the officer stepped back. "I was just heading out anyway. We're about done talking to Detective Jackson about the two missing corporals."

"Not fast enough," Liliana muttered into his chest, inhaling the familiar scent of canine and chemicals.

"Is she a friend of yours?" Officer West asked. His hands were surprisingly long fingered and slender with neatly trimmed nails. Liliana realized she had unintentionally opened her second eyes that she reflexively opened in combat situations to see enemies coming from any direction. She quickly shut them before they were spotted, making herself blind again.

Pete said, "Yeah, she's a friend."

"She said she had important life or death information for a case." Officer West's deep voice came from just above Pete's shoulder. He must have moved around to the other side. "Is she all right?"

"She's just a little lost, I think," Pete said.

"Well, that seems like life or death information," Sergeant Giovanni commented.

"Life or death," Liliana mumbled into Pete's chest. Her helplessness frustrated her. Doctor Nudd and Siobhan might die because she couldn't handle crowds well or drive a car. She took a deep breath. "Life or death. Seconds count. We have to go now." She pushed Pete, not sure if it was in the right direction, but at least it would get him moving.

Sergeant Giovanni chuckled. "You heard your new girlfriend, Pete. What are you waiting for?"

"We can swing by Lilly's place on the way back to base and drop her off."

"Hold on a second there, Mr. Teague." Detective Jackson gently touched the back of Liliana's hand, where it worried the edge of her sleeve. Her dark face at the same height as Liliana's blocked most of the staring eyes in the room. "Was there something you needed to tell me?"

Liliana turned away from Pete's chest for a moment. "My friends, Doctor Nudd and Siobhan, are going to die. On base. Very soon."

Pete squeezed her tighter. "That's what you were trying to tell us. Zoe and I will take care of it, Lilly."

Liliana shook her head. "Pete won't get there fast enough to save them. We need your help, Detective Jackson."

The detective's eyes narrowed. "Can you tell me where exactly? Fort Liberty is damn near as big as Fayetteville."

"A lab. With chemicals and machines and a cot on wheels, like a hospital but not." She looked up at Pete. "Near where Siobhan got her new arm."

"You're not taking her seriously, are you?" Sergeant Giovanni said.

"Any reason why I shouldn't?" Detective Jackson asked the soldier.

Pete didn't give his friend a chance to answer. "If Lilly says something's going to happen, you can believe her."

Sergeant Giovanni's dark brows went up, then her mouth twisted suspiciously. "If you think something's up on base," she asked Liliana, "why didn't you go to the authorities at Liberty?"

Liliana opened her mouth to say that she had spoken to their colonel, but he wouldn't allow her onto his base, and closed her mouth again. That information would not be helpful. She looked at the gun on Sergeant Giovanni's belt. "You are a police officer for the Army base, aren't you?"

Pete grinned at the MP. "She's got a point."

Detective Jackson asked, "Sergeant, do you have any idea how valuable it could be to know about a murder before the victim is a corpse?" Her face lit from within with a kind of wicked glee. "If it's a wild goose chase, so what? If there's any chance to stop two murders today, I'll take it."

"We have to go! NOW!" Liliana shouted, then cringed when all eyes turned to her again. "Seconds count," she mumbled into Pete's chest.

Detective Jackson nodded crisply. "West, I need a black and white unit with four-wheel drive. We're going lights and sirens. Speed is important."

When Detective Jackson snapped out the order, things moved fast.

The big officer disappeared with a crisp, "Yes, ma'am."

Liliana let herself be swept along into the stairwell, the underground police parking garage, then the passenger seat of a squad car only a little smaller than the colonel's car. Detective Jackson drove, and Sergeant Giovanni and Pete took the back seat.

The heater made the dash glow, and the seat warmed under

Liliana, both trying valiantly to steam the cold water from her clothes.

Detective Jackson took the wheel to drive manually, just as Colonel Bennet had done. Her driving starkly contrasted with the colonel's steady progress through the wet, windy streets.

The siren wailed while the rain beat a hard rock rhythm, accented by the deep base of thunder and strobe of lightning. The detective danced with her car to the manic rhythm, hydroplaning around curves. Her tires still grabbed enough pavement to squeal in protest as she avoided obstacles and traffic that didn't get out of the way fast enough to suit her.

The auto-drive flashed yellow near-collision alerts almost as constant as the lightning. The polite disembodied female voice kept offering to take over until Detective Jackson put it on mute.

With the way the detective drove, hands moving controlled and fast on the wheel, they were highly likely to arrive in time to alter the outcome, assuming they didn't die getting there. Future paths flashed and changed and changed again in the spider seer's mind too rapidly to follow.

The future was in flux.

Liliana couldn't tell if the detective's help would accomplish her goal.

Sergeant Giovanni speed dialed her wrist phone. "I'll get us emergency clearance through the nearest gate."

Liliana shivered and huddled in the seat, knees pulled up and arms wrapped tightly around them, even though that made the seatbelt cut into her waist. She opened her fourth eyes.

Who is Sergeant Giovanni calling to get permission for them to enter the Army base?

Oh no.

"Do not tell him I am with you, Sergeant Giovanni!" Liliana said quickly.

"What the hell? You want me to lie to my commanding officer?"

"Trust her," Pete said. "Do what she says."

"Like Hell. The last time I saw this woman, she was a murder suspect. She's not even human." The line clicked open. A tiny hologram of Colonel Bennet's head and shoulders appeared, hovering above Sergeant Giovanni's wrist.

"Giovanni here, sir. Detective Jackson wants emergency access to one of the base buildings. She got a tip on two possible attempted murders: the goblin doctor and the cyborg fairy."

"Is a woman named Liliana with you?" he asked, face stern and blank of expression.

Pete shook his head frantically at the sergeant, but she pursed her lips and ignored him. "Yes, sir."

Detective Jackson swerved hard around a limb fallen in the middle of the road, throwing them all to the side for a moment.

Sergeant Giovanni braced her hand against the lowered barrier between the front and back seat, making it easy for Liliana to lean into the tiny camera's range and speak to her wrist where the prince could see her.

"I am here, Colonel Bennet," Liliana said. "But I will get out of the car at the gate."

"I'll accept your word on that." The semi-transparent image of his face looked straight at her.

"Thank you." She did not think there were many people whose word the prince would accept after such a short acquaintance. His miniature image gave her a tiny nod, a barely perceptible movement, but it felt as if he had bowed to her again in respect. Apparently, saving the prince from being hit by a car had earned her more than just a ride to the police station.

"Emergency access for the detective is granted. Where will it happen?"

Pete answered. "From Lilly's description, it sounds like the cybernetics research lab in Womack med center."

"I'll inform the gate guards and meet you there." The line clicked dead.

"Why did you tell him you'd get out of the car, Lilly?" Pete asked.

Liliana started to answer, but her teeth clacked together as

Detective Jackson hit a curb. The entire car jolted to a slant with two wheels on the sidewalk. The street was clogged with traffic ahead, backed up behind an accident.

Detective Jackson drove around it. The detective's face sparkled with delight. She honked the horn, adding to the noise of thunder and the already wailing siren and shouted, "Get out of the way!" for good measure, even though the windows were sealed.

The few people on the sidewalk, walking while huddled under their portable umbrella fields, leapt to the side.

"The Colonel does not trust me," Liliana answered when she could get the words out. That was a balanced state. She did not trust him either.

"Which makes me wonder even more why the hell we should trust you," Sergeant Giovanni commented.

"Because she saved your life, Zoe." The soldier looked at her friend like Pete had sprouted flowers out of his ears. "She saved both our lives," Pete added. "More than once."

Detective Jackson took her eyes off the road for a quick glance at the spider-kin. "That true?"

Liliana shrugged and nodded. "We protected each other when we fought the widow spiders."

Detective Jackson added, "She saved my life too."

Sergeant Giovanni snorted in the back seat. "Did she tell you that?"

Pete sighed next to her. "Zoe, did you think the liver-eating stone giant just happened to trip when she was chasing you?"

There was no answer, but Liliana wasn't really surprised. Sergeant Giovanni did not trust Others. And she knew Liliana was Other, while she did not know that Pete was.

Siren still blaring, the detective skidded to a stop at the entrance gate checkpoint for Fort Liberty.

The detective caught the spider-kin's wrist for a moment before she was fully out of the car. "Sorry about this," she shouted over the noise of the siren and storm.

The rain soaked the spider seer to the skin as soon as she opened the car door. The siren and thunder that built and rumbled competed to see which could assault Liliana's eardrums the hardest. "Just save my friends," she shouted back.

The detective's jaw tightened with determination, and she stomped on the gas. The door slammed shut as she accelerated.

Pete looked back at Liliana apologetically through the rear window as they left her behind in the pouring rain.

CHAPTER 16

SOGGY SPIDER, BLEARY BADGER, AND LIVID LION

LILIANA DIDN'T REALLY CARE ABOUT THE RAIN OR THE wind cutting through her soggy clothes. At least the hail had stopped. She turned away from the gate, putting her back to the cameras, then opened her fourth eyes. She kept her human eyes open as she started walking home so she could see the cold puddles even as she put her feet in them. She could not be any more wet if she had gone swimming in her clothes. Fortunately, she did not live far from this entrance into Fort Liberty.

She searched for the series of events leading to Doctor Nudd's death. Some things came sharper and clearer now that it was closer in time and she already knew some of it.

Why would the pride-king kill Doctor Nudd?

Holding that question clear in her mind allowed her to see even more of the near future.

Her vision showed a large examination room as big as her entire house, with three complex microscopes and other unknown scientific-looking equipment on a long counter along one wall. Black office chairs with wheels sat in front of the equipment. Glass-doored cabinets above the bench held an odd combination of beakers, computer chips, test tubes, and electrical wire. Workbenches with granite tops held Bunsen burners and soldering irons, with bottles of chemicals on shelves above, and wooden cabinets that opened on both sides of the bench below. Several types of 3-D printers sat in the corners. Office doors lined the wall opposite the counter with the microscopes. Brass plaques indicated the owners of the offices.

It looked like a place where many doctors and scientists like Pete might all work together, but in Liliana's vision, the place was nearly deserted, all the workers gone. The clock on the wall showed it was twenty-two minutes into the future. The people who worked there must have already gone home.

Near the center of the big open space waited a gurney. On it lay an American badger-kin in his brown and white-furred, pointy-nosed, demi-badger form, wearing a lieutenant's uniform. Liliana looked at the name badge. As she'd suspected, Runningwolf was stitched on the front. An IV ran into the young beast-kin soldier's arm.

She'd never seen a beast-kin asleep in his demi-beast form. Beast-kin normally shifted to human form when sleeping.

Doctor Nudd walked past the door and did a double take, as if also surprised to see the gurney with Lieutenant Runningwolf on it in demi-badger form. He walked over and checked the information printed on the IV bag. His brows wrinkled in puzzlement.

After knocking on the office door with the brass plaque that read "Dr. Andrew Periclum" and getting no answer, he went in. On the desk lay a folder labelled "Other Physical Enhancement Nanite Model 14." The goblin picked it up, then stepped back out to the exam room. He pulled one sheet of paper from the folder and held it up beside the IV bag. The long scientific words on the paper in his hand matched the ones printed on the IV bag.

The goblin doctor mumbled softly, "Remove the needle from the badger. Right. It makes sense now."

Liliana felt a wash of pleasure to know that her friend remembered her warning.

He removed the IV needle from the young badger's arm carefully, holding a cotton ball over the hole to keep it from bleeding into Lieutenant Runningwolf's fur. He waited expectantly for a few minutes, but removing the needle had no immediate effect. The badger-kin soldier remained deeply asleep. "Hmph. Or perhaps not."

Liliana nodded to herself. It was all right. Doctor Nudd didn't know it yet, but he had bought himself a few important moments of life.

He picked the folder back up and read through more of the information, mumbling things under his breath as he read like, "What was he thinking?" and "This is madness."

Andrew Periclum entered the large room and saw the goblin holding the folder.

They argued, shouting a lot of scientific words Liliana did not understand. The words "side-effects," "toxic," "unethical," and "human experimentation" from Doctor Nudd made the meaning reasonably clear. The essence of Andrew Periclum's argument seemed to be "power." Power for all Others, power for himself, and power that would impress Princess Aurore with his genius. He mentioned her again as a sponsor of his experiments, but the way he said her name made Liliana wonder if he wanted more than just power from the beautiful Fae princess.

Andrew Periclum seemed to think that ended the discussion and walked into his office.

Doctor Nudd followed. "Princess Aurore has no authority to give orders on this side of the ocean, and furthermore ..."

Liliana skipped ahead in time to the end of the argument, perhaps a half hour in the future, when the fight would progress beyond words.

The argument ended with the honorable goblin drawing himself to the full height of his slim human form in Periclum's office and swearing, "This could kill people. I'm surprised half your subjects aren't already dead."

"More than half of them are," Periclum said with a wave of his hand as if that were unimportant.

Doctor Nudd's face was a picture of shock. "I insist you put a stop to this outrage immediately."

"I am the king of lions, and my word is law. Are you challenging me?"

"Absolutely I am. Your rank is no more an excuse than Aurore's. This is wrong."

"Do you know how the North Carolina pride chose me to be king?" Periclum asked calmly, as he opened a large, classified equipment locker behind his desk with his thumbprint and retinal scan.

Doctor Nudd spluttered, "Do you think you can simply change the subject and I will forget that you are poisoning ..."

The locker door opened. Periclum swung it wide so Doctor Nudd could see that it was filled with ancient weapons: swords and shields, axes, maces and knives. Periclum picked up a mace and tossed it at the goblin doctor. In surprise, the goblin dropped the folder full of papers he was carrying and caught the weapon.

Periclum chose a sword for himself. "For thousands of years, the pride-king has been the one who can claim kingship and defeat all challengers." He turned to face the goblin. His shirt and lab coat ripped along the seams. His military-buzzed, black hair lengthened and straightened into a thick, shaggy, golden mane.

Doctor Nudd swallowed, the mace slack in his hand, staring at the seven-foot-tall, four-hundred-pound demi-lion. "We could simply discuss this, like civilized men."

Fangs so long his mouth couldn't contain them pushed from between Periclum's lips as he completed the transformation. He smiled at the goblin, an entirely unfriendly gesture.

"Right. Well, then." Doctor Nudd hefted the mace up into a proper guard position. "I'd like a shield, as well, if you please."

Periclum was already in the process of picking up a shield from the still open locker. He tossed it at the goblin. While Doctor Nudd fumbled to catch it with a mace in one hand, the lion-kin's voice echoed in a rumbling growl inside the tiny office. "I am the King of Lions, and my word is law," he quoted the ancient ritual challenge as if Doctor Nudd had called challenge against him for his position as pride-king. It made the attack sort of legal under beast-kin tradition, since Doctor Nudd was challenging an order Periclum had given as king. Human law, of course, wouldn't condone the murder, but he didn't seem to care about that.

The pride-king lunged. His huge, clawed feet shed scraps of boot leather and dug deep grooves into the wood as they propelled the lion over the desk.

Doctor Nudd jumped back out of the office. He slammed the door in the lion's face with his elbow, while he fumbled with the weapons.

The lion-kin burst through the door, not bothering to open it. Wood splinters flew everywhere.

Nudd ducked his face behind the shield, holding it by the edge. Most of the door fragments struck the shield, and he staggered back against a shelf full of beakers, spare electronic parts, and various tools.

Some of the flying shards of wood struck the badger-kin on the gurney. Lieutenant Runningwolf woke abruptly, growling and swiping out blearily with his claws.

Those formidable six-inch claws forced the demi-lion to halt his charge and dodge to the side.

Doctor Nudd made good use of the crucial moments that the badger's unexpected attack bought him. He got his left arm through the shield loops and put the mace in his left hand along with the second shield loop. He used his free hand to hurl a large microscope. The cast steel instrument caught the lion on the shoulder while he was off balance from dodging the badger's claws.

Pressing his advantage, the goblin heaved a rolling office chair at the lion's head, knocking him down completely.

With his enemy's charge stopped, the oak goblin doctor took a moment to shift to his own eight-foot-tall demi-tree form with the tough barky skin. He hefted the mace and shield and attacked.

Liliana squealed with delight and bounced on her wet toes

splashing in a puddle as she watched the goblin use the training she had given him to fight back ferociously.

The old-world monsters armed with ancient weapons crashed and smashed their way around the modern lab, shattering expensive equipment and cabinetry.

The badger-kin soldier coughed and rolled off his gurney. Too drugged to stand, he collapsed on all fours, his black eyes blinking sleepily.

Doctor Nudd's longer reach and ferocity seemed to have Periclum on the run.

Then the lion ducked under the mace and shoved against the shield with a powerful shoulder, hurling Nudd into the workbench where his woody head impacted the cabinets with a *thunk* that left him dazed and the cabinet dented. The lion kicked hard against the wheeled gurney. It flew across the room and hit Doctor Nudd's hip. The oak goblin grunted in pain and was knocked to the ground next to Lieutenant Runningwolf.

Periclum swung his sword in an arc that would have passed through Runningwolf's neck and Nudd's arm.

From his knees, the goblin deflected the blow, protecting both himself and the demi-badger with a well-executed shield defense, but his counterattack was weak.

With skill earned in years of combat practice that the goblin hadn't had enough time to match, the pride-king contemptuously swept his opponent's mace aside with his sword tip. The mace flew across the room and smashed into a cabinet door, splintering it.

The goblin doctor hefted his only remaining defense: his shield.

The lion feinted to the right, as if to stab Lieutenant Runningwolf.

Doctor Nudd desperately extended the shield beyond his center of balance to protect the young soldier.

With a powerful clawed hand, Periclum ripped the shield off the goblin's arm, nearly taking the arm with it.

Nudd cried out and cradled his injured arm against his chest. Rather than scramble to escape, the unarmed goblin placed his own unshielded body between the raging lion and the groggy, defenseless lieutenant.

Liliana stopped still at the side of the road, as the future fight she watched, reached the the crucial moment. The rain beating on her head, and the wind tearing at her clothes didn't matter. She held her breath, expecting once again to see the sword plunge into her favorite goblin's chest.

A pistol shot cracked instead, echoing through the lab. The were-lion jerked, and his sword paused in its path to the goblin's heart. Another shot, and another flinch.

Blood spread in a stain from two small holes in the back of Periclum's shredded lab coat. The lion's "RRROAR!!" rattled the shelves, knocking glass containers off to shatter on the floor. He turned on his new attacker, fangs bared in a snarl of rage.

"Damn," Siobhan said from the doorway. She tossed aside the two-shot pistol and pushed the pressure plate to close the panel in her upper arm where she kept it hidden. "I hate it when they make me leave the Kel-Tec behind."

She ran away down the corridor as fast as her four-foot human form would carry her.

The were-lion roared as he pursued in feline fury, goblin forgotten in the primal hunger to kill the one who hurt him.

Doctor Nudd helped the badger-kin soldier to his feet and righted the slightly mangled gurney so he'd have a place to sit. "You all right, Lieutenant?"

Two slow blinks followed by a nod of the long dark nose answered him. "The doc said I needed some kind of extra tweak to keep the cybernetics working right," the badger grumbled. "Why did he try to kill me?"

"Excellent question, my boy. You stay here where it's safe, and I'll go ask him." Doctor Nudd ducked back into Periclum's office. He grabbed the slimmest sword in the weapons locker and ran down the corridor.

Liliana nodded to herself and continued walking. She had foreseen this possible future already. In this future, Siobhan would die instead of Doctor Nudd, or possibly with him. She had no way to change that future path directly now, but she had sent Pete, Sergeant Giovanni, and Detective Jackson to help. Colonel Bennet was also on his way. Maybe that would be enough.

Her fourth eyes focused a few more moments farther ahead in time on another large lab, filled with Bunsen burners, and solid granite workbenches with the storage cabinets underneath that opened on both sides. The walls were lined with shelves filled with glassware and bottles of various chemicals. This lab seemed dedicated to chemistry without the soldering irons or parts for electronics.

Siobhan jumped nimbly out of the way of a reaching hairy arm. She landed on a workbench. As she ran along the granite tabletop, she hurled beakers and glass jugs full of chemicals at the lion's head.

Chemicals spilled and mixed on the floor, some foaming and smoking, as she knocked over racks of beakers and test tubes in the lion's path.

With an inhuman growl, Periculum shook bits of glass out of his mane and stalked the sprite.

"Hey, Doc." Siobhan waved at Doctor Nudd as he poked his head around the doorway. "You know that favor I owe you?"

"Look out!" Doctor Nudd shouted.

The sprite dropped off the table.

The lion's sword brushed the tips of her bright red spiked hair as it swished past and embedded itself in a wooden cabinet.

Siobhan rolled across a floor littered with broken glass, wincing at the sharp cuts in her skin. "I consider that favor paid in full," the little sprite said.

"Agreed." Doctor Nudd coughed through chemical fumes.

While the lion ripped his sword loose from the wood, sending slivers flying, the sprite opened a cupboard under a stone-topped workbench, grabbed a jug labelled "ACETONE" and tore the lid off.

Siobhan whirled around to fling a stream of clear liquid out of the top of the jug, angling it up, so it hit the charging lion in the eyes.

"GRRAAGH!!" the lion roared again and clawed at his face.

"Catch!" Doctor Nudd called and threw the sword in his hand, hilt first.

Siobhan dropped the chemical bottle with a wrinkled nose for the smell, neatly caught the sword by the handle, and saluted with it. "Thanks!"

She ducked into the cupboard under the workbench and closed the door, effectively disappearing while the were-lion was blinded. Before the lion got his vision clear, she slipped out the other side of the workbench and hid in another of the multi-door cabinets.

Doctor Nudd ducked behind the doorway, just outside the room, also effectively disappearing from their adversary.

What will be the outcome of the new path? Will my friends survive?

The spider seer's view jumped farther ahead in time.

She saw...fire and death.

Oh no.

Liliana had not saved anyone. She made it worse.

I've killed them all.

Her friends were going to die. They had listened to her, and all gone to the laboratory. They would all die. Her actions had involved the prince as well. Now, he would die today too.

No, no, no.

She had to get there. She had to change this.

She stopped on the side of the road in the rain, looking over a tall fence into the vast expanse of Fort Liberty. Her fourth eyes showed her the path and direction to get to where her friends fought, but it was so far.

There was no time.

CHAPTER 17

RACE WITH DEATH

THE SPIDER-KIN PELTED OFF THE ROAD INTO THE WOODS on the edge of the Army base. She scurried up a tree, then drew a long line from the spinneret on her wrist and swung out as far as possible. She barely cleared the eight-foot electrified fence with the razor wire. She landed in a roll to spring back up in a run.

A siren sounded somewhere, some sort of alarm. The camera drones that normally patrolled the border of the Army base were probably grounded due to the terrible weather, but the stationary cameras could still track Liliana's petite form.

Somewhere, no doubt, patrols were scrambling in the pouring rain. She couldn't slow down to avoid them. If she ran any slower, she might as well go home and get used to not having any friends again.

The drenching rain beat at her. It made her ballet shoes slippery in the grass and leaves. Brambles caught in her skirt. The wind blew icy in her face, and rain dripped in her eyes.

Tracked vehicles crunched into the brush on her trail.

Up ahead on a four-foot barbed wire fence, a sign read:

DANGER
Restricted Area

UNEXPLODED ORDNANCE
Authorized Access Only

Liliana hurdled over the fence and ran through an open field with rolling hills. She watched with her fourth eyes for metal hiding in the tall grass to make sure she didn't trip over anything dangerous. Stickery grass and burrs tore at her tights in the untamed field, slowing her down. She hopped up and sideways to avoid a metal cannister and kept running.

The tracked vehicles she heard earlier stopped at the fence. The barrels of weapons that looked like elongated radar dishes swiveled toward her as she ran, tracking her until they caught up. A strange, low-pitched sound hit like a huge pillow, knocking her off her feet. She felt it vibrate in her belly as much as heard it. Blood ran from her nose. She couldn't think with the overwhelming noise.

The spider seer struggled up to her hands and knees, but she couldn't make it to her feet. A metal canister in the grass near her shaped like a huge bullet exploded, showering the area with shrapnel. Fiery heat seared her left thigh in streaks.

The weirdly heavy air pressed her down. She struggled against it. She wanted nothing more than to lie down and slam her hands over her ears, but she couldn't stop.

She had to keep going.

As her limbs gave out beneath her, she gave one last push and rolled behind a low hill, blocking the direct line of sight between her and the sonic weapon. The sudden cessation of gut-vibrating pressure felt like a boulder had been lifted off her.

To avoid the sound weapons, she loped like an animal in a low crouch with her hands on the ground. Following the natural curve of the rolling hills, she kept earth between her and the sound weapons while still moving as fast as she could in about the right direction. The horrific sound vibrations continued behind her. She heard another explosion, but it was far behind by then.

Liliana risked using her fourth eyes to check on Siobhan,

wondering if she managed to not die while fighting a lion-kin five times her size.

Her fourth eyes showed the future vision of Siobhan dodging the enraged were-lion in the lab with the chemicals. The sword Doctor Nudd had given her danced in her skilled hands, deflecting with finesse and speed the powerful strikes of the lion's long sword. The lion had the advantage of size and strength, but Siobhan had the edge in speed and skill. Hurled glass jars, lab equipment, and insults kept the lion-kin too enraged to think straight.

A grin crossed Liliana's face. She should have known that Siobhan with a sword could hold her own against pretty much anyone

That moment was still in the future. Liliana did not have her clocks, so she wasn't sure how many minutes she had. Perhaps fifteen or twenty, or was it ten? All too soon, time would catch up with the seer's visions.

She still had half of Fort Liberty to cross.

Liliana's teeth chattered from the cold even as the muscles in her legs burned, and a suspiciously hot liquid trickled down her thigh. The wet, cold air clogged her lungs along with a sharp smell like after a match has burned. The sound weapons were far enough behind that she could stand again and run full out. She clenched her teeth so they wouldn't chatter and ran as if a pack of wolves nipped at her heels.

If only she could run faster. She had to run faster.

The spider-kin ran by things she never would have expected to see on an Army base, like a baseball diamond. A siren blew the base alarm from the speakers above the empty stands. She jumped the chain-link fence near third base and pelted across the neatly trimmed grass to first, glad for the open, easy ground, but concerned about the lack of cover if anyone came after her. She made it across and hurtled over the next fence without breaking stride. If she kept running at this rate, she would make it. She was going to get there in time.

She passed a building with a statue of a soldier and a big sign that read, "82nd Airborne Division War Memorial Museum," just as three soldiers—two men and a woman—rounded the corner of the building. They shouted at her, voices unintelligible in the deluge of rain and wind. The guns they pointed at her made their message clear, though.

Desperately, Liliana dodged between two buildings, out of sight of the patrol, then leapt up, caught a windowsill, jumped again, and climbed to a roof of what looked like a two-story apartment building with red brick framed by yellow. She ran across the peaked roof past the ear-splitting siren mounted on it. She attached a line to the edge, before swinging out as far as it would take her.

The three soldiers searched far behind her as she kept running.

Liiana splashed her way through ankle deep puddles in a broad park-like space that left her frighteningly exposed to weapons fire as sirens blared from every building. No new patrol had found her yet. Her heart hammered as she raced across, expecting a challenge or a bullet at any moment. She ducked gratefully behind another building.

Just as she ran onto the hard blacktop of a parking lot, four more soldiers came out of the building in front of her that read Special Warfare Museum. They pointed guns straight at her and ordered her to "Halt!"

She put her hands up for a moment, as if giving up, but she couldn't. Not really. If she stopped, everyone she cared about would die.

As the soldiers relaxed, she dove between two cars, then rolled over her shoulder. In an instant, she regained her feet. They fired as she ran in a crouch, dodging between cars. They chased her, shouting and shooting, but their bullets all missed her darting form in the pouring rain.

Their pursuit forced her off the direct trajectory toward the medical center. Those four soldiers chased her into a narrow strip of forest. Here, she was better able to avoid pursuit. She leapt into the tree branches and ran, just as fast on narrow branches as on flat ground. The soldiers searched through the forest, calling out to her over loudspeakers to give herself up, as she doubled back to get on the right path. She ran directly above their heads, ballet-slippered feet carefully silent. The rain that battered her also aided her by confusing the pursuing soldiers. Thunder and the many sirens hid the sound of rustling leaves.

The loudspeakers kept calling after her as she jumped and climbed over another fence, this one six-feet tall and made of wood. She landed in someone's backyard with a swing set.

Detective Jackson had not been exaggerating when she described the base as another small town, nearly as big as Fayetteville itself. Liliana had so far still to run.

She wondered where her friends in the car were.

When will they arrive?

With her fourth eyes, she followed the course of the patrol car that Detective Jackson drove. The spider-kin knew she would cross their path soon. Even while Liliana hoped they would get to the lab in time to save Siobhan, she desperately wished they would slow down. She had only entered the base a few minutes after them, but she could not run as fast as a car, especially not with Detective Jackson driving.

She watched the car with her fourth eyes while her second eyes watched all around her for obstacles or more security patrols. The weird colors her second eyes saw washed out to white every time lightning flashed. She hated running while using her second eyes. The shifted color spectrums made her feel like she was living a nightmare. If she did not run fast enough, the nightmare would be real.

A few military vehicles felt their way carefully along the streets through the deluge. Visibility was limited to only a few feet by the driving rain. She had to stop, panting at the side of the road, hidden by a hedge in what appeared to be someone's front yard. Sirens mounted on the corner street light poles screamed about her invasion of the base.

She sobbed for breath as vehicles with big knobby tires crept slowly down the road, search lights shining all around. She had to wait until they were out of sight, or she would be caught, but every moment felt like forever. Seconds could make the difference.

She couldn't save them, though, if she were caught. She panted, trying to catch her breath as the big cars rolled by.

Go faster, go faster. Please go faster.

As they finally rounded the corner, she burst from hiding and ran again, fighting to ignore the pain in her leg that made her want to limp. She couldn't limp. She had to run faster.

For a while, she didn't see any more foot patrols. Apparently, even soldiers didn't like to be out in a thunderstorm if they had any choice in the matter. Or maybe they still thought she was hiding in the little patch of woods. She didn't have enough eyes to check.

Her fourth eyes watched her friends.

Pete and the others arrived at the medical center in the middle of the base. They jumped out of the police car into the rain and ran for the medical center's back door, sirens blaring in the parking lot. The Fae prince met them there.

"Colonel," Sergeant Giovanni said and saluted properly, ignoring the pouring rain as if unaware it was there.

The prince gave her a crisp acknowledgment of the salute and drew his sidearm. "Why did you order the base alarm to sound?"

Sergeant Giovanni looked confused. "We thought you did that, sir."

Colonel Bennet's lips tightened. "Liliana."

"She got out of the car at the gate just like she said she would," Pete told him.

"Of course she did." Colonel Bennet put his wrist phone up to a sensor, and it popped open a door in the back of the huge medical complex. "Detective, this is a military matter. It might be best if you stayed behind."

Detective Jackson snorted and drew her pistol from a holster under her jacket. "Not a chance."

"She knows about Others, sir," Pete told him.

Colonel Bennet shrugged. "Well, then. Welcome to the party. Don't shoot any of my people, or I'll shoot you."

Detective Jackson shrugged. "That's fair."

As her friends started down the long corridor with caution, a loud roar and crash made the direction of the danger obvious.

What caused the crash?

Liliana's fourth vision re-focused. The sprite stood on a table by a window, grabbing things off high shelves and throwing them at the lion.

Andrew Periclum lifted a massive centrifuge and hurled it at the sprite.

Siobhan jumped aside in time, but the heavy piece of equipment caught her sword, knocking it out of her hand and through the window out onto the medical center lawn. The broken window let in the rain, the wind, and the sound of blaring sirens.

Now, the little sprite had no weapon but her wits.

She rolled under a table to avoid flying glass and debris and dodged through the two-sided cabinets to another bench.

The lion roared and ripped thousand-pound stone-topped tables loose from their bolts in the floor, shoving them aside. Glassware and chemicals atop them added to the chemical soup on the floor.

Liliana ran toward them from too far away. She hurdled a few chain-link fences as she passed the middle school where Pete's beloved worked and Janice's children learned. In the distance, from too far away, she heard the window break as the centrifuge flew through it.

Less than a minute after she saw it in her visions.

She had to run faster.

Would Pete, Detective Jackson, Colonel Bennet, and Sergeant Giovanni arrive soon enough to save Siobhan?

Her fourth vision shifted again.

In that moment, her vision passed from the overbright visions of the future into the sharper certainty of the present.

She had no more time. Everything she saw was happening as she saw it.

Her friends ran into the room where the sprite fought the lion.

The spilled chemicals in the big room had filled it with acrid fog. It made the newcomers cough and struggle to make sense of the trashed lab and the life-or-death battle inside.

Siobhan dodged between the legs of a table on the other side of the lab by the big window as the massive lion-kin tried to catch her with his claws, then tore the solid wood table itself apart to get to her.

They made it in time. Siobhan's still alive!

Tumbled furniture, broken lab equipment, and a chaotic, intermittently smoking and bubbling mix of random chemicals filled the once-orderly lab. Driving rain from the spring storm diluted the chemicals into rapidly growing puddles by the large, broken window. The wind whipped and swirled through the chemical fog.

"Freeze!" Detective Jackson shouted, pointing her gun at the big lion-kin.

Periclum turned to face them with a snarl, sword up in a guard position.

Siobhan took advantage of his distraction to do a flying tackle with all her weight into the back of the lion's knee. It would have been an effective attack if she had had a little more weight to throw.

As it was, the lion man merely staggered. His clawed hand grabbed the collar of her leather jacket and lifted her up, as if showing Siobhan to her friends.

"OY! Let go of me, you big ball of clatty fur!" The sprite twisted and struck out wildly but couldn't get free. Blood ran down her face from a claw scratch on her forehead.

The point of the lion's sword came to rest in the center of her back. Siobhan stopped struggling. Her lips flattened in an expression of irritation.

"Put your guns down or the little bitch dies." The wind whipped the lion's mane, and rain driven through the window soaked him and Siobhan both. Thunder rumbled after another flash lit the clouds behind him.

Pete, who had a knife in each hand, sheathed them and raised his empty hands. "Please, don't hurt her."

Detective Jackson said calmly, "You might as well put her down and give up. There's no place to go." Her gun stayed trained on Periclum's head through the blowing chemical fog.

The lion laughed, showing a whole lot of pointy teeth. "You don't scare me, little human. I could eat you for a snack." He licked his lips.

"She's right," the Fae colonel backed up the detective. "This is over. Drop the sword, or I will drop you where you stand." His gun with the wide barrel never wavered.

Liliana had no doubt that whatever weapon Colonel Bennet had would be effective against the were-lion. She was afraid that the unseelie prince wouldn't care if that gun killed both lion and sprite. A seelie Fae sprite was probably not someone he felt responsible to protect.

The spider seer raced across the front of the neatly landscaped grounds of the medical center, ballet slippers squelching through mud. Seconds after she ran past the center, four armed men ran out of the main entrance.

In the lab, Sergeant Giovanni followed her commanding officer's lead and kept her gun up.

"Don't think I'm bluffing, Colonel," growled the lion. "I will kill this irritating little bug."

"Regardless of what you do," Colonel Bennet answered, "you're done here."

The lion-kin seemed to consider his options for a moment. No one had a clear shot at him with the sprite held up in front of him like a shield and overturned granite tables blocking a shot at his legs.

The colonel jerked his chin at Sergeant Giovanni, widened his eyes, and tilted his head.

She nodded, as if that had been a clearly spoken order.

They edged in opposite directions around the sides of the room. In a few more steps, they would each have a shot. The lion couldn't protect both his flanks at once.

Detective Jackson talked to the lion-kin. "You're not in a good position here. Just put her down, place the weapon on the floor, and no one has to get hurt."

Pete edged closer, empty hands held out, carefully not blocking Detective Jackson's shot.

"Stop now, all of you, or she's dead!" the lion growled. He dug the sword tip into the back of Siobhan's leather jacket. It pushed her forward and arched her back enough to change her facial expression from anger to pain. Only the thick leather kept the sword from piercing her.

Pete froze in place, but saw the Fae prince and Sergeant Giovanni still creeping closer along each wall. "Colonel, please!" he begged.

The prince's jaw tightened, and his nostrils flared in anger, but he stopped creeping closer to the lion.

Sergeant Giovanni stopped when the colonel did.

"You're going to be okay," Pete said softly to Siobhan. "Don't worry."

Siobhan rolled her eyes, despite the pinch of pain around her lips. "I hate being the damn hostage."

At the obvious standoff, Doctor Nudd came in from around the doorjamb. "He killed soldiers from your SET unit," he told the colonel, voice shaking with rage. "The first two died slowly over a period of days. After that, when he saw the first signs of toxic reactions to his nanites, he got the widow spiders to eat the soldiers to hide the evidence. Their acid venom destroyed the nanites completely. It wasn't just six soldiers either. Ten are dead. He shot and buried some in the forest and the last two are dying."

"You knew." Nudd held up the folder, shaking the proof at Periclum like a weapon. Everyone else was frozen, but Nudd walked down the center of the room in front of the big lion, crunching broken glass under his shoes. "You knew the nanites were deadly, and you just kept doing it anyway!" Nudd set the folder down with shaking hands on a wrecked work bench. "I don't think I can save the last two." He rubbed his hand through his messy hair. "When you realized one batch was killing your subjects, you just changed the nanites slightly and went right on. You put them in Lieutenant Runningwolf less than an hour ago, and I don't even know if I can save him." He pointed a shaky finger at the big werelion. "You are no doctor. You sicken me."

Periclum eased the pressure on the tip of his sword against Siobhan's back, as if forgetting that he held her. "That's rich, you telling me I'm not a doctor. I use science, not hand wavey mumbo jumbo to heal. You're nothing but a witch doctor pretending to do medicine."

While they yelled at each other, Liliana kept running. She was almost there. She might make it.

"Stop where you are, ma'am, or we'll shoot!" a soldier shouted behind her.

No, no, no.

She couldn't stop now.

Bullets splashed a trail by her feet as she ran around the corner of the sprawling complex. She could see the centrifuge on the wet lawn by the broken window a half block away. She didn't think it was possible to run even faster as her breath sobbed through her lips and burned her lungs, but she tried.

Lightning flashed, blindingly white, followed rapidly by a bone-shaking crack of thunder.

While they were blinded by the lightning, the lion-kin hurled Siobhan past Nudd and jumped out the window, shifting to full lion form in mid-air.

Pete leapt up to catch the hurtling sprite. The force of impact slammed into his chest and smashed him and Siobhan back against a wall of shelves. The wolf-kin curled protectively around the small woman.

Periclum ran into the storm on four feet, leaving his sword behind.

Liliana saw the huge lion with the tattered remains of a lab coat flapping like a cape disappear into the gray of the rain, but she ignored him, sprinting all out for the window he just escaped through.

The soldiers pursuing her rounded the corner.

Inside the room, Pete uncurled from around Siobhan. "Are you okay?" The shelving units they'd slammed into tottered. Shelves collapsed forward, broke completely, or tilted. Cardboard boxes and plastic storage containers slid, some crashing to the ground around them.

The sprite ran her hand through her soggy red hair, wiped blood that was dripping into her eye, then climbed to her feet. "Right as rain. You seem to have a habit of saving me from hairy beasts." She grinned down at Pete and offered him a hand up. "And how are you feeling this fine day?"

"Like I got hit by a flung fairy?" Pete smiled up at her and rubbed his chest in obvious pain where her small body slammed into him.

After sidestepping a falling box, she slugged him in the shoulder. "Keep up the name callin', and you'll be back in the doghouse."

"Sergeant, get the SET squad mobilized immediately," Colonel Bennet ordered. "Find Periclum, and either take him in, or take him down. He doesn't leave this base." Colonel Bennet winced. "And turn off the damn base alarm."

"Yes, sir." Sergeant Giovanni punched buttons on her wrist phone and spoke into it rapidly.

"I'd sure like to know what exactly was going on here," Detective Jackson said.

The Colonel gave her a hard glare.

Jackson raised her hands in a placating gesture. "When you've got a few minutes to spare, of course, whatever isn't too classified."

Liliana made it to the window just as the soldiers chasing her opened fire again.

A bullet slammed the spider-kin sideways as she jumped.

Liliana landed badly in the lab as Pete struggled to his feet, groaning, one hand in Siobhan's and the other braced on the damaged shelf behind him.

The spider-kin staggered to her feet, holding her bleeding side just above her hip where the bullet hit.

"NO!" the spider seer shouted at Pete as he stood. She ignored her wounds, stumbled across the broken glass and caustic chemicals, leapt over the broken tables, and dodged under the colonel's long arm as he reached for her.

She stepped on Pete's bent knee, making him yelp, then leapt and caught the open-topped box marked "ELEMENTAL METALS" as it fell from the top shelf. The glass containers inside rattled together.

As Pete had curled protectively around Siobhan, Liliana curled around that box, praying she could cushion the landing with her body.

"Oof." The wind exploded out of her as she landed on her back on the ground, the big box cradled carefully. Pain shot through her injured side, but that didn't matter. Thick glass bottles clacked hard against each other when she hit. She tensed every muscle, waiting to be immolated in chemical flame.

Nothing happened.

She risked a quick look. Two of the bottles had chips and spiderweb cracks, but they were all intact. She closed all her eyes and dropped her soaking head back on the chemical-covered floor littered with glass shards.

I made it.

For a while, she just lay there, panting for breath and shivering in a slowly spreading puddle of her blood. Not only did her side hurt, but her thigh felt like it had been seared with a hot fireplace poker. Or three.

After a few seconds of silence aside from her own labored panting, she cracked one human eye. Everyone stared down at her, looked at each other, then back down at her.

She was too tired and sore and cold for the staring to even make her uncomfortable. Or maybe it didn't matter as much being stared at when her friends were the ones doing it.

"Stand down," Colonel Bennet ordered when the men who shot Liliana reached the window. "Sergeant Giovanni and I have the situation under control. And turn off that damn siren!"

Doctor Nudd stepped forward and took the box out of the exhausted spider-kin's hands. "Oh my," he said. "Good thing that didn't fall and break in here. If the elemental sodium had come in contact with the water and acid on the floor, it would have set fire to the entire lab."

Pete peered at the labels on the bottles. "Actually, once ignited, the phosphorous, potassium, and magnesium powder would probably have blown this entire section of the building up. What idiot stored these together?" He grinned down at the spider-kin and extended a hand. "Glad you could join us, Lilly."

CHAPTER 18

BLANKETS, HOT COCOA, AND MURDER

LILIANA SAT ON ONE END OF AN EXAMINATION TABLE IN A small room and sipped hot cocoa, her injuries clean and bandaged. The shrapnel had been removed from her thigh. The bullet had passed through the skin and muscle just above her hip relatively cleanly. The wound would heal in a few days. She was nearly buried under blankets that had been warmed in a special oven. Her wet clothes had been replaced with borrowed military fatigues that were several sizes too large.

Pete and Doctor Nudd fussed over her at least as much as they fussed over Siobhan, who sat next to her on the examination table, similarly dressed in dry but ill-fitting clothes and covered in warm blankets. The little Fae had a few minor cuts, including a deep claw scratch on her forehead. A white band held the gauze pad over the taped wound, pushing her red hair straight up on the top like a woodpecker's crest.

Doctor Nudd had been in and out, caring for them and for Lieutenant Runningwolf. Nudd's healing gift seemed to be helping the badger recover from the toxic nanites still circulating in his system. He'd only gotten half of the nanites in his system before Doctor Nudd had removed the needle from his arm. Nudd had little hope for the others who had been infected. While he had no idea how to get them out, his talent directly mitigated the nanites' toxic effects, in Runningwolf at least.

Liliana found she rather enjoyed being fussed over. Siobhan grumbled a lot, but Liliana's third eyes showed her that the little Fae enjoyed it just as much as the spider-kin.

Siobhan caught her looking and winked.

Liliana smiled into her cup.

When their injuries were completely cared for and they were as comfortable as possible, Doctor Nudd opened the door to allow the others access. "One at a time, please."

Pete left to give them space.

Colonel Bennet was the first to visit.

Liliana quickly closed her third eyes.

After a brief, cold nod to Siobhan, he focused on Liliana. "The next time you need access to the base, it's granted. I'll get you a pass for the gate," he told her. "That's the second time you saved my life today, and the third time since we met. I should have trusted you."

"You didn't know me, so you had no reason to trust me." Liliana shrugged. "Just like I don't really know you."

The dark prince finished her thought, "So you have no reason to trust me."

"I need to know you better." Liliana considered how she might accomplish that. "May I visit your home? Doctor Nudd tells me that it is a social rule to inform someone before visiting."

"I look forward to it." He bowed to her slightly.

He turned to leave. The prince had barely acknowledged Siobhan's existence, even though Liliana recognized the sprite's work in the unique weapon he carried in the holster on his hip.

Siobhan and Colonel Bennet were of opposite courts. Enmity between seelie and unseelie Fae had existed for millennia, and the spider seer suspected from what she had seen inside him that Colonel Bennet had a personal grudge against the seelie as well.

But the flower sprite had fought so bravely, and Liliana did not like seeing her friend snubbed. "It was Siobhan who saved Doctor Nudd's life," Liliana said. "He would not have survived until you or I got here if she had not chosen to fight the pride-king alone."

Colonel Bennet turned back. He looked to Doctor Nudd for verification.

"That is true, actually." Doctor Nudd tucked his clipboard inside the sling that held one arm, and drew himself to his full height, even taller than the prince. "I would have died long before help arrived if not for Siobhan."

The prince glanced at Siobhan. "I understand you owed Nudd a favor." He had seemed formal when he spoke to Liliana, but with the little Fae, his tone turned icy. He spat the word favor as if it were an insult.

Siobhan nodded, face closed and wary. "He saved my life. I saved his. We're even now."

Doctor Nudd tapped his pen but didn't add to that.

Liliana sighed. So much bloodshed in the past could have been avoided if the Fae did not insist on dividing everyone into opposing camps. Bridges had begun to be built across previously uncrossable lines. The first Sidhe court in North America would not begin by burning those bridges, not if Liliana had any say in the matter.

The prince told her himself that he didn't intend to let those old lines define or restrict him. She would see to it that he kept that oath.

"Regardless of the reason, she saved a Fae under your protection that you would have failed to protect without her aid."

The prince turned his dark glare on the spider-kin, but Liliana kept her eyes down on the cup in her hand. This prince seemed to follow the old rules of fealty that had been ignored by so many Sidhe. Rules mattered to him. Order mattered. Honor mattered. But Sidhe tended to interpret the rules to their own best advantage, and many of them would ignore honor when it suited them.

She wondered if this prince would honor his obligations in an age when so many did not.

"I told Siobhan that she would probably die if she came here. Doctor Nudd did not ask her to come, and her obligation to him would have died with him if she had done nothing. Siobhan chose to protect one who serves you, knowing the price could be her life."

Anger narrowed Colonel Bennet's dark eyes. A muscle in his square jaw jumped as he clenched his teeth. He frowned at Liliana for a moment, then he seemed to grow larger, crowding the tiny space in the examination room.

Doctor Nudd swallowed and backed his lanky body as far as he could into a corner.

The prince didn't shift to his Fae form, but dark power flowed up from the earth. Silent snakes of smoke in a dozen shades of green so dark they were nearly black crawled around his body until he glowed with an aura of flickering shadow. A ghost of silver spikes wreathed his head like a white flame crown.

Doctor Nudd went down on one knee.

Siobhan's eyes got very large. If she hadn't known before what Colonel Bennet was, she did now. She lifted her tiny chin in defiance, but she pulled the blankets around herself more tightly as the unseelie Fae prince turned his full attention on her.

Then the towering prince wreathed in the aura of his power surprised them both. He gave Siobhan a very slight, minimal bow. "I am in your debt."

Siobhan swallowed and licked her lips. "The debt is paid."

He shook his head. "Your debt to my Merlin is paid. However, as the spider-kin reminds me, I am personally indebted to you for shielding one of mine with your life." His lips twisted as if he didn't like the way the next words tasted. "I owe you a favor."

The sprite in human form glanced at Liliana, blue eyes huge. A favor from a Sidhe prince was priceless. Siobhan could ask for virtually anything, and the prince would be required by his honor to use his considerable power to grant her request.

Liliana reached over and squeezed the sprite's hand. Siobhan had earned it.

"What would you ask of me?" the prince said.

Siobhan handed her cup of hot cocoa to Liliana. She straightened her back and looked up at the prince wreathed in shadows of power.

His eyes glimmered red like hot coals in the dark glow of his power, the only sign of anger he showed.

"Look, just...just keep him safe," Siobhan said. "I don't want you to give me anything for watching Nudd's back. Just, if he's one of yours, then, watch out for him, yeah?"

Some of the red fire from the prince's eyes faded as his brows pinched in confusion. "Why?" he asked the sprite, towering over her. "Why would a seelie Fae use a prince's favor to protect a goblin?"

Siobhan's small body tensed as if preparing to run or defend herself. "Because I don't let any feckin' court or any royal toffs tell me who my friends are." Her faint Irish accent went thick. She trembled under the blanket, but she still spat the words in the face of the unseelie prince glowing with raw power.

Liliana realized that the people she had come to call friends shared one trait. They were all imbued with gargantuan amounts of courage.

The dark prince blinked and took a half step back, stoic face completely failing to hide his surprise. His dark power faded to a less intimidating presence. "Nudd has the full protection of earth and fire." He bowed a little more deeply to the sprite. "But the debt remains. He was mine to protect already."

It was Siobhan's turn to look surprised. "Only a land-bonded Sidhe can offer the..." She swallowed. "You rule both earth and fire?"

The prince shrugged one shoulder minutely. "Within the borders of Fort Liberty, but my influence has been spreading. Some of Fayetteville and the wilderness in this area is mine now as well. I cannot protect him beyond my borders, but you can, and I see now that you will. For that alone, I would be in your debt."

Siobhan scratched at the dried blood in her short red hair. "I've lived nearly two centuries, and no royal of any court has ever said a word to me, much less offered me a favor."

"One has now," the prince told her. The ice thawed from his voice, and the red disappeared from his eyes. "It was honorably earned, and it would please me to grant it."

"If I may, sir?" Doctor Nudd said.

Alexander Bennet nodded permission for the goblin to speak.

Doctor Nudd directed his words to Siobhan. "Colonel Bennet knows about Pete, what he is, and he knows about me taking care of a Celtic wolf since he was a boy. In spite of that, he still offered me a place, and he treats Pete like one of us, even though he doesn't know what the Colonel is. He's not cruel and capricious like the Goblin King or Queen Mab. In the nine years since the land chose him, I have never regretted pledging my fealty."

The prince placed a hand, with its attendant living shadow, on the kneeling goblin's shoulder with an expression of pride. Some of the shadow of raw Green played over Doctor Nudd's skin and sank in.

Doctor Nudd shivered. His face, often scrunched with worry, smoothed into an expression of peace that made him look centuries younger.

The edge of that shadow brushed the little sprite where Nudd's hand rested on her knee.

Siobhan's face turned speculative, looking down at the connection. "Can I carry my Kel-Tec on base?"

Colonel Bennet's lip quirked slightly at one corner. "Is that how you would use your favor?"

"Nah, I'll have to give the favor some thought. That's not something to waste." She bounced up onto her feet on the examination table, making her a bit taller than the prince. She tossed the blanket to Liliana and gestured widely. "See, I was thinking I could help you keep Nudd and Pete and your soldiers out of trouble better if I had my weapons with me all the time. I mean, if you want me to protect your people properly, that is?"

The prince watched her pace back and forth on five feet of exam table. "Are you offering me your service as a guardian for my court?" His lips twitched again. Unseelie Fae court guardians were usually terrifyingly powerful Others like rock trolls or dragon-kin.

"Well, I supply your SET unit with custom weapons effective against Fae and beast-kin already." Her pretty face turned wry, and she waved away a comment the prince didn't actually seem inclined to make. "Yes, I know about the secret Special Enemies and Tactics force you're in charge of." She rolled her eyes. "Every Other in Fayetteville knows."

"I did not know," Liliana pointed out. It had never occurred to her to look for such a thing.

Siobhan waved her cybernetic arm at Liliana. "Well, except for Lilly, who was practically a shut-in until recently. The thing is, I always keep an eye on your soldiers, especially at the bars off-base, so I could––" She broke off and looked at the prince with his aura of raw power who was watching her, his handsome face unreadable.

Her shoulders slumped. "I mean I could do it sort of... unofficially. I know you wouldn't want a cyborg flower sprite to serve you publicly." She scoffed. "People would probably laugh at a prince with a sprite for a guardian." She laughed, ugly and bitter.

"I am honored to accept you in my service, Guardian," the prince said solemnly.

Siobhan blinked once, and a grin dawned in place of the bitterness on her pixie face. "So you'll give me a permit to keep the Kel-Tec with me on base?"

"Of course." The prince nodded to the sprite.

"Yes!" She punched the air. "And can I get real grenades for the grenade launcher?"

Alexander Bennet's mouth curved up a tic at the corners. "Don't push your luck." His aura of oppressive power faded into the floor. He appeared, once again, to be an ordinary human, although Liliana thought he was still quite impressive.

She smiled into her cocoa. This prince of shadows was definitely a man worth getting to know more deeply.

"If you ladies will excuse me, I have something pressing I need to take care of."

Liliana tilted her head and opened her fourth eyes for a moment to see what the prince was referring to.

Oh. Right.

"Don't stand too close," she told him.

He gave them each a small bow and left.

Doctor Nudd got up. His face split with a wide grin. "Welcome," he said to Siobhan and gave her a formal bow. "To the Court of Earth and Fire."

"Does this mean I'm unseelie now?" the sprite asked. "Will I feel stronger at night?"

Doctor Nudd did not seem to know the answer to that question for certain. "Well, the prince is unseelie. Normally, unseelie rulers don't choose seelie Fae for their court. The land gives power according to its traditions, and if the peak of its power is at night..." He scratched his stubbly beard thoughtfully. "But the land doesn't usually change your nature."

Liliana considered that, looking into the past. "No land in North America has ever chosen a non-native Fae before." Liliana considered some images of ancient Fae courts in North America that flashed before her fourth eyes. She couldn't understand any of the conversation and many of the native Others were unknown to her. "I don't think this land has any concept of seelie or unseelie. I see no separation between Fae and beast-kin either. Even Normals who were wise or had extraordinary skills were accepted in the land's service. The Green peaks and ebbs with the seasons, neither at noon nor midnight, but it seems to have worked well to nourish all Others in the past."

Doctor Nudd's grin nearly split his face. "That means that our prince has the freedom to choose who he will accept without restriction."

"He told me as much, with the power of an oath behind it. I wonder if that is part of why this land chose him." Liliana glanced at her sprite friend sidelong. "I think you have chosen the one court where you truly can belong and let your heart choose your friends."

Nudd grinned at the little sprite. "And you have been chosen right back. I've got a bottle of three-hundred-year-old mead I've been saving. Tonight seems like a great time to open it."

Siobhan whooped. "Now, that's a Fae who knows how to celebrate!"

Her friends' joy made Liliana happy, but she had seen the prince's near certain death in less than a year. "The new court may be very short-lived," she warned her friends.

The tall goblin shrugged. "I know he's half human and mortal, but some of the great kings and queens of legend were mortal. If it only lasts a few years, then..." He shrugged. "Then I believe they'll be good years. And I would rather live fifty years in the court of a good king than another thousand alone."

Siobhan nodded agreement. "You don't know what it's like for a Fae to have no court, no tie to the land," she told Liliana. She rubbed the spot on her leg where the barest edges of the prince's power had touched her, not like it hurt, but like she wanted to rub the sensation in deeper. "It feels like being...uprooted. You can survive for a while, but you can never grow or thrive."

"And yet, you both came to this continent because there were no Fae courts here."

The two Fae shared a look. The smiles left both their faces. Doctor Nudd's deep voice rumbled low. "Some things are worse than being uprooted."

Liliana's decision whether or not to save the prince was now even more important. The land of her home had chosen him to lead. If Colonel Bennet would make a good king, then it would give her friends great joy to serve him. If he would become a bad king, then she should let him die. It would be better than putting her friends through the same horrors that drove them from their homes in the British Isles in the first place.

A knock on the door made them all look up. Detective Jackson leaned in. "My turn?"

"Yes, Detective Jackson, you may come in now," Liliana said.

She handed Siobhan back her no longer hot cup of cocoa, and the sprite settled cross-legged on the exam table next to her to drink it.

The smile on the detective's face was triumphant. "We did it! We stopped a murder from happening."

"Thank you for believing me," Liliana said.

The detective chuckled. "You just made my homicide detective's heart happy. No one got murdered!"

"But the would-be murderer got away," Liliana pointed out.

Detective Jackson made a rude noise. "We know who he is, and he held a hostage at the point of a weapon right in front of multiple witnesses. He'll get his. If you have any more visions like that, you keep right on coming to me. Promise?"

"I will, Detective Jackson. If you can help, I will make sure that you know." Liliana had already foreseen several deaths. Her mind wandered, pondering the possible future paths, looking for ways that the detective's help might save lives.

Detective Jackson offered Siobhan and Liliana a ride home. Siobhan declined, opting to go home with Doctor Nudd to share a bottle and companionship. She could put her bike in the back of his pickup. Doctor Nudd invited Detective Jackson and Liliana to join them.

They both accepted.

Liliana peeked forward a bit and saw all four of them making music together, drinking and laughing until dawn.

She smiled. It would become quite a party.

Not since she was a child in the circus had Liliana attended a party. She had never in her adult life had so many friends.

The bullet wound would, once again, prevent her from dancing, but that would be okay. She had friends now who loved to make music. She would have many other chances to dance as much as she liked.

Detective Jackson gave her a ride to Doctor Nudd's house. She still ignored the auto-drive's suggestion to let it take over with the bad weather adaptation application, but she drove at a far more careful and sedate pace. During the ride, Liliana's thoughts and fourth eyes wandered, turning to the escaped killer.

Periclum had fled in full lion form. Tracking a lion on an Army base would normally be a simple thing, but the pride-king knew the location of all the cameras, and the bad weather still grounded the drones and greatly limited visibility.

Sergeant Giovanni reported to Colonel Bennet that Periclum had eluded capture. The prince accepted the report, then drove northeast in his car with the big tires.

Liliana's vision was not greatly affected by the rain. She found the wounded lion in one of the empty places on base that were used for weapons testing, the same one the spider-kin ran across when the sound weapons nearly killed her. Here and there, unexploded shells lay around in the place where soldiers tested the larger artillery.

Periclum in lion form made slow, limping progress through the pouring rain toward the tall fence on the border of the Army base. The car that had nearly run over the prince in the parking garage waited on the other side of the fence. At the wheel was the lion-kin with the scarred face that the Fae colonel called Bradley.

She also found, unsurprisingly, Colonel Bennet parking his car a short distance away and getting out in the rain. A land-bonded Sidhe with command of the earth could easily track anyone on his land.

While Liliana watched, Colonel Bennet walked into the path of the bleeding lion, just out of range of the lion's claws. He stood in between Periclum and the fence with the waiting car on the other side.

Periclum shifted to demi-lion form so he could speak. One long, furry arm still touched the ground where he hunched. The other was held in tight to his body to slow the flow of blood from two small bullet holes. "You can't touch me, Bennet. Aurore gave me a spell of protection against you." He lifted a furry-maned chin toward the car. "Even if you could, you wouldn't. If you killed the pride-king in front of a witness, you'd make enemies of the entire beast-kin community."

"I have no intention of touching you," the prince answered calmly. "I also have no intention of allowing you to leave my land alive after you killed a dozen of my soldiers and tried to kill my Merlin."

The lion-kin snarled a scoff. "Nudd is no Merlin." Pink puddles formed at his feet as the rain sheeted across his bloody fur. "He couldn't cast a spell to save his life."

"He gives good advice, and he has the gift of healing." The prince shrugged. "Your opinion is irrelevant anyway."

Liliana wondered why the prince bothered to speak to Periclum, since he did not appear to care about anything the lion-kin said. Motion in the scrub and wet grass behind the pride-king caught one of Liliana's eyes. A cylindrical metal thing bigger than a football with a cone shape on one end like a giant bullet rolled toward the king of lions from behind him. It was twice as large as the cannister that exploded from the sound weapons leaving shrapnel in Liliana's leg. The earth gently swelled behind it like a ripple in water, pushing it closer and closer while the prince distracted the lion with conversation.

Bradley, the lion-kin champion by the car, was too far away to see the shell rolling toward his king through the rain and the tall grass.

Periclum's attention was focused with wary caution on the prince. He showed no sign of noticing as the shell rolled to a quiet stop a foot behind his rear paws.

"I'm leaving, Bennet. And there's not a damn thing you can do about it." The lion-kin started limping toward the fence again, ignoring the prince's existence as if he would walk right through him. The shell followed at his heels like an obedient dog.

"Actually, there is something I can do," Colonel Bennet said. "But there's something else I want to do first."

The lion-kin paused, golden eyes narrowed, fangs showing in a contemptuous snarl. "What's that?"

The Colonel turned his back on the lion and took three long strides away. Liliana thought it unlikely that either Periclum or Bradley were close enough to see the prince's hands tremble from the effort of the powerful magic he'd used to make the earth itself move in such a carefully controlled manner.

Detective Jackson drove to Doctor Nudd's house and walked with Liliana to his lovely hand-carved front door at the same moment the prince walked away from the lion.

Liliana remembered to say, "Hello," as required, when Doctor Nudd and Siobhan welcomed them, but most of her attention was on the battle of wills taking place back on base.

Colonel Bennet turned back to the lion-kin to continue the conversation. "Someone warned me not to stand too close." In a louder voice, which would carry to the fence, he shouted. "Look out!"

Andrew Periclum looked around puzzled and finally noticed the shell at his feet.

The shell exploded.

Dirt, flame, and shrapnel flew in every direction. Burning bloody pieces of the pride-king rained down as far away as the fence.

Colonel Bennet raised his arms to shield his face. His uniform got some mud and blood splattered on it, but the Fae prince was unharmed.

The explosion was loud enough that Liliana heard it from Doctor Nudd's front porch a few miles away.

Liliana bounced on her toes and smiled with fangs. She was tempted to shout, "Yes!" and punch the air like Siobhan would.

Her friends all looked up curiously at the sound.

"What was that, Lilly?" Pete asked.

"Andrew Periclum is dead," Liliana said, careful to keep the prince's secrets. "He encountered an unexploded shell on the testing range."

Siobhan jumped up, put a fist in the air, and pulled it down. "Oh yeah. Now, this really is a celebration."

The handsome prince of shadows commanded both earth and fire within his bonded domain. Liliana suspected that not everyone understood the implications of that power on a firing range littered with old explosives.

Clearly, the pride-king had not.

As far as the lion-kin champion watching from the fence, Bradley, knew, the Fae prince hadn't come anywhere near his king. Colonel Bennet had even shouted a warning just before Periclum died in an unfortunate accident.

The beast-kin community would have no reason to find fault with the Fae prince.

Clever, fierce, and deadly.

All intensely attractive traits.

And also, all very dangerous traits.

The prince would make a formidable ally, or a fearsome enemy. If he would be a good king, then one day, he might become a great king.

As she watched from the shelter of Doctor Nudd's welcoming living room with the old grandfather clock and the crackling fire, the violent storm outside faded to a gentle, soaking spring rain. The spider seer considered what she should do next.

She no longer simply drifted through her days.

Liliana had friends. Friends made the days and nights come alive in brilliant colors.

Nudd brought out a bottle covered in dust, brushed it off with great fanfare, and broke the red wax seal. He poured some in glasses and made sure everyone had one.

Friends were worth any price, even if the price might be the spider-kin's own life.

Siobhan was right. It was Lilana's life. She could decide who was worth the risk of it. At this time, that list included Pete, Siobhan, Doctor Nudd, and Detective Jackson. The pride-king had threatened and endangered all her friends and hurt Siobhan and Doctor Nudd.

Now, he was as dead as the widow spiders.

If the prince had not killed Andrew Periclum, then the spider-kin would have had to find the pride-king and kill him herself. She would not allow anyone to harm her friends.

Colonel Bennet had simply saved her the trouble. And shown again how deadly he could be.

She lifted a glass of incredibly good mead to join in a toast, her fourth eyes supplying a vivid image of the handsome Fae in her mind, that moment when a sparkle of mischief lit his eyes and his lips touched her palm. She could see the raw desire mixed with distrust in his face.

Nudd said, "To good friends, good music, and good times!"

Liliana drank with the rest, smiling more than she had in decades.

Siobhan sipped the mead and feigned passing out on the floor. "That is the finest thing I've ever tasted, Nudd. Bury me here. I can die happy now." She clutched the glass to her chest. "Of course, I'll be taking this with me into the underworld."

Everyone laughed.

Liliana opened all her eyes and looked around the room at the dear faces that had become more precious to her than her life.

Danger threatened all their futures.

But for tonight, there was music and laughter, and Liliana gloried in it.

Thank you for reading! Did you enjoy? Please add your review because nothing helps an author more and encourages readers to take a chance on a book than a review.

And don't miss the next book of the Liliana and the Fae of Fayetteville series coming soon!

Until then read <u>CALLED TO THE DEEP</u> by City Owl Author,
Desirée M. Niccoli. Turn the page for a sneak peek!

Also be sure to sign up for the City Owl Press newsletter to receive
notice of all book releases!

Sneak Peek of Called to the Deep

By Desirée M. Niccoli

Little remained of *The Osprey*.

One of her masts, once a towering white pine, snapped clean off in last night's storm. Its canvas sails floated adrift, rippling upon the waves amongst splintered wood. The ocean had swallowed the ship in its gaping maw and spat back out just enough to taunt Captain Killian Quinn with the stark knowledge of how easily his crew could have shared this fate.

As much as the ocean was a mariner's greatest joy, the ever-looming threat of a watery grave also made it his greatest fear.

Steering his fishing trawler through the other vessel's wreckage, two-hundred nautical miles from shore, was a cruel reminder of this fact. Not even a modern hunk of metal like his *Dawn Chaser* was impervious to the raging sea.

Static crackled over the radio, interrupting that dismal thought. "I don't have a good feeling about this, Captain," Will Branson said. Normally unflappable, the lead deckhand's voice shook. "We found a torn immersion suit in the water. Stained with blood. There's no sign of anyone, living or otherwise."

Peering out into the grey early morning haze, Killian pressed his lips together. He reached to turn off the station that was quietly playing the news, left on for the off chance something useful about the storm or *The Osprey* might be said.

"The U.S. cod fishery hit an all-time low in 2016..."

He paused, compelled to hear what followed.

"...but this year's total for the state of Maine is projected to be even

lower. Scientists are attributing the decline to past years of overfishing and warming oceans."

Exactly why they avoided fishing for cod. He turned off the news broadcast, more of a distraction than a help.

Fog had rolled in when the storm passed, reducing visibility to less than a mile. It pressed in from all sides, curtaining the vastness of the ocean beyond, a claustrophobic, isolating shroud. As far as the eye could see, the world did not exist outside this fishing boat, his crew, and *The Osprey's* ghostly remnants.

And this bloody immersion suit...

The one thing that could keep its wearer warm, dry, and afloat for extended periods of time.

Even if the person survived whatever tore them from it, the water was cold for mid-September. A frigid forty degrees. It only took one or two hours to die of exposure in that temperature, and four had already passed since *Dawn Chaser* received *The Osprey's* 3:00 a.m. distress call. If by some miracle this person was still alive, bleeding out in the open ocean without the fluorescent orange suit, Killian and his crew might never spot them in the water.

The ocean swallowed all other color.

Killian lifted the pilothouse communications radio. "The Coast Guard should be here soon. Just keep your eyes peeled for any survivors. We can at least do that much until help arrives."

They were all just simple, offshore fishermen, hailing from small town Haven Cove, Maine. Keeping his crew alive, ensuring they caught enough to pay them well, returning them home to their families, that's all he wanted. That was his job, his responsibility as captain. While their jobs were never "safe," and they'd fought storms before, this one had been *bad*. It had taken every ounce of his skill to get them through it.

He wanted to bring the other crew home, too, if he could, but he and his band of fishermen were as far from prepared to conduct a proper search and rescue operation as *The Osprey* had been to weather last night's storm.

Before meeting its end, *The Osprey* had been an exact replica of a tall ship, one of the ones that traversed the seas two hundred years ago, resurrected to train modern maritime students and adventure-seeking hobbyists in historic sailing craft. Even knowing that she was essentially a moving museum exhibit, built sometime in the 1980s, Killian felt out of place, out of time, staring at her broken remains.

As he strained to catch a sign of life in the gloom, he glimpsed a dark shadow darting just beneath the surface near a tangle of line. He tracked its path toward the mast where five deep gouges sliced into the fractured wood. Someone must have clung to it with desperate, adrenaline-fueled strength, just before the sea ripped them away.

Or perhaps a shark had dragged them under.

"What will we do with a drunken sailor?"

A chill breeze skated across his skin through the cracked open windows. Though he appreciated a little fresh air to help clear his head, goosebumps prickled the back of his neck.

There it was again. A whispered voice across grey, choppy water, a little louder now than when he'd first found *The Osprey's* remains, but still just quiet enough that he struggled to make out the words. He'd heard bits and pieces of the sea shanty all morning, the normally upbeat tune made eerie by the voice's hushed tones, as if carried in on the wind.

Killian turned to his helmsman McAdams. The man was bent over a navigational chart, tracing a path across it with his finger. "Do you hear that singing?"

Dawn Chaser's foghorn blasted, a deep, trembling bellow that raised the hair on Killian's arms. Though it was a common enough sound in his line of work, nothing about today was normal.

McAdams shrugged. "My ears ring every time the foghorn goes off. Wouldn't call it singing though."

The lilting voice continued. *"Put him in the bed with the captain's daughter."* McAdams rubbed his ear, and Killian waited for him to comment further, because he had to have heard it this time, but the helmsman said nothing more.

Auditory hallucinations then. *Great.* Must be from the lack of sleep.

Draining the dregs of his coffee, Killian tuned out the song. His crew relied on his ability to focus under pressure and this search and rescue operation required his full attention. He had to push past these symptoms, especially if they were to have any hope of success.

And yet, exhaustion or not, he couldn't shake the uneasy, nauseating feeling that hours of searching would yield little, if any, rescuing. There was no sign of the rest of the ship or its crew; it seemed more likely that they'd all sunk to the bottom of the sea.

Remembering the five gouges clawed into the broken mast and the dark shadow darting through the debris, his uneasiness deepened.

A piercing whistle shattered Killian's thoughts and commotion erupted on the decks below. Both he and McAdams whirled around to look out the stern-facing pilothouse window. A second whistle blared, and the rest of the crew rushed port-side. "We've got eyes on someone in the water!" Crackling static punctuated Branson's message over the radio.

"Okay, I'm coming down," Killian replied. Sharing a brief look with McAdams, he handed over the pilothouse radio. "Take the helm."

Switching to his hand-held radio, Killian dashed down the stairs and grabbed a life ring, joining Branson at the gunwale. The lead deckhand pointed one pale, calloused finger to an orange immersion suit bobbing in the distance. Well, how about that. They'd found someone, despite the odds. A surge of adrenaline raced through his limbs, and he gripped the boat's railing to steady his shaking hands. Thrill of the find. Or maybe it was jitters from too much caffeine.

As they drew near, he noted that the person had smooth, feminine features. They'd found a young woman.

Cupping his hands over his mouth, he shouted, "Hang on! We'll get you out!"

Relief wasn't a strong enough word to describe the expression that flooded her face. It was a moment of knowing—that she'd stared utter devastation in the eye, but came out on the other side, living to tell the harrowing tale.

Killian threw the life ring to her, and she kicked her way over to where it splashed in the water. Looping an arm through its center, she gave a weak wave. He hauled her in, hand over hand along rough line, but his palms suffered no chafing. It had been years since he was a deckie—most of his work as captain involved driving and running day-to-day operations—but time hadn't softened the callouses on his hands.

As Killian pulled her in close, Branson lowered a sling, a thick leather strap hooked up to a winch. The next part would be tricky.

Bumping against the side of the boat, the woman released the life ring and reached for the sling. "Try to get it under you," Killian called down. The lines of exhaustion on her face deepened as she struggled to wriggle herself onto it, her movements stiff and clumsy, encumbered by the puffy immersion suit. A bright orange Michelin Man of the Sea. Leaning over the railing, he considered how he might climb down to help her. Maybe rig up a bit of line and rappel over the side...

Gripping the sling, the woman hoisted herself up with one great floundering heave but managed to seat herself. That short burst of adrenaline would only last so long. They needed to get her on deck quickly, but safely, before its absence sapped all remaining energy from her body. Then he really would have to figure out how to get down there and help her up.

Nodding to Branson, whose thumb hovered over the control panel, he said, "As quick as you can but keep her steady."

"You got it, Cap." With the press of a button, the winch kicked into gear.

Killian monitored the woman's ascent. She stared up at him, holding his gaze, barely even blinking. Her eyes reminded him of green sea glass, like the bottles that wash up on shore with messages secreted away inside. While echoes of despair still haunted their depths, a clearer message roiled to the surface: S.O.S. *Help.*

He didn't dare break eye contact; this must've been the first bit of human connection she had in hours, a damn-near eternity out on the open ocean, all alone with nothing but hundreds of miles of sea all around. And until now, no hope of rescue.

"You're almost there," he said, keeping his voice steady and calm, hoping it would be the emotional lifeline she needed.

Tears streaked her cheeks. "Thank you," she managed through chattering teeth. The blue tinge to her lips was worrying. Either the suit had a leak, or she wasn't dry when she put it on, and that made her more susceptible to hypothermia.

As soon as she rose to deck level, he said, "I'm going to put an arm around your waist and one under your legs and pull you in."

She cast a nervous glance down at the ten-foot drop, the twist of her body too sharp, too sudden.

And slipped.

He shot forward, grabbing her around the waist, and held on tight, anything to keep her from plunging to the waves below. The crew behind him inhaled with a collective gasp and a few muttered curses. Despite Killian's firm hold, the woman clung to the sling with a death grip. What little color she had left in her cheeks completely drained, as white as the inside of an oyster shell.

"No looking down. Look at me." His heart thundered in his chest, only settling itself when she nodded, complying despite the cold fear in her eyes. "I've got you," he soothed, hooking his arms around her more firmly. "Now grab onto me."

Shaking violently, either from cold or nerves or both, it took her a moment to let go and lock her arms around his neck. But once she did, he whisked her onboard. "You appear to be borderline hypothermic, so we need to get you out of this suit and into some dry clothes. I can help with the suit and check you for injuries, but then you can do the rest privately if you are stable enough. Do you understand?"

The woman nodded.

In the distance, Killian heard a plane's *burring* propellors. The Coast Guard probably. Maybe they'd have more luck and find others in the water, but for now, the woman's wellbeing was his primary concern.

Sharing a brief look with his lead deckhand, he said, "Take command of the boat and radio this in. I'm taking her inside where it's warm."

Branson turned and shouted across the deck, "Ian, stop messing with the lines and grab a spare blanket from the crew's quarters for the lady." Nearly jumping out of his skin, their newest and youngest crew member dropped the rope he was coiling and darted inside. "Everyone else, I want your eyes on the water."

The rest of the crew returned to their lookout positions on either side of the boat, rubbing their bleary eyes and squinting out into the fog.

Ushering the woman inside, away from the cold sea wind, Killian closed the deck door. "Are you hurt?" he asked, pulling open the Velcro to her hood and unzipping the suit. Trapped scents of salt and seaweed drifted between them.

"No. Just sore."

"Sore how?" he pressed.

Her lips trembled. "My muscles ache. I'm cold. Exhausted. Maybe a little bruised."

"That's pretty good, all things considered." He drew the suit over her shoulders and peeled it down the length of her body. Crouching to pull her feet out, he instructed her to hold onto his shoulder. She reached for him with a pale hand, icy to the touch, but at least her fingers weren't blue like her lips. When he tugged on the immersion suit, the woman's boot caught on the material, throwing her off her balance. She grabbed onto his shoulders, her grip surprisingly tight. A little painful even as his bones creaked and joints cracked beneath her fingers.

Damn, this woman was strong.

Masseuse or chiropractor training? Or just more of that good ol' adrenaline?

Once she steadied herself, and eased up her hold, he suppressed the urge to roll the soreness from his shoulders. Throwing her off her balance again wouldn't be wise. While he wasn't old, he wasn't a young man either, and another bone-crushing grip from her might do some damage.

"Sorry," she muttered, a shade of rosy color returning to her cheeks. "I don't know where that came from."

"It's all right." He freed one foot and then the other. She didn't appear hurt, as she'd said, but seawater soaked her auburn hair and clothes.

Half a beat later, Ian opened the door with a wool blanket in hand and traded it for the discarded immersion suit. The woman shrank against the rush of cold air.

Sputtering apologies, Ian closed the door. "Captain." His voice lowered. "Should I stow this with the other one?"

Killian nodded curtly, glancing over at their rescuee. The woman's expression hadn't changed, so she'd probably missed Ian's question. Thank God. She didn't need to know they'd found another suit—bloody, torn to shreds, and without a body.

* * *

Don't stop now. Keep reading with your copy of <u>CALLED TO THE DEEP</u>

Don't miss the next book in the Liliana and the Fae of Fayetteville series coming soon, and find more from Paige E. Ewing at www.paigeewing.com

Until then, discover CALLED TO THE DEEP by City Owl Author, Desirée M. Niccoli!

First comes desire. Then hunger.

When Killian Quinn, captain of offshore fishing boat *Dawn Chaser*, receives a distress call from a sailing ship caught in a terrible storm, he and his crew rush to provide aid. But when they arrive, all that's left of the ship and its crew is splintered wood and a borderline hypothermic woman who can't remember how she survived. His attraction to her is instantaneous, and maintaining a professional distance proves to be a struggle, especially when she needs a place to stay that's far from the press and curious townsfolk, and his idyllic cottage by the sea is the perfect sanctuary.

What was supposed to be a thrilling once-in-a-lifetime opportunity for Lorelei Roth, turns into a seafaring tragedy. As Lorelei struggles to accept that she's *The Osprey's* only survivor, she's plagued by strange dreams and sleepwalking episodes that draw her into the ocean. And if the grieving process wasn't hard enough, Lorelei also grapples with guilt from developing feelings for the captain who rescued her. But worst of all, is a new, unsettling hunger for raw flesh that's eating her from the inside out. The handsome captain begins to look like a tasty snack in more ways than one.

Discovering she's descended from the people-eating mermaids who devoured her crew, Lorelei struggles to accept her identity knowing her entire existence relies upon its secrecy and devouring human flesh. What happens if Killian finds out? The world at large? What if Lorelei answers the ocean's call to the deep?

Please sign up for the City Owl Press newsletter for chances to win special subscriber-only contests and giveaways as well as receiving information on upcoming releases and special excerpts.

All reviews are **welcome** and **appreciated**. Please consider leaving one on your favorite social media and book buying sites.

For books in the world of romance and speculative fiction that embody Innovation, Creativity, and Affordability, check out City Owl Press at www.cityowlpress.com.

ACKNOWLEDGMENTS

Thanks first and foremost to my agent, Michelle Hauck, who believed in me and my work. I also owe a lot to my publisher and editor, Tina and Lisa G. at City Owl Press. Thanks for giving my work a chance.

ABOUT THE AUTHOR

PAIGE E. EWING writes about superheroes and sentient cities, were-spiders and gun-loving fairies, werewolves and fighter pilots. For her day job, she gives speeches and writes about big data analysis and data architectures, a subject which also doubles as a sleep aid for many.

For fun, she shoots arrows, and throws axes. She lives in the middle of nowhere, Texas, and will show you far too many pictures of her garden if you let her. She once invented a way to grow food on Mars that NASA liked, and has a cute trophy to show for it. Her dogs and horses are unimpressed.

www.paigeewing.com

X x.com/PaigeEwing
  mastodon.social/@PaigeEwing
  instagram.com/paigeewing_author

ABOUT THE PUBLISHER

City Owl Press is a cutting edge indie publishing company, bringing the world of romance and speculative fiction to discerning readers.

Escape Your World. Get Lost in Ours!

www.cityowlpress.com

f facebook.com/YourCityOwlPress

X x.com/cityowlpress

instagram.com/cityowlbooks

pinterest.com/cityowlpress

Made in the USA
Columbia, SC
06 November 2023

25257583R00136